I0846589

The Dream Diary:

Rise of the Shadowborne

David Comer

ISBN: 979-8-218-92575-8

Cover art and illustrations designed by David Comer

Interior formatting by David Comer

Published by the author

Printed in the United States of America

First Edition

To my family, who chose love over judgment.

And to anyone who has ever felt different, out of place, unseen, unsuccessful, or even alone —

This story isn't just for you.

It **is** you.

And when you find your light, the darkness can no longer keep you hidden.

Winnie

The air was crisp and carried the fragrances of autumn leaves and dampened earth. The moon cast an eerie glow amongst the silhouette of trees much like a campfire at night. A veil of mist crept over the landscape, shrouding the grounds of Darkspire Academy in an impenetrable fog. Tendrils of damp air twisted around the trees, their branches like skeletal fingers reaching for the moon. As the fog swirled, it revealed glimpses of the academy's foreboding architecture: turrets and spires that pierced the darkness like shards of bone, and walls that seemed to absorb the faint light, radiating an aura of malevolence.

Within this mist-shrouded world, Winnie stepped through the creaking gates of Darkspire Academy, a school for witchcraft nestled deep within the monster world of GrimWood. With her long, wavy autumn-colored hair rustling in the misty breeze, Winnie walked with purpose, her purple dress fluttering around her knees beneath a black, tailored, double breasted jacket. A witch's hat adorned her head, and a leather satchel slung over her shoulder, usually home to her feline companion and familiar, Jynx, who on this occasion sauntered beside her. Jynx's collar, boasting an emerald gem, seemed to mock the dull atmosphere around her as it swayed back and forth due to her movement, while Winnie's sheer black stockings peeked out from beneath her dress as she walked.

Darkspire Academy loomed before them, its intensified scale stretched towards the moon. The buildings seemed to absorb the faint light, casting long, ominous shadows on the ground. Winnie shivered, despite the thickness of her cloak and paused on the school's grounds. Jynx, who never seemed to be bothered by much at all it seemed, tilted her head and stared along the school's horizon. Lightning pierced the midnight sky like a harpoon entering its prey, making Winnie slightly jump with unease.

Tonight was Halloween. In the mortal realm that meant a night of fun and candy gathering but in GrimWood it meant open enrollment for the witch's Academy. Students in each of the monster realms were expected to master the dark arts of intimidation and fear manipulation in order to control the mortal realm. Winnie's parents, whom were very powerful and esteemed witches in their own right, had enrolled her in Darkspire to follow in their footsteps. Winnie, being a first year would not only have to live up to her parent's expectations but would also have to prove worthy enough to maintain her spot within the school.

However, Winnie's heart just wasn't in it. She'd rather learn about healing and protection spells, not how to scare mortals half to death, and a dark witch from GrimWood learning the arts of divination were absolutely forbidden.

Jynx, sensing Winnie's discomfort, let out a dismissive snort, narrowed her eyes, and flopped onto the grass. Winnie couldn't help but smile at her familiar's antics.

Their first class was Dark Arts 101, taught by Professor Orion Black, a tall, gaunt figure with eyes that seemed to suck the light out of the room as well as any enjoyment. He droned on about the art of psychological warfare, illustrating his points with examples of mortals' deepest fears. Winnie listened but her mind wandered to the mortals she'd rather help than harm.

As the class ended, Jynx stood, stretched, and trotted after Winnie, her tail swishing back and forth with amusement as well as eagerness to be leaving. They had a few more classes to get through though, including Spell-Casting and Fear Inducement. Winnie hoped she'd find a way to use her magic for good, despite the school's sinister focus.

"Hey, Jynx," Winnie whispered, "Think we can find a way to make this place work for us, instead of the other way around?" Jynx blinked, her emerald glinting with mischief, as if to say, "As long as I'm still getting fed."

The halls of Darkspire were overwhelming to say the least. It appeared every turn always revealed two more turns, that turned into two more after that. Winnie stopped inside of a four way split corridor to try and gather herself within her new surroundings. "Which way do we go to get to our Spell-Casting class, Jynx?" Winnie questioned as she looked at her school schedule. Jynx, ever the helpful companion, slowly started turning towards each corridor and finally decided that it was time to just lie down and take a nap instead." "Big help you are." Winnie replied with a sardonic smirk. "Let's make this easier on at least one of us," she said as she reached down, picked up Jynx, and placed her inside the satchel she was carrying across her shoulder.

Winnie gazed down each hallway, the flickering torches casting eerie shadows on the walls, but none of the door signs seemed to match the one she was looking for. "Spell-Casting... Spell-Casting..." she muttered to herself, trying to recall any hints Professor Silvermist might have dropped about the classroom's location.

Frustration mounting, Winnie decided to take a different approach. She had been practicing a locator spell over the summer, and this seemed like the perfect opportunity to test it out. Rummaging through her satchel, she found the small piece of parchment with the spell's incantation and diagram. "Valea ostendo," she whispered, tracing the intricate symbols with her finger.

Suddenly, the corridor around her blurred, and she found herself racing down the hallway at an alarming speed, her feet barely touching the ground. Jynx, who had been dozing peacefully in the satchel, let out a startled yelp as Winnie zipped around corners and through doorways, the satchel flapping wildly. Jynx tumbled out of the bag, her paws scrabbling to grip the strap as she clung to it for dear life, her fur ruffled by the wind and bouncing around like a pogo stick. Winnie's laughter echoed through the corridors as she finally skidded to a

stop in front of a door marked " Spell-Casting 101".
Panting, she struggled to keep a straight face as she gazed
over and saw Jynx's disheveled appearance. Jynx glared
at her, her fur standing on end, as if she had just licked an
electrical outlet, and let out an annoyed hiss. Winnie bit
her lip, trying not to giggle. "You look... um, very
distinguished, Jynx." Jynx's glare deepened and she
turned her head away, tucking her tail beneath her.

A few moments passed by allowing Winnie and Jynx
to freshen up some before entering the classroom. Winnie
made her way to an empty workstation. Their instructor,
Professor Lysandra Silvermist, suddenly emerged from
the doorway and said, "In this class we'll be learning the
fundamentals of magic. This isn't going to be a class you
can just sleep through. You will have to prove to me that
you can in fact hone your skills if you ever intend to move
on from this class. All magic, not just dark, is much more
than just reading an incantation or waving a wand. In this
class you will learn how to cast it, how to harness it, and
how to avert it when necessary."

Winnie's eyes enlarged with every breath her
professor spoke. Her hands began to tremble as she
nervously started looking around the room. Winnie
started to quietly mutter under her breath "I don't think I
can ..." but before she was able to finish her sentence she
felt a large thud in her side. Jynx, nudging her in the side
of her ribcage, was reassuring her that she was stronger
than she gave herself credit for. Winnie, at that moment,
was extremely grateful for her companion, not only
because she was her familiar but also because she was her
friend. Familiars weren't seen in the dark world as
companions or friends, they were seen only as a masters'
minion, there to do their biddings. You could even see the
difference in Jynx's personality versus the ones around
her. They all looked like robots; just sitting there showing
no emotions or interacting with anything around them.
Winnie fell in love with Jynx the moment her parents
gifted her to her and she knew it was the love she had

shown Jynx that made her the exceptional companion she was today.

"Let's stop dawdling and just jump right in." Professor Silvermist asserted. "Everyone should have at least a basic sense of magic by this point, otherwise your parents wouldn't have felt you were ready to enroll here." Winnie's eyes widened again. Professor Silvermist continued, "Today we'll be casting a shadow spell. Shadow spells are considered not only part of dark magic but also illusion. Does anyone happen to know why?" Winnie saw a hand dart up from the corner of her eye. She turned her head and saw a confident presence begin to speak. Her hair was black as midnight, long and silky, like a web. She had eyes of crimson red that looked as though they could pierce the thickest of armors. Her look was absolute perfection from the leather jacket, to the black feather skirt, all the way down to her black boots. "Yes, Ravyn" called out Professor Silvermist. Winnie quietly gasped and mumbled "Oh, so that's Ravyn! It's only the first day here but already I've heard so much about her." Ravyn retorted with a smug tone that dripped with condescension, "That's because shadows can be manipulated into any form that one desires." Jynx, trying to sit patiently beside Winnie, rolled her eyes. "You are correct" Professor Silvermist said, her voice measured with approval.

Winnie was greatly intimidated by her classmate Ravyn but she was also extremely fascinated as well. Ravyn's past was shrouded in mystery, but it was whispered that she came from a long line of powerful sorcerers who had mastered the dark arts. Her parents, renowned for their mastery of shadow magic, had taught Ravyn the intricacies of manipulation and deception from a young age, so it was no wonder she was familiar with the manipulation of shadows.

It slowly started to make sense to Winnie now about everything revolving around Ravyn. Her family revered the darkness of the night. Her familiar was an oil slick colored raven named Midnight, and every witch in her family had one just like it. The raven was more than just a symbol to Ravyn's family; it was a reflection of their own values: intelligent, cunning, adaptability, and a sharp insight that pierced through the veil of uncertainty. They saw themselves in the bird's enigmatic gaze, its sleek black feathers, and its sharp, discerning mind. Ravyn's magic and Midnight's sharp eyesight made them a force to be reckoned with.

Ravyn had quickly established herself, at Darkspire, as a force to be feared, her sharp tongue and quick wit making her a popular, if somewhat intimidating, figure among her classmates.

"Let's go ahead and set up our workstations for the shadow spell" requested Professor Silvermist. "There will be no spell easier than this one and everyone in here should be able to master this very quickly. I mean, even a candle can do it." she scoffed with a chuckle.

Professor Silvermist stood before the class and gave a quick demonstration on how to conjure a shadow. One by one each member of the class performed the task with little to no issues but now it was Winnie's turn. As she attempted to conjure her shadow her magic began to falter. Jynx sat beside her, watching with curious eyes and hopefulness. Winnie's magic was failing, producing only a faint ripple in the air.

Professor Silvermist strode past Winnie's station; her eyes expressed a sense of disappointment. "Concentrate, Winnie. You must focus your will." But before she could offer further guidance, a voice cut through the room. "I'm almost worried for you, Winnie. Would you even be able to handle a shadow if you did manage to conjure one? I mean...you're already trembling like a leaf – I can only imagine what would happen if you actually had some real power at your fingertips. Maybe it's better this way for everyone's sake, really. I bet you'd give a whole new meaning to – running from one's own shadow." Midnight held her eyes closed for a brief moment and let out a formidable "caw" as if to agree with Ravyn's remarks and mock Winnie at the same time.

Winnie's face burned with embarrassment as the entire class fell into uncontrollable laughter. Jynx stood up, her fur bristling, and claws emerging, as if ready to defend Winnie against the verbal jabs. Winnie took a deep breath, trying to calm her racing heart. "Maybe I'm just not trying to scare the living daylights out of everyone," she said, her voice steady.

Ravyn raised an eyebrow. "That's exactly the problem. You're not trying hard enough. This isn't about being nice or gentle. It's about power." Winnie met Ravyn's gaze, her determination growing. "I can learn power without losing myself in the process."

Professor Silvermist intervened, her voice calm and authoritative, "Enough, Ravyn. Winnie's struggles are her own to overcome as ridiculous as they may be. Let's focus on mastering the shadow spell." As the class continued, Winnie redoubled her efforts, Jynx watching with supportive eyes while instinctively wanting to murder that bird. Despite Ravyn's jabs, Winnie felt a spark of determination ignite within her. She would master the dark arts, but on her own terms, it just may not be today.

Winnie left Spell-Casting class that day with a sense of self doubt in her abilities but also a feeling of alienation from her peers. Feeling down on herself and only wanting to go back to her room she knew she had one more class to get through before the day's nightmare would end. Winnie, rechecking her school schedule, as if it had miraculously changed from the first time she looked at it today, said with a sigh "Well Jynx, let's get this over with. Maybe the Fear Inducement class won't be as bad as the last one."

Winnie and Jynx made their way down the corridor towards the next classroom. They knew where they were going this time as they could see the sign above the door. As Winnie approached the door she started to quietly read the name along the plaque on the door, "Professor Lucas Blackthorn." She peered inside the room through the diffused glass inside the door to try and get a better sense of who was inside but didn't have much luck. "I

can't see through the glass Jynx." she said. "What if I'm
walking right into another moment of utter
embarrassment carrying over from the last class?" Jynx,
looking out from the satchel, took her paw and tapped
Winnie's arm and began to purr. Winnie realized at that
moment that she already had one friend in the school, no
matter what happened on the other side of that door and
walked inside the classroom.

As she walked into the room the class immediately
erupted into a fit of laughter. Winnie began to panic and
started feeling nauseous. It wasn't until she happened to
realize that none of the students were actually looking in
her direction but instead towards a man doing
handstands at the front of the class. She slowly began to
feel a moment of ease again and made her way to an
empty seat.

"I'm Professor Lucas Blackthorn everyone and I
welcome each of you to Fear Inducement class," the
middle aged man announced. Winnie, now completely
confused, with how this class has started in comparison
to all of her others, begins to let her guard down a little
more and smiles with an even more reassurance.

"As newcomers to this school, you're likely still
finding your footing. I should warn you, my teaching
methods may be...unconventional," Professor Blackthorn
said with a hint of a smile. "To truly grasp the nature of
fear, we need to explore its opposite: happiness. By
understanding what drives and fulfills a person, you'll
gain insight into the human psyche. This class won't be
about exploiting weaknesses, but about developing a
strategic advantage. Empathy isn't vulnerability; it's a
tactical edge. You'll learn to read people, anticipate their
moves, and outmaneuver your opponents."

Winnie's thoughts drifted away from the chaos of the
day, and she felt herself becoming fully immersed in the
class. As Professor Blackthorn spoke, she sensed a
connection to the material that she'd yet to experience
elsewhere in her first day. It was as if she'd stumbled
upon a hidden doorway, and she couldn't wait to see

where it would lead. As for Jynx though, she was relieved that she could just finally lie down to finish taking her nap. The two hour class seemed to just whiz by when the bell rang and Professor Blackthorn finally concluded with "and that will be it for today I supposed!"

As night descended, the day drew to a close. GrimWood's academic schedule deviated from the normal traditions of the mortal realms. Classes convened only once a month, with students expected to refine their skills through self-directed practice. Homework took a backseat to personal growth, as pupils focused on cultivating their strengths and addressing their weaknesses in their own time. The monthly classes served as milestones, where students were expected to demonstrate progress and improvement from the previous session.

As Winnie and Jynx crossed the Darkspire Academy campus, the fading light of day cast long shadows across the grounds. Winnie quickened her pace, anxious to reach the safety of her dorm room. Suddenly, she spotted Ravyn surrounded by her friends, their laughter and chatter carrying through the evening air.

Ravyn's face lit up with a warm smile as Winnie approached. "Oh hey, Winnie, I'm so glad we're running into one another actually! I was thinking, maybe we could study together for Silvermist's class? I'm really struggling with part of the incantation," Ravyn said, her voice friendly. Winnie's guard dropped slightly, but before she could respond, Ravyn's expression shifted. "Though, I have to say, your... interesting outfit today really makes you stand out. That dress looks like it's straight out of the mortal realm's thrift store and I have absolutely no idea what you were thinking about that hat; a witch's hat!? Honestly Winnie, that's so cliché."

Winnie felt a surge of anxiety but chose to ignore Ravyn's taunts, picking up her pace to hurry past the group. Ravyn's friends snickered and made snide comments, but Winnie kept her head down, focusing on reaching her dorm.

Jynx didn't seem to share Winnie's desire to avoid confrontation this time though. She shot Ravyn a warning glance, her eyes flashing with a mixture of amusement and annoyance. Jynx's tail flipping back and forth, and with a swift swipe of her paw, she raked her claws across Ravyn's arm. Ravyn bellowed out in pain, clutching her arm. "Ouch! You stupid little beast, you're going to regret that!" Ravyn's voice rang out, her eyes flashing with challenge as she glared down at Winnie's satchel, where Jynx was half-poking out with a mischievous glint in her eye. Jynx, clearly entertained, shot Ravyn a sassy stare, her eyes slowly dropping to a sly gaze. Winnie, startled by the sudden exchange, took off running, dashing back towards her dorm room as fast as she could. "You and your demon cat can't intimidate me, Winnie!" Ravyn shouted after her, her tone dripping with an impending doom.

Winnie didn't dare look back, her feet pounding the ground as she fled from Ravyn's wrath. But with each step, the angry shouts grew fainter, and Winnie's racing heart began to slow. She breathed a sigh of relief, her senses still on high alert, but the distance between her and Ravyn growing wider with every passing moment.

Winnie finally made it to her dorm room. Feeling a sense of relief wash over her from narrowly escaping, she pushed the door open and entered the room. She was finally safe from Ravyn's taunts and teasing. She slipped off the satchel from around her neck and set it down on her desk, letting out a gentle sigh. Jynx, who had been riding shotgun in the satchel, hopped out and promptly face-planted onto the floor, sprawling out into comical poses.

Winnie couldn't help but giggle at the sight of her cat, which looked like she'd been knocked out cold. "You're such a drama queen, Jynx," Winnie said, shaking her head in amusement. Jynx, still splayed out on the floor, gave Winnie a lazy blink before stretching out her long, black body and arching her back in a sluggish motion.

As the night wore on, Winnie became completely absorbed in her notes, her scribbled handwriting and hastily drawn diagrams a testament to the whirlwind of events that had unfolded earlier that day. Jynx, meanwhile, wandered lazily around the room, pausing to sniff at the shelves, paw at the curtains, and investigate the soft rustle of papers on Winnie's desk. Every so often, she'd jump up onto a nearby chair or table, only to leap down again a moment later, as if drawn to some invisible thread of curiosity that only she could see. As Winnie's pen scratched across the page, Jynx's gentle explorations provided a soothing background hum, a reminder that even in the midst of intense focus, there was still room for gentle companionship.

While Winnie was a clever little witch she was nowhere near a seasoned one let alone a confident one. She found herself hunched over her desk, surrounded by stacks of tomes, encyclopedias, and scattered notes from the day's events that took place. Jynx lounged in the windowsill, chasing the fading sunlight with lazy swipes of her paw. The emerald on her collar glinted, casting a tiny green glow on the wall.

Winnie's attention began to wane as she pored over her notes from the day's classes. The scribbled words and diagrams started to blur together, and she found herself struggling to focus. Just as she was about to yawn, a memory suddenly surfaced - her parents had given her a gift before dropping her off at Darkspire Academy, telling her to open it when she was alone in her room. Winnie's eyes lit up as she rummaged through her satchel, her fingers closing around a small, intricately wrapped package. The wrapping paper was a deep, midnight blue, adorned with tiny, silver stars and moons that seemed to shimmer in the dim light of her room.

As she began to un-wrap the package, Jynx, who had been lounging nearby, perked up and sat up straight, her ears twitching with curiosity. She tilted her head to one side, watching with interest as Winnie revealed the gift. The wrapping paper fell away, revealing an ancient tome bound in worn, black leather. The cover was embossed with intricate, golden filigree along with a strange golden symbol which she'd never seen before. Winnie's eyes widened as she ran her fingers over the cover, feeling a strange energy emanating from the book.

Winnie's mind began to fill with questions. What was this book, and why had her parents given it to her? She knew her parents were powerful witches, but she had never really understood what type of magic they specialized in. Was this book a clue to their mysterious past? Winnie's heart swelled with excitement and curiosity as she opened the book, revealing yellowed pages filled with strange symbols and illustrations. Jynx, sensing her mistress's fascination, leaned in closer, her whiskers twitching as she sniffed at the pages. Together, Winnie and Jynx studied the book, eager to uncover its secrets.

As the hours turned to days, and the days to weeks, Winnie's study of the mysterious book continued, her mind lost in theories and interpretations, but the book's true nature and purpose remained a puzzle she was still trying to solve. Despite her prolonged study, she still couldn't shake the feeling that she was only scratching the surface of the book's secrets. The more she read, at least what she was able to read, the more questions she seemed to have. Winnie's eyes scanned the pages, her fingers tracing the intricate symbols and illustrations that danced across the parchment. As she thumbed through the book, she stumbled upon a section that looked unlike anything she'd seen before - an ancient ritual, perhaps, or a forgotten incantation. The pages were yellowed and crackling with age, the text written in a language she didn't recognize. "What is this?" Winnie murmured, turning to Jynx with a questioning gaze. Jynx, who had been lounging nearby, turned her head towards Winnie showing interest in the mysterious passage as well.

"I don't even know how to read this Jynx," she said in bewilderment. "Nothing in this book seems to make any sense." she said in frustration. "Maybe, there's some kind

of information in another one of these books that can
help me understand what we're dealing with here," she
says as Jynx continued to ignore her. There was
something about these pages that seemed to fascinate
Winnie though; so much so they would not allow her eyes
to divert themselves away from the book. As she
continued staring at the page she began to slowly slide
her finger down the words written in the mysterious ink.

As Winnie's finger touched the first word, it began to
shimmer and dissolve, only to reappear in English. The
mysterious phrase "Quomodo accedere ad
Umbramortem" transformed into "How to access The
Shadowfel." Winnie's eyes widened as she whispered,
"What's The Shadowfel?" She hesitantly ran her fingers
over the pages, and the ancient text continued to
translate itself. "The Shadowfel is the land of nightmares
within a mortal's dreams." Winnie's voice rose in alarm
as she repeated, "Land of Nightmares?" As she read on,
her eyes scanned the passage, and her face grew pale.
"The Shadowfel allows a group to access the fears,
nightmares, anxieties, and traumas of a mortal being."
Suddenly, the pieces clicked into place, and Winnie's
voice rang out, "Jynx, I think this ritual was used by
witches and monsters to torment mortals within their
own dreams!" Her mind and heart grew heavy with the
weight of her discovery.

As Winnie's fingers traced out each of the words, they
came to rest on an incantation that seemed to pulse with
an otherworldly energy. A shiver ran down her spine as
she touched the final word, and the text shifted, revealing
the underlying message. "Jynx, look at this!" Winnie
whispered, but her enthusiasm was evident. She held up
the book, and Jynx meandered over, her tail swishing
gently behind her. Jynx batted at the pages, and Winnie
laughed, dodging the playful swipes. "Okay, okay, serious
face again," Winnie said, composing herself as she
studied the incantation. According to the text, six beings
would need to stand on six symbols to unlock the magic,
and then they could channel its power into any object of

their choosing. Winnie's eyes sparkled with curiosity. "What kind of object could we use, Jynx?" she mused, her mind began to wonder as her eyes scanned the room. Suddenly, her face lit up with glee. "I know, my crystal ball!" she exclaimed in a delightful tone.

Winnie, unlike many in the monster world, felt a sense of compassion towards those around her. "You know Jynx," Winnie said inquisitively, "If my ancestors used this book to stir up nightmares within the mortal dreams, I bet we could use it to stop them too!"

As Winnie studied the incantation for a second time, another shiver ran down her spine. "Six beings, six symbols...but who are they?" she whispered to Jynx. The cat meowed and batted at the pages, as if trying to offer suggestions. Winnie laughed. "I wish it were that simple, Jynx."

"I need to find five others who would be willing to stand with me; who share my sense of empathy," she muttered. "But where do I start?" Jynx jumped onto the desk, knocking over a pile of books as well as knocking the mysterious book out of Winnie's hands. Winnie sighed, "I guess we'll just have to figure it out together, huh?" she said as she started picking up the books. As she reached down and flipped over the mysterious book, she realized that Jynx in fact had knocked a page loose from within it. Another page was stuck to the back of the ritual page. It was an illustration of some kind but revealed ancient markings of what seemed to be the six symbols the incantation was referring to and an empty space for another resting in the center of them all.

With a determined expression falling upon her face, Winnie decided to begin her search. She had no idea who the others were or where to find them, but she was ready to assemble a team and face the nightmares that lurked in the shadows. Jynx, sensing Winnie's resolve, stood up straight, her eyes beaming with a warm glow of partnership. Together, they agreed to embark on a journey to find and gather the unknown team members as well as unlock the secrets of The Shadowfel.

Vaughn

In the shadowy alleys of The Midnight Sector, where moonlight struggled to penetrate the darkness, Vaughn stood atop a crumbling mausoleum, his black cape fluttering behind him like a dark wingspan. His bright, curious eyes scanned the rooftops, and for a moment, he felt like a superhero, not a vampire. His cape, with its bold red lining, made him feel invincible, like he could save the world from the shadows that enveloped the city's horizon.

But beneath his youthful enthusiasm, Vaughn struggled with the weight of his legacy. As a very young vampire, he grappled with the expectations placed upon him by his kind. The tales of old spoke of blood as sustenance, but Vaughn knew the truth: drinking blood wasn't about sustaining life, for their immortal hearts beat strong without it. Instead, it was a means to unleash their true power, to tap into the raw strength that coursed through the veins of the living. With each sip, a vampire's senses heightened, their muscles swelled with vitality, and their will became almost unbreakable. Yet, this potent elixir came at a terrible cost, for it was also a tool of domination, a way to assert control over the weak and subjugate the worthy. The idea of wielding such power over others made Vaughn's skin crawl, and he wondered if he could really follow in the footsteps of his elders. Vaughn's gaze fell upon the city below, its twisted spires and Gothic architecture a testament to the darkness that lurked within its heart.

He knew that soon, he would be expected to take his place among the vampire elite, but Vaughn wasn't sure if he was ready. He felt like a kid, not a monster. The question was, would he conform to the cruel traditions of his kind, or forge his own path, one that defied the legacy of bloodlust and dominance? The weight of his decision hung heavy in his heart, like the shadows that shrouded the city, waiting to swallow him whole.

Vaughn had a pretty keen view of the city from where he was positioned atop the mausoleum. He treated it like his safe space at times, a place to escape the pressures of his world. He could see much of the city from this viewpoint, and would sometimes sit for hours watching the "Abandoned" rummage inside the city walls. The term "Abandoned" seemed fitting for these fragile creatures, a reference to the way they'd been left to survive in the shadows. The Abandoned themselves were pale, almost translucent beings, their skin a deathly, pale bluish white from years of living in the dark. Their features were humanoid, yet eerily fragile, as if the very light of the world had been drained from them. Vaughn's gaze lingered on the Abandoned as they scurried about, their movements a mix of fear and resignation. He knew that to his kind, the Abandoned were little more than playthings, vessels for their power and sustenance. Yet, as he watched them, Vaughn couldn't shake the feeling that there was more to the Abandoned than met the eye.

Vaughn's curiosity got the better of him as he gazed out at their city below. He'd never seen one up close before, and the more he watched them, the more he wanted to know. What were their lives like, living in the shadows and scrounging for scraps? What drove them to keep moving, to keep surviving? The questions swirled in his mind, and he felt an overwhelming urge to get a closer look.

Tonight, of all nights, seemed like the perfect opportunity. Halloween was a time when the vampires of the Midnight Sector would flock to the city walls, reveling in the chaos and fear that came with the night. The Abandoned would be on high alert, and Vaughn figured that his presence might go unnoticed amidst the commotion.

Without thinking twice, Vaughn slid down from the mausoleum, his eyes fixed on the city walls in the distance. He'd never ventured inside before, but

something about the Abandoned drew him in. He wanted
to see them up close, to understand what made them tick.
And maybe, just maybe, he could learn something new
about the world beyond the Midnight Sector's narrow
view of the Abandoned being mere playthings.

With a sense of wonder and apprehension, Vaughn
set off towards the city walls, the shadows swallowing
him whole as he disappeared into the night.

Vaughn navigated through the darkness, his eyes
adjusting to the faint moonlight as he made his way down
the mountainside. The city walls loomed before him, a
sprawling structure of crumbling stone and twisted iron.
The stone boulders, once sturdy and imposing, now wore
the scars of time and neglect, their surfaces weathered
and worn. The iron bars that topped the wall seemed to
stretch on forever, a jagged latticework that cast long,
ominous shadows on the ground.

Vaughn's gaze lingered on the wall, his mind working
out the best way to gain entry. Climbing the tall structure
wouldn't be easy, and he wasn't yet skilled enough in the
art of transformation to slip through the bars unnoticed
as a bat. His kind could transform into the winged
creatures with ease, but for Vaughn, it was still a tricky
process. He'd attempted it before, a handful of times, but
he wasn't confident enough to risk it here, not when
stealth was crucial. Besides, drawing attention to himself
wasn't part of the plan. He wanted to observe, to learn,
without being seen.

As he scanned the wall, Vaughn's ears picked up the
distant sounds of laughter and screams. His elders, the
vampires of the Midnight Sector, were already indulging
in the night's festivities. He watched as a pair of them
swooped down, their dark silhouettes stark against the
moonlit sky. They taunted a group of The Abandoned
huddled together in a corner, their pale faces upturned in
fear.

Vaughn's eyes narrowed, a mixture of fascination and
discomfort stirring within him. He'd seen such scenes
before, but tonight, something felt different. Maybe it was

The Abandoned's desperate gaze, or the way they seemed to shrink away from the vampires' cruel words. Whatever the reason, Vaughn felt a pang of curiosity, a desire to understand these fragile creatures better.

He began to move along the wall, searching for a weak point, a place where he might slip in unnoticed. The stone boulders seemed to offer the best chance, their weathered surfaces providing potential handholds. Vaughn's eyes scanned the wall, his mind calculating the risks and benefits of making a move.

Vaughn's fingers grabbed at the iron bars, testing each one for weakness, searching for a spot where he could slip through undetected. The cold metal bit into his skin as he applied pressure, his senses heightened as he worked his way along the wall. The loose rocks crumbled beneath his touch, and he paused, holding his breath, each time, waiting to see if the sound would attract unwanted attention.

Finally, after what felt like an eternity, he found a spot where the structure had given way, creating a narrow opening just large enough for him to squeeze through. The gap was hidden behind a vacant building, its crumbling facade seeming to lean drunkenly against the adjacent structure. Vaughn's eyes lit with radiance as he realized he'd found his way in.

He crept around the building, his footsteps silent on the dusty ground. The windows, once bright and cheerful, now stared back at him like empty eyes, their panes cracked and broken. Vaughn's curiosity got the better of him and he peered into each window, trying to catch a glimpse of the building's past life. The rooms were bare, stripped of any furniture or fixtures, leaving only the echoes of memories behind.

As he approached the rear of the building, Vaughn heard a sound that made his heart skip a beat – the scream of a child, shrill and terrified. The sound grew louder, and Vaughn's instincts kicked in. He scrambled towards a broken window, hoisting himself up and through the jagged opening just as the screaming figure came into view.

Vaughn landed awkwardly on the dusty floor, his ears ringing from the sudden noise. He waited, frozen, expecting the screaming to stop, for the child to be comforted or silenced. But the sound only grew louder, more frantic, and Vaughn realized with a start that it wasn't a child at all – it was one of the Abandoned, and it was running straight for the building.

Vaughn's heart pounded in his chest as he crouched in the shadows, holding his breath and waiting to see what would happen next. The Abandoned's screams grew louder still, and Vaughn could hear the sound of footsteps pounding the ground, heavy and urgent. It was clear that the creature was being pursued, and Vaughn's mind started racing with worry; worry for the creature and worry that he'd be caught.

Vaughn's heart still racing, he slowly peeked out of the broken window, his eyes scanning the alley below. The childlike Abandoned was running down the narrow passageway, its tiny legs moving as fast as they could. The creature's face was contorted in fear, its eyes streaming with tears as it wailed in terror.

Vaughn's gaze followed the creature, his mind working overtime to understand what was happening. But as he watched, he realized that he couldn't see anything chasing the Abandoned. It seemed to be running solely out of fear.

Without thinking, Vaughn acted on instinct. He rushed to the door of the vacant building and flung it open, grabbing the Abandoned as it reached the entrance. He pulled the creature inside, slamming the door shut behind them.

As the Abandoned struggled in his grasp, Vaughn and the creature locked eyes. For a moment, they simply stared at each other in shock. Then, simultaneously, they both let out a blood-curdling scream and released each other. The Abandoned scurried to one side of the room, while Vaughn stumbled backward, his back hitting the wall as he frantically tried to put distance between himself and the creature.

Both Vaughn and the Abandoned cowered in opposite corners of the room, their eyes wide with fear as they stared at each other.

Vaughn's head slowly emerged from behind an old desk, where he'd taken cover after their initial terrified encounter. He peeked over the edge, his eyes locking onto the Abandoned child, who still cowered in the corner. Although he wasn't entirely sure, the child seemed to resemble a young girl, with features that were delicate and fragile. Vaughn's gaze met hers, and he stammered, trying to sound gentle. "H...h...hello?" he said softly. "Are you...ok?"

The Abandoned child didn't respond, her cries continuing persistently. She remained huddled in the corner, her small body shaking with each sob. Vaughn watched her, his curiosity getting the better of him.

"What were you running from?" Vaughn asked as he tried to comfort her and conceal himself at the same time. He ducked back behind the desk slightly and then popped back up, trying to gauge the child's reaction. "Did something scare you?"

The child's sounds were raw and animalistic, devoid of any discernible language. Vaughn's eyes remained fixed on her, searching for any sign of what she might be thinking or feeling.

"Can you understand me?" Vaughn asked, his voice softening. "Do you know where you are?"

The Abandoned child's gaze flicked up, her eyes meeting Vaughn's. For a moment, they simply stared at each other, the only sounds being the child's labored breathing and sniffling. Vaughn tried to smile, hoping to reassure her, but his lips trembled, and the smile faltered.

"I'm not going to hurt you," Vaughn said, trying to sound convincing. "I just want to...understand." He trailed off, unsure of how to finish the sentence. The silence between them was oppressive, heavy with unspoken fears and questions but before Vaughn could try to bridge the gap, a new sound echoed through the room – the soft thud of footsteps landing on the roof above. Vaughn's heart sank as he recognized the weighty, deliberate stride of one of the elders.

The Abandoned child's eyes flashed with terror as the footsteps echoed above, her small body tensing in anticipation of the worst. Vaughn's gaze met hers, and he saw the fear in her eyes spike, her pupils dilating as she cowered further into the corner. The elder's voice called out, muffled but unmistakable, searching for the child.

Vaughn sprang into action, rushing over to the girl's side. "Don't worry, I won't let him take you," he whispered urgently, trying to reassure her. "I know a way out. I can get us out of here. I just need a distraction first."

The child's eyes locked onto Vaughn's, her gaze filled with a desperate plea for help. Vaughn's thoughts were all over the place trying to think of ways to create a diversion. He glanced around the room, in search for something he could use to distract the elder but only noticed a broken window and a pile of debris.

As the elder's voice grew louder, Vaughn knew they had to act fast. He leaned in closer to the child; his voice became heroic yet comforting. "Get ready. We'll get out of here together."

Vaughn's mind was racing as he searched the room for something, anything, that could be used as a distraction. His eyes landed on a nearby piece of broken pipe, half-hidden under the pile of debris. He gestured to the child to stay put, and then crept over to the pipe, his movements silent.

As he picked up the pipe, the elder's voice grew louder, calling out to the child in a tone that was both commanding and cruel. Vaughn's grip on the pipe tightened, his heart pounding in his chest. He knew he had to act fast.

He turned to the child, his eyes locking onto hers. "Ready?" he mouthed, trying to convey a sense of calm despite the turmoil brewing inside him.

The child didn't respond, but her eyes seemed to bore into Vaughn's soul, as if searching for reassurance. Vaughn took a deep breath, gripping the pipe tightly, and nodded to himself. It was time to create the distraction.

Vaughn carefully positioned himself near the door, the pipe at the ready. He took a deep breath, preparing himself for what was to come. As the elder's voice grew louder, Vaughn knew it was only moments before he would burst through the door.

With a swift motion, Vaughn slammed the pipe into the nearby wall, creating a loud crash that echoed through the room. The elder's voice faltered, and for a moment, there was silence. Vaughn seized the opportunity, gesturing to the child to follow him.

"Come on!" he whispered urgently, already moving towards the window he'd used to enter the building. "We have to go, now!"

The child hesitated for a moment, her eyes darting towards the door as if expecting the elder to burst through at any second. Then, seeming to trust Vaughn's urgency, she scrambled to her feet and followed him towards the window.

Vaughn helped the child up to the windowsill, and she awkwardly climbed out into the alleyway. He quickly followed, dropping down beside her. Grabbing her hand, he whispered, "Follow me," and took off in a sprint.

The child stumbled to keep up, but Vaughn's grip on her hand kept her upright. They ran down the alley, Vaughn's eyes fixed on the crumbling wall ahead, the opening that had led him to this spot now serving as their escape route.

Meanwhile, the elder vampire had fallen for the distraction. He entered the abandoned building through the door, his eyes scanning the empty space. A sly smile spread across his face as he scraped his fingernail against the doorframe and his voice dripping with ill intent. "I know where you are, child," he taunted. "You escaped my clutches the first time but you won't be so lucky the next."

The elder's voice echoed through the empty building, unaware that his prey had already escaped.

As they crawled through the opening in the wall, Vaughn and the girl emerged on the other side, gasping for breath. They continued their frantic pace, dashing up the mountainside towards the mausoleum. The trees blurred together as they ran. The only sounds they could hear were those of their own as they struggled to catch their breath as they climbed the terrain.

Finally, they reached the top of the mountain and entered the graveyard, the mausoleum looming before them like a stone sentinel. Vaughn slowed to a stop, his chest heaving with exertion. "I think we're safe now," he said, trying to capture his breath again.

The girl didn't respond, but instead threw her arms around Vaughn's neck, hugging him tightly. The girl's hug caught Vaughn off guard, his unfamiliarity with emotional displays causing him to stiffen in response. However, as he felt her warmth and vulnerability, something shifted within him. He began to relax, his arms slowly wrapping around her in a gentle return of the embrace. The world around them faded into the background as they stood there, suspended in a moment of awkward yet tender connection.

As they sat side by side on the hilltop, the city below them a chaotic mess, Vaughn's gaze drifted out towards the darkness. "I'm really sorry about your home," he said softly, his voice nearly drowned out over the distant sounds of screams and shattering glass. "I wish things were different here for you... and me."

The girl turned to him, her eyes shining with a quiet admiration. Vaughn's words seemed to have touched something within her, and for a moment, she just looked at him, her gaze filled with a deep appreciation.

Vaughn's eyes met hers, and he smiled slightly, feeling a sense of connection he hadn't experienced before. "I don't even know your name," he said, his curiosity getting the better of him. "What do I call you?"

The girl's face lit up, and she bent down, picking up a stick from the ground. She began to sketch out her name in the dirt. As she finished, she looked up at Vaughn, her eyes sparkling with a hint of pride.

"Auri," the letters read, scrawled in the dirt before them.

Vaughn's eyes widened slightly, a sense of wonder crossing his face. This was the first time he'd known for certain that Auri understood him, that she was more than just a silent, frightened child. A real connection had been made, and Vaughn felt a sense of joy and curiosity at the prospect of interacting with one of The Abandoned in a way he'd never done before.

As they sat in the graveyard a little while longer, Vaughn felt a sense of connection he had never experienced before. He talked to Auri, sharing his thoughts and feelings, and was met with her silent understanding. He felt seen and heard in a way that was new to him.

As the night wore on, Vaughn glanced out at the city below. "It looks like the elders are starting to head back to their crypts," he said. "I think it's time I got you back home. Are you ready to head back into the city?"

Auri nodded, and Vaughn helped her to her feet. They descended the mountainside, making their way back to the crumbling wall where they had escaped earlier. As they reached the opening, Vaughn ushered Auri back through the gap, following closely behind her.

As they stood on the city side of the wall, Vaughn looked at Auri with a determined expression. "I don't know how yet, Auri, but I'm going to figure out a way to make a difference for others, like you and your family," he vowed. "Today helped me realize – YOU helped me realize, that there's more to life than just existing. I'm going to do my best to find out what that something is."

With that, Vaughn bid Auri farewell. Auri threw her arms around him once more, leaving him feeling a sense of purpose and direction that he had never known before but was now eager to pursue.

Freddy

In the quaint village of Brindlemire, a centuries-old well stood proudly in the center of the village, its stone walls bearing witness to generations of stories and secrets. Legends said that magic dwelled within its waters, and the villagers had long believed that the well was a source of wonder and enchantment.

For generations, the villagers had believed that the well held the power to grant wishes, heal the sick, and bring good fortune to those who visited with a pure heart. While many dismissed the notion of its magic as mere fantasy, the well remained a beloved landmark and a symbol of the village's rich history and folklore.

All Hallows' Eve and Halloween were special days in Brindlemire, a time of celebration and merriment to honor the magic of the well. For two days and two nights, the villagers would come together to feast, play games, and make merry. Nearly every villager would present a token to the well, making a wish in exchange for good fortune, health, and happiness. The air would be filled with laughter and music, and the village would be aglow with candles, lanterns, and fireflies.

The villagers would gather around the well, sharing stories and legends of its magic, and the children would toss coins into its waters, making wishes and dreams come true. It was a time of joy and wonder, a time to connect with the past and look towards the future.

For the village's only tailor, Ethan Sutorre, and his son, Freddy, this annual tradition held a special significance. They were inseparable, and their visits to the well had become a highlight over the years. As they stood before the well, Freddy's smile lit up with pure joy and Ethan would lift him up so he could toss a coin into the water, making a wish with all his heart.

This particular All Hallows' Eve, however, would prove to be different. Freddy fell gravely ill and Ethan's world began to unravel. Desperate to grant his son one last wish, Ethan carried Freddy in his arms, determined to reach the well in time. As they arrived, Freddy's condition worsened, and with a final breath he whispered his final wish: "Daddy, please be okay when I'm gone." His small hand, weakened by illness, released the token it held, and it dropped into the well's water with a soft "dip." The sound was followed by a gentle ripple that spread across the surface of the water, as if the well itself was responding to Freddy's plea.

Before Ethan could make his own wish, Freddy's eyes closed, and he went limp in his father's arms. Ethan held him tightly, tears streaming down his face as he cried out for his son to come back to him. His tears fell into the well, mingling with the water and the magic that lay within.

The next day, Ethan laid Freddy to rest in their family cemetery, his heart heavy with grief. He was still numb from the loss when an old woman appeared at his doorstep. Ethan answered, his eyes red-rimmed from crying, and muttered a somber "yes?"

The old woman's eyes, while different in color, seemed to hold a deep understanding, and began speaking in a gentle rhyme:

> *"I heard the call and I come with a gift,*
> *from a token that fell inside of the rift.*
> *Mixed with a tear that pure love had shed,*
> *to grant the wish your boy once led."*

Ethan stood before the woman, dazed and unsure what she meant, but the woman continued,

> *"Three things you must do before tonight's end,*
> *complete them in time to bring back your friend.*
> *A heart, a brain, a new body from four,*
> *shall begin the steps to open the door.*
> *Then place this toy upon his chest,*
> *to awaken said child from eternal rest."*

26

She handed Ethan a small teddy bear and began to leave, but not before turning back to say,

"One day a debt will come due, to which you'll answer when I call upon you."

And with that, she vanished into the shadows.

Ethan was left standing in his doorway, the teddy bear clutched in his hand, wondering if this was some kind of cruel joke or a genuine chance to bring Freddy back. But the pain of his loss and the love he had for his son drove him to consider the old woman's words. He would do anything to bring Freddy back, no matter the cost.

Ethan's mind reeled as he replayed the old woman's rhyme in his head. "Three things you must do before tonight's end..." He glanced at the clock on the wall: 6 pm. The sun had begun to set, casting a golden glow over the room. If he was going to follow through with this madness, he had less than six hours to complete the tasks.

With his grief commanding his actions, Ethan repeated the rhyme to himself, focusing on the first line: "Three things..." He felt a surge of adrenaline as he turned to rush out the door, heading towards the family cemetery where Freddy lay.

As he ran, the darkness gathering around him, Ethan couldn't shake off the feeling that this was either a wild goose chase or a chance at redemption. He pushed aside the doubts and focused on the task at hand, his heart pounding in his chest.

When he arrived at the cemetery, Ethan stood before Freddy's grave, his eyes welling up with tears. He took a deep breath and began to recite the rhyme again, trying to make sense of the words. "A heart, a brain, and a body from four..." What could it mean? And what was he supposed to do?

Despite the uncertainty, Ethan felt a spark of hope ignite within him to accept the challenge he'd now been presented with. He would do whatever it took to bring Freddy back, no matter how impossible it seemed. Now with a new focus, Ethan decided to begin search for the first item on the list: a heart. But what kind of heart was the old woman talking about. She couldn't have meant a real one could she?

Ethan's mind pounded with questions and doubts, but he pushed on, driven by his desperation to bring Freddy back. He thought about the old woman's words, trying to decipher their meaning. A heart, a brain, and a body from four... What kind of heart was she talking about? Was it a literal heart, or something more symbolic?

As he stood there, frozen in thought, Ethan's eyes wandered to the graves around him. His gaze fell upon his wife's grave, where a small, intricately carved wooden heart lay. He remembered helping Freddy create it from an old piece of wood on the day they laid her to rest. The memory of Freddy's words came flooding back: "This way I know my heart will always be with her." Ethan's emotions welled up as he admired the wooden heart, and in that moment, he was struck by the realization of just how pure and full of love his son's heart had been. He felt a deep sense of pride and love for Freddy, and the pain of his loss felt even more overwhelming. The wooden heart, though roughly carved, was a testament to Freddy's innocence and capacity for love.

Suddenly, a spark of inspiration struck Ethan. Could this be what the old woman meant; a symbolic heart rather than a literal one? He approached the grave and gently picked up the wooden heart, feeling a sense of hesitation and hope. Was this the first item on the list? He turned the heart over in his hands, studying it carefully. It felt... right.

With the wooden heart clutched in his hand, Ethan's driven purpose began to wash over him. He had one item down, two to go but what about the brain and the body from four? What exactly was he supposed to do for a brain? Ethan's mind was filled with more questions the more he focused on the task at hand. He had less than six hours to complete the tasks, and he wasn't going to waste any more time.

Ethan focused his attention on the second item on the list: a brain. He had no idea what it could be or mean, and the search was proving to be frustrating. Minutes turned into an hour as he scoured the house, searching for something, anything that might fit the old woman's rhyme.

As he tore through Freddy's room, Ethan's eyes landed on a small, worn-out notebook. It was Freddy's favorite sketchbook, filled with drawings of their adventures together. Ethan's heart skipped a beat as he flipped through the pages, memories flooding back. Freddy's scribbles, his laughter, his imagination... it was all there, captured in the notebook.

The notebook seemed to resonate with Ethan on a deep level, and he wondered if this might be the key to fulfilling the old woman's riddle. Was it possible that Freddy's thoughts and dreams, captured in these sketches, were the "brain" she had spoken of? As he held the notebook close, Ethan felt a deep connection to his son, and the familiar scribbles, drawings, and short stories transported him back to moments with Freddy, making it feel as though he was standing in the room with him once again.

With the wooden heart and the sketchbook in hand, Ethan felt like he was finally making some real progress. He had two items down, and now he just needed to figure out the body from four. Just like the other two clues though, he had no idea what that even meant? Ethan's mind was spiraling out of control with questions and he knew his deadline was almost up, but he was determined to find a way to finish what he had started. He glanced at the clock, relieved to see that only an hour had passed, and he still had a few hours left to complete the tasks he had been given.

Ethan's mind wrestled with the challenge of "body from four." He knew he couldn't use Freddy's actual body, so he had to interpret the rhyme literally - a body created from four components. As a tailor, Ethan had an idea. He could sew a body together using four different fabrics. He envisioned the project unfolding: a yellowish-green fabric for the bulk of the body, which he had in abundance from an unfinished project; black fabric for the suit and his hair, reminiscent of Freddy's favorite outfit; white for the shirt, crisp and clean, just like the ones Freddy used to wear. Ethan thought to himself, "But what about the fourth fabric?" as his eyes scanned his workshop, filled with rolls of colorful materials. He thought about Freddy's bright personality, his sparkling eyes... and suddenly, it clicked—blue for Freddy's eyes. "That's it!" Ethan exclaimed. "I'll use blue for his eyes, and that'll make a new body from four!"

With a surge of focus, Ethan began cutting out the fabric pieces, his scissors moving swiftly as he worked against the clock. Time flew by as he sewed the body together, carefully crafting every detail. He measured, pinned, and stitched with precision, pouring all his love and longing for Freddy into every seam. The hours ticked by, but Ethan didn't notice, consumed as he was by his task. Finally, after what felt like an eternity, the body began to take shape. Ethan's fingers moved deftly, stitching together the limbs, torso, and head. When he finally finished, he inserted the notebook into the head and the wooden heart into the chest. To his relief, he still had nineteen minutes to spare before midnight.

Ethan stepped back to admire his handiwork, his eyes welling up with tears once again. The sewn body looked nothing like his real son but still possessed a sense of being ... almost human. It was at least the same size as Freddy, and the fabrics seemed to capture his essence or would at least have to, seeing it was all he had to work with. Ethan's heart swelled with hope as he placed the teddy bear on the chest, just as the old woman had instructed. The familiar plush toy seemed to bring a sense of comfort to the makeshift body, and Ethan felt a pang of nostalgia. He sat down beside the body, his eyes fixed on the clock, waiting for the hands to strike twelve. The anticipation was unbearable and Ethan's heart pounded with angst but also skepticism. Would this really work? Would Freddy come back to life? He sat there staring at this oversized pile of fabric thinking how crazy he must be to go through all of this. The minutes ticked by, each one feeling like an eternity, as Ethan waited with bated breath for the clock to strike midnight.

The clock's final chime approached, and Ethan's anticipation grew. He sat upright in his seat, his eyes fixed intently on the sewn body, his heart racing with expectations. The air seemed to vibrate with tension as the clock's mechanism could be heard grinding, counting down the final seconds. Ethan's breath caught in his throat as the clock's seconds hand moved to eleven fifty-nine... eleven fifty-nine and fifty seconds... and then, the chime struck; it was midnight.

The twelfth and final chime resonated through the room, its echo fading away into silence. Ethan's gaze remained fixed on the sewn body, waiting for something, anything, to happen...but nothing did. The body remained lifeless, slumped on the table, its fabric limbs still and unmoving. Ethan's anticipation turned to confusion, and then to frustration. He felt like he'd been duped, like the old woman's promise had been nothing more than a cruel joke.

As the reality of the situation sunk in, Ethan's frustration boiled over into anger. He slammed his fist on the table, making the sewn body jolt. "Why?" he shouted, his voice echoing through the room. "Why would you do this to me? What kind of sick game is this?" His anger turned to rage, and he felt himself losing control. He thought of all the pain and suffering he'd endured, all the tears he'd shed for his son and for what? So some old woman could play a heartless trick on him?

As the anger burned itself out, it left behind a deep, aching sorrow. Ethan slumped forward; his body racked with sobs, and buried his face in the fabric leg of the sewn body. The weight of his grief crushed him, and he let out a primal wail, releasing all the pain and frustration he'd been holding in. He'd already lost his beloved and to come to terms with losing his son now was too much for him to bear. Tears streamed down his face, soaking into the fabric as he wept uncontrollably.

In that moment, Ethan felt like he'd hit rock bottom. He'd given up everything, risked everything, for a promise that had turned out to be nothing more than a lie. The old woman's words echoed in his mind, taunting him with their emptiness. He felt like he'd never be able to escape the pain, like it would consume him whole.

Just as his emotions seemed to reach a breaking point, Ethan felt a gentle touch on the back of his head. A soft, small voice whispered, "Don't cry, Daddy, it'll be okay." Ethan's body jerked upright, his eyes wide with shock, as he stared at the sewn body through his tear filled eyes. It was still slumped on the table, lifeless... or so he thought. Suddenly, the fabric body began to shift, its stitched limbs unfolding as it sat up. Ethan's gaze locked onto the face he had so carefully sewn together. He was at a loss for words.

The blue fabric eyes transformed into the most vibrant, sparkling orbs Ethan had ever seen. They shone with warmth and kindness, and the stitched mouth now wore a gentle, loving smile. Ethan's mind struggled to comprehend the transformation unfolding before him. The fabric body had taken on a life of its own, its stitched limbs and torso now possessing a soft, almost lifelike quality. As he gazed into the figure's eyes, Ethan felt his emotions surge out of control. Was this really Freddy, resurrected in a new, wondrous form? The possibility overwhelmed Ethan. His voice cracked as he called out, "Freddy?" The figure's stare locked onto his, and Ethan's breath caught in his throat, waiting for a response.

For a brief moment, they simply stared at one other. Then, the figure's smile grew, and it nodded its head. "Daddy," it said, its voice soft and gentle.

Ethan's heart swelled with joy. It was Freddy. It had to be. He reached out a hand, and the figure didn't flinch as Ethan's fingers touched its cheek. The skin was soft and warm, like real skin. Ethan's eyes, still welled with tears, studied softly the figure before him, his son, alive and smiling at him once again.

"Freddy, is that really you?" Ethan asked, his voice shaking with emotion.

The figure nodded again, and its smile grew wider. "I'm here, Daddy," it said. "I'm home."

Ethan pulled the figure into a tight hug, tears streaming down his face. He didn't care that Freddy wasn't exactly the same; he was alive, and that's all that mattered. As they hugged, Ethan felt a sense of peace wash over him. He had his son back and in that moment the world seemed to quiet around them.

As they pulled away from one another, Ethan looked into Freddy's eyes and saw a spark of recognition there. Ethan asked, "Do you remember me?" his voice full of hope.

Freddy's smile faltered for a moment, and then it returned. "I remember being with you, Daddy," Freddy said. "I remember playing and laughing. But it's all a little fuzzy."

Ethan smiled, relief washing over him. It didn't matter if Freddy's memories weren't perfect. "That's okay, kiddo," Ethan said. "We'll make new memories together. I'll help you remember."

Freddy nodded, and his smile grew wide again. "I'd like that, Daddy," he said.

As they hugged again, Ethan felt the truth settle in his chest: this was not only the beginning but a new beginning; one of a new journey, filled with second chances, fragile hope, and the promise of something brighter than what came before.

Wraps

Aridia, the City of Eternal Rest, stretched across the dunes like the shattered shell of something once mighty. Its buildings, crafted from crumbling stone and weathered wood, seemed to lean in, as if sharing macabre secrets. The streets were filled with the shambling undead, their tattered clothes and wrappings flapping in the breeze. Zombies lurched along, their vacant eyes fixed on some unknown horizon, while mummies wrapped in tattered linen shuffled along and their bandages unwinding like the threads of a frayed rope.

In this city of the dead, a young mummy named Wraps lived a life of quiet chaos. He was a clumsy, cheerful adolescent, always tripping over his own feet or knocking over objects with his gangly arms. His wrappings were constantly in disarray, and his eyes had a vacant, clueless stare that made him look like he was forever lost in thought. Despite his appearance, Wraps was a whiz with machines and gadgets, able to cobble together complex devices from scraps and parts.

Wraps' parents, the rulers of Aridia, looked upon their son with a mixture of pride and concern. They expected great things from their only child and heir, who would one day take the throne and rule over the city of the undead. To prepare him for this role, they had hired a new royal tutor, a stern-looking skeleton named Professor Grimmins.

Professor Grimmins stood tall, his bony frame imposing as he greeted Wraps in the palace courtyard. "Ah, young prince, I see you're... uh... enthusiastic," he said, eyeing Wraps' tangled wrappings and vacant stare.

Wraps beamed, his face splitting into a wide grin as he introduced himself, "Hi, I'm Wraps. It's nice to meet you, Professor Grimmins."

The professor nodded curtly. "Let's focus on your studies, shall we?"

Wraps nodded eagerly, trying to hide displaying signs of the faux happiness he felt from within. As he followed Professor Grimmins to the palace library, his mind began to wander. He thought about the gadgets he could build, the machines he could invent, and the wonders he could create if only he were free to pursue his own passions.

The problem was, Wraps' parents would never approve. They expected him to take the throne, to rule over Aridia with wisdom and honor, and despite his clumsiness and goofy demeanor, knew better than to defy his parents' wishes. He would have to find a way to balance his duties as future ruler with his own desires, all while keeping his true interests hidden from prying eyes.

As Wraps sat down at the library table, Professor Grimmins began to drone on about the history of Aridia's rulers. Wraps' eyes glazed over, his mind drifting to the workshop he had set up in secret, hidden away inside the castle walls. He couldn't wait to get back to his projects, to tinker, invent, and create. But for now, he would have to pretend to be the dutiful son, the future ruler of Aridia.

As Professor Grimmins lectured on, Wraps' attention wandered further and further. He doodled in the margins of his notes, sketching out designs for a new gadget that would revolutionize the way the undead did laundry. His mind was only focused on gears, pulleys, and levers, and he couldn't wait to get his hands on some materials to start building.

But every time he looked up, Professor Grimmins was staring at him, his bony face stern and disapproving. Wraps quickly snapped back to attention, trying to look interested in the lesson. He nodded along; pretending to take notes ...but beneath the calm, his mind was unfolding like one of his blueprints — each idea clicking into place, piece by piece.

The hours dragged on, and Wraps found himself growing more and more restless. He listened to the humdrum sounds of Professor Grimmins' voice, but the words themselves didn't register. His attention drifted off as Professor Grimmins turned to the chalkboard, scribbling notes about the rulers of Aridia from centuries past. Wraps' eyelids began to droop, and before he knew it, his head, wrapped fully in bandages, slumped forward, slamming down onto the desk, in front of him, with a loud thud.

For a brief moment, Wraps was out cold. But then, as Professor Grimmins turned back around, Wraps' head shot back up, his eyes wide awake and alert. Professor Grimmins' stare anchored on him, his eyes flashing with annoyance. "Pay attention, Wraps," he said sternly.

Wraps rubbed his bandaged head, trying to shake off the drowsiness. He nodded hastily, trying to look alert and interested, but his mind was still foggy from the sudden nap. He glanced around the room, trying to gather his wits, and then focused on Professor Grimmins, who was now glaring at him expectantly.

"The weight of this city's history is crushing, Your Highness," Grimmins said, his voice a mixture of reverence and despair. "Centuries of progress and conflict have shaped Aridia, including the wars with Queen Akhet's scarab legions, which have left an unforgettable mark on our city. Her dark magic has twisted the bodies of ill-fated tomb raiders, merging them with the sacred scarab beetles she reveres. What emerges is an army of grotesque, human-sized creatures that stalk the sands, armed for battle and capable of taking to the skies on buzzing wings. Through said magic these abominations are bound to her will, driven to serve her every whim or desire."

Wraps' gaze drifted out the window as Professor Grimmins spoke of Queen Akhet's scarab legions, his mind absorbing the weight of the threat. He understood the gravity of the situation - the potential destruction, the lives at risk, the city's uncertain future. Yet, the idea of leading the city's defense felt suffocating. Wraps felt out of place in the palace, where every move was scrutinized and every decision carried weight. Give him a quiet workshop, surrounded by gears and wires, and he was in his element.

In solitude, Wraps found freedom. No expectations, no obligations, no piercing eyes judging his every move. He could lose himself in the intricate tangling of gears and pistons, creating something new, something beautiful. The thought of trading this peaceful existence for the burdens of kingship was daunting. As he walked alongside Professor Grimmins, Wraps' thoughts bounced between his conflicting scenarios—to do what was expected of him or to follow his own heart.

The dire scenario presented by Grimmins wasn't lost on Wraps, but his introverted nature yearned for the simplicity of his workshop, where the only voice that mattered was his own. Queen Akhet's army might be a formidable force, but Wraps' true battle lay within—balancing his duties as a future ruler with his passion for engineering.

But for now, he had to put on a good face. He smiled and nodded along as Professor Grimmins discussed their next lesson, trying to look like the dutiful son and future ruler.

As they walked, Professor Grimmins seemed oblivious to Wraps' inner turmoil, launching into a detailed explanation of the upcoming lesson's topics. Wraps continued to play along but he felt trapped being forced into a role that didn't suit him. The palace's grand corridors and ornate chambers felt like a gilded cage, confining him to a life he truly didn't want.

As they approached the palace's central courtyard, Wraps spotted a group of courtiers and guards gathered near the entrance. They seemed to be waiting for the young prince, their faces somber and concerned. Professor Grimmins followed Wraps' gaze and cleared his throat, his expression turning serious.

"Your Highness, it seems your presence is required," he said low and measured. "Perhaps we can continue our lesson at a later time?"

Wraps' heart sank, sensing that something was amiss. He nodded, and Professor Grimmins bowed slightly before taking his leave. As the professor departed, Wraps turned to face the approaching group, his smile quickly melting from his face. What new challenge or responsibility was coming for him now? He steeled himself, preparing to face whatever duty called him.

The courtiers and guards approached Wraps, their faces solemn. "The king and queen request your presence in their chambers, Your Highness," one of them said, bowing slightly. Wraps nodded with curiosity and a touch of apprehension rising within him. He followed the guards through the palace's winding corridors. The ornate tapestries and sandstone floors a blur as he wondered what his parents wanted to discuss.

Upon entering the chamber room, Wraps was struck by the unusual sight of two elaborately decorated sarcophagi propped up against a sandstone wall. His parents, the king and queen, emerged from them, their faces regal and composed. The queen and king thank the guards before sending them on their way. The guards bowed and departed, closing the door behind them. The king and queen then turned their attention to Wraps.

"Ah, son, we're glad you're here," the king said in a warm tone. "We've been discussing the preparations for your upcoming coronation. It's going to be a grand affair, and we need to make sure you're prepared."

The queen smiled, her eyes sparkling with such enthusiasm, "...and the decorations! We'll have garlands of flowers draped across the city walls, and the citizens will be dressed in their finest attire. It will be a spectacle unlike anything Aridia has ever seen!"

The king nodded, his expression turning more serious. "And, Wraps, as king, you'll need to project strength and authority. I've arranged for you to begin training with the local army, to build your character and brute strength."

Wraps' eyes darted back and forth between his parents, feeling increasingly panicked. He couldn't take it anymore. "I don't want to be king, I want to be an inventor!" he blurted out.

His parents stopped mid-sentence, their faces frozen in shock. "What did you just say?" the king asked, defiance burning in his voice.

The king's face darkened "No son of mine is going to dismiss his—"

But the queen interrupted, speaking over him. "Honey, how do you know that you don't want to be king? You're still young, and—"

Their words were cut off by the sound of the door bursting open. The guards rushed in, their faces urgent. "My apologies, my liege, but this could not wait. Queen Akhet and a small army of her forces were seen just past the sand dunes of Aridia's outer territory, and it appears she's heading this way."

The queen's gasp filled the chamber as the king's face turned stern. "Gather our forces, now!" he barked at the guard. The guard hesitated, his expression grim. "Sire, our army is not at full strength. Part of our forces were sent out on expedition today and have not returned yet."

The king's panic turned to alarm. "Gather what troops we have, then! We must do what we can and hope the rest of our army returns soon." He turned to Wraps, who was trying to interject. "Dad, maybe I can—"

But the king cut him off, his voice firm and impatient. "We are not finished discussing what we were just talking about, but I do not have time for any more of your foolishness or nonsense right now. Go to your room and lock the door immediately!"

Wraps tried to protest, but his father wouldn't let him finish. "But—"

The king's voice rose to a shout. "NOW! I SAID MOVE!" He turned to the guard. "Escort my son to his room and lock the door from the outside. See that he stays there until I say otherwise."

The guard nodded, his face impassive, and grasped Wraps' arm. Wraps felt a surge of frustration and helplessness as he was led away from the chamber, the sound of his father's angry voice echoing behind him. As the door to his room closed, he heard the guard turn the key in the lock, trapping him inside. Wraps was left alone, with thoughts and fears of Queen Akhet's army and his own desperate desire to do something to help.

Wraps paced back and forth in his room, his thoughts tangled in a knot of frustration and worry. He knew he was trapped, with a guard stationed outside his door and no way to climb out the window. But he couldn't just sit idly by while his father faced Queen Akhet's army. He thought back to his workshop, where he had been tinkering with a new invention that might just be useful in the current situation.

If he could get to his workshop, he might be able to build something that could help his father's army. But first, he had to get out of his room without the guard noticing. Wraps' eyes scanned the room, searching for any possible means of escape. He knew it wouldn't be easy, but he was determined to help his father, even if it meant keeping it a secret.

The thought of his parents' disapproval stung, and Wraps felt a pang of anxiety from their dismissal. He had already angered them with his outburst about not wanting to be king. The idea of disappointing them further was unbearable. If he was going to help, he would have to do it without them knowing. The risk was worth it, though, if it meant protecting his father and the city.

Wraps' determination hardened, and he began to think of a plan. He would have to be careful and resourceful if he was going to escape and make it to his workshop undetected. But he was ready to take the risk. For his father, and for the city, he would do whatever it took.

Wraps' eyes scanned his room, searching for anything that might aid in his escape. He spotted a tiny smoke bomb on his workbench and picked it up, hoping to use it to disorient the guard long enough to escape. He planned to cast it underneath the door, creating a cloud of smoke that would give him the opportunity to pick the lock.

Wraps lit the fuse, expecting a billowing mist of smoke. Instead, a small stream of smoke and ash trickled out, and the device became wedged under the door. Wraps groaned, trying to retrieve it, but it was of no use. The smoke wafted up from under the door, but it was hardly enough to create the diversion he had hoped for. "Maybe the guard outside won't even notice?" He thought to himself.

Undeterred, Wraps continued his search for another way out. His eyes landed on a complex contraption, he was tinkering with earlier, with springs and gears. He examined it, thinking it might be useful somehow. As he tried to use it, the tool suddenly came apart, springs and gears flying off in all directions. One spring ricocheted off the wall and smacked him in the face, making him wince.

Wraps groaned, tossing the mangled tool aside. "That didn't go well," he muttered. He turned his attention to a large box at the end of his sarcophagus, rummaging through its contents. "There has to be something in here," he said, digging through the assortment of gadgets and tools.

As he searched, he pitched aside various items, his urgency growing. "A crossbow!" he exclaimed, holding up the weapon. "I didn't invent this, but it still gives me an idea!" Wraps took the crossbow to the window, loading a bolt and tying a rope to it. He fired the bolt at a statue in the palace courtyard, hoping to create a makeshift zip line.

The bolt hit its mark, and Wraps tied his bandages together, planning to slide down the rope. However, as he leaned out the window, he realized his bandages weren't long enough. They hung partway out, and as he started to lower himself, they began to unravel, leaving him dangling in mid-air like a yo-yo. Wraps' stomach dropped as he felt himself being slowly pulled back up, his bandages unwinding with a maddening slowness.

The guard outside his door was reeling him in like a fish on a line. The guard's face appeared in the window, a mixture of surprise and amusement on his features. "Your Highness, I was instructed to keep watch on you and to not let you out of this room for any reason," the guard said, his voice firm but slightly amused. "So, please, stop trying to escape."

Once back inside his room, Wraps, feeling a bit of false remorse, nodded vigorously, promising the guard, "I won't try to escape again, I swear. I was just... really anxious." His words trailed off as he continued to scan the room for an escape route, all while maintaining a sheepish grin. His gaze landed on a small vial on a nearby shelf, containing a potent sleeping potion he had invented. The potion, designed to induce deep relaxation and sleep, was perfect for his situation. With a contrite expression, Wraps shuffled towards the shelf, apologizing to the guard for his previous behavior. As he reached the shelf, he swiftly grabbed the vial and smashed it onto the floor in front of the guard, releasing a gentle cloud of vapor into the air. The guard, unaware of the impending danger, inhaled the fumes, which would soon take effect.

The guard's eyes began to water, and he started to cough violently, falling to one knee. Wraps watched with anticipation, thinking the guard was about to pass out. But to his surprise, the guard struggled to his feet, still coughing, and stumbled towards the door. Just as he reached the door, he turned to Wraps, his eyes streaming with tears, and raised his hand as if to speak then suddenly dropped fast and hard to the floor, knocked out cold.

A sly grin spread across Wraps' face as he mumbled, "Delayed but still effective," before stepping over the unconscious guard. Wraps took the opportunity to grab the key from the guard's belt and let himself out of the room. With a spring in his step, he made his way to his workshop, his excitement fueled by the thrill of outsmarting the guard and the prospect of pulling off a secret mission. The city was in peril, and Wraps saw this as his chance to prove himself. He slipped into his workshop, driven by a singular focus: to craft a solution that would help his father and the city, all without revealing his involvement.

Wraps' hands moved swiftly as he rummaged through his workshop, the dim light illuminating rows of half-finished projects and scattered tools. His eyes scanned the shelves, searching for the specific design he had been tinkering with. It was a defensive mechanism, one that could potentially repel Queen Akhet's soldiers and give the city's defenders an upper hand. The blueprints were tucked away in a dusty corner, covered in scribbled notes and crossed-out ideas.

As Wraps unfolded the plans, his mind began working through the challenges he knew lay ahead. He wasn't sure if the design would work as intended, but he had to try. The fate of his father and the city hung in the balance. Queen Akhet's military strategy seemed clear: she would rely on her soldiers to breach the city walls, while she, herself, remained at a safe distance. Wraps' priority was to thwart the soldiers' advance, buying time for his father's army to regroup and counterattack.

With his new plan in mind, Wraps set to work, his hands moving with a purpose as he began to refine his design. The clock was ticking, and every minute counted. He knew that if he could perfect his invention, it might be the turning point the city needed to survive the siege — or at least the one pressing down on them today.

With the blueprints in hand, Wraps began to refine his design. The light refractor, a device that could manipulate light to create illusions, was exactly what he needed to deceive the scarab soldiers. He worked tirelessly, his hands moving swiftly as he assembled the device.

As the sun began to set, casting a warm orange glow over the city, Wraps finally completed the machine. He carefully carried it to the roof of the palace, the highest point in the city, where it would have the greatest impact.

The roof offered an unobstructed view of the outer city, and the sunlight would amplify the effect of the refractor.

With a deep breath, Wraps activated the device, and a brilliant light burst forth, refracting and bending in a complex pattern. The city army, positioned below, seemed to grow larger and more formidable, their numbers appearing to swell. Wraps held his breath, hoping that the scarabs would fall for the illusion.

As the scarab soldiers approached, their ranks seemed to falter, their advance slowing. Wraps watched anxiously, his heart pounding in his chest. Would it work? Would the scarabs believe the illusion and retreat? The fate of the city could go either way at this point, and Wraps could only wait and watch as the scarabs hesitated, seemingly unsure of how to proceed.

The guards stood frozen, their shields at the ready, as they watched the scarab soldiers retreat into the distance. The sudden change in the enemy's behavior left them perplexed, and they exchanged uncertain glances. Some whispered among themselves, speculating about the reason behind the scarabs' abrupt withdrawal.

As the minutes ticked by, the guards remained vigilant, expecting a potential trap or counterattack. However, the silence that followed was deafening. The scarabs did not return, and the city army stood before the gates, confused and wary.

One of the guards, a grizzled veteran, cautiously approached the gate's edge, peering out into the distance. He saw nothing but the receding figures of the scarab soldiers, disappearing into the horizon. The guard turned back to his comrades, shaking his head in bewilderment.

"It seems we've been spared," he said, his voice carrying both relief and confusion. "...but why? What trickery is this?"

The guards continued to discuss the sudden turn of events, unsure of what to make of it. Meanwhile, on the palace roof, Wraps let out a sigh of relief, a broad smile spreading across his face. His plan had worked, and the city was safe – for the time being.

With the immediate danger passed, Wraps began to consider his next move. He knew that Queen Akhet would not take kindly to her soldiers' defeat, and she would likely regroup and plan an even more devastating attack. Wraps realized that he needed to continue working on his inventions, preparing for the next battle, and finding ways to protect the city from the queen's wrath.

With the city safe, Wraps knew he had to act quickly to cover his tracks. He carefully dismantled the light refractor, his thoughts consumed by the need for secrecy. He hurried back to his workshop, storing the device and blueprints away; ensuring no evidence of his involvement remained.

Next, Wraps rushed back to his room, his heart pounding in his chest. He turned the key, eased the door open, and let out a quiet breath— the guard was still sprawled in the same spot he'd left him. He pushed the guard, still dazed from being knocked out, out of the room and against the door frame, propping him up to make it seem like he had been standing guard the entire time. He placed the key back on his belt and closed the door behind him. Although the door couldn't be locked from the inside now, he waited patiently, pretending to have been confined to his room all afternoon.

Just as Wraps was holding his breath, the guard outside his door stirred, rubbing his head in confusion. Before he could piece together what had happened, the king appeared in the hallway, instructing the guard to unlock and open the door.

The guard, still disoriented, obeyed the king's orders, unaware that the door was already unlocked. As the king entered the room, Wraps remained motionless, curled up in his sarcophagus, pretending to be asleep.

The king's expression transformed from frustration to relief as he gazed upon his son, who appeared to be sleeping. Without a word, he turned and exited the chamber. The ruse had worked, and Wraps had managed to keep his secret safe – for now.

The door began to creak as the door shut, Wraps let out a sigh of relief, his eyes fluttering open. He felt a mix of emotions: pride, guilt, and frustration. Today had been a roller-coaster—he'd outsmarted the guards, built a working invention, and saved the city from Queen Akhet's army. Yet of all the emotions he bore, his parents' expectations weighed the most.

Wraps thought about the world outside his window, full of possibilities for everyone else, but narrowly defined paths for him. His life was already mapped out. He would follow in his father's footsteps, marry well, and maintain the family legacy.

The more he thought about it, the more suffocated he felt.

In his sarcophagus, surrounded by the darkness, Wraps made a silent vow. Today might be a good day, but he wouldn't let it be the last day he pursued his passion. He'd find a way to balance his love for inventing with the demands of his royal life. The thrill of creation coursed through his veins, and he couldn't imagine living without it.

As he lay there, an idea began to form. Perhaps his inventions could be more than just tools for survival; maybe they could be a means to freedom; freedom to choose his path, to follow his heart, and to forge his own destiny. The thought sparked a fire within him, and Wraps knew that he would continue to create, no matter the consequences.

As Wraps drifted off, a sense of purpose settled within him. The city may have been quiet, but his mind was ablaze with possibilities. The future was unwritten, and he was ready to shape it with his own hands. The night held its breath, unaware of the storm that was about to unfold.

Wyatt

In the small town of Lunara, surrounded by dense forest, myths and legends of shape-shifters have been passed down through generations. One popular tale that's been told and retold is the story of the Baraffinx, a terrifying creature said to roam the woods under the light of the full moon. According to legend, the Baraffinx is a shape shifter with the power to take on many forms, from a menacing beast to a seductive stranger.

The story goes that many years ago, a group of travelers ventured into the forest during a harsh winter, ignoring the warnings of the townspeople. As the days passed, the travelers vanished one by one, and the townsfolk whispered about the Baraffinx's involvement. Some claimed to have seen a figure lurking in the woods, its eyes glowing with an otherworldly light. Over time, the legend of the Baraffinx had become a cautionary tale, reminding residents of the dangers that lurk in the unknown and the importance of respecting nature.

As the years went by, the town of Lunara grew and prospered, but the legend of the Baraffinx remained a part of its fabric. The townspeople would often gather around the fireplace, sharing stories of strange occurrences and unexplained events. In the midst of these whispered warnings and eerie tales, Wyatt's family made their home, nestled in a secluded house on the town's forest border. Wyatt, their young son, grew up listening to the stories of the Baraffinx, his curiosity piqued but not yet stirred to action.

Wyatt's days were filled with school, sports, and hanging out with friends. He was a popular kid, and his life seemed pretty normal. But at night, he'd often lie in bed, listening to the sounds of the forest outside his window. The creaks and groans of the trees, the hooting of owls and the occasional howl of a distant animal all blended together to create a symphony of sounds that both fascinated and unsettled him.

As he drifted off to sleep, Wyatt would sometimes wonder if the stories of the Baraffinx were true. Was there really a shape-shifter lurking in the woods, waiting to pounce? Or were the stories just mere fantasy, meant to scare kids into behaving?

One night, as Wyatt was falling asleep, he thought he heard a strange noise outside his window – but on the second floor? It sounded like someone was scratching on the glass. He sat up in bed, his heart racing, and listened intently. The scratching stopped, and an unsettling silence fell over the house.

Wyatt mustered the courage to get out of bed and approach the window. The moonlit night revealed nothing out of the ordinary – just the gentle sway of tree branches in the distance. Convinced it was just his imagination, he returned to bed, determined to catch some rest before the morning alarm.

The next thing he knew, his mom was knocking on his door, calling out a cheerful "Good morning!" Wyatt groggily got out of bed, feeling the weight of his sleepless night. He shuffled to the bathroom to wash his face, hoping the cool water would revive him.

As Wyatt stood in front of the mirror, scrubbing his face with soap, he caught a glimpse of something peculiar in the reflection – a shape that vaguely resembled a wolf, though it was far-off and indistinct. Wyatt's heart skipped a beat as he quickly turned toward the window behind him, but there was nothing there, just the forest's trees standing tall and still.

Shrugging it off as a trick of the light, Wyatt finished washing up and headed downstairs to grab some breakfast before catching the bus. The familiar routine of morning chores and family chatter provided a comforting distraction from the strange occurrences of the night before.

As Wyatt walked through the school gates, the chatter of his classmates filled the air. Many called out his name, waving or nodding in greeting. Wyatt smiled and returned the greetings, his friendly demeanor making him a beloved figure in the school. Despite being part of the jock crowd, Wyatt's kind nature and genuine interest in others made him approachable to everyone.

As he made his way to his locker, Wyatt couldn't shake off the feeling of not quite belonging. Despite being popular and well-liked, he often felt like an outsider looking in. He knew the social dynamics of his school like the back of his hand, but he never quite felt like he fit into any one group.

Wyatt's thoughts were interrupted by the sound of his friends calling out to him. "Hey Wyatt, what's up?" "Yo, Wyatt, you ready for the game on Friday?" Wyatt smiled and responded, playing along with the banter, but his mind kept wandering back to the strange occurrences at home.

The bell rang, signaling the start of class. Wyatt grabbed his books and headed to his first period, the familiar routine of the school day providing a sense of comfort and normalcy. But as he walked down the hallway, he couldn't help but feel like something was off, like he was being watched.

As Wyatt returned home, he walked through the front door, his backpack slung over his shoulder. "Mom, Dad, I'm going to go hang out with my friends tonight," he said, trying to sound casual. "There's a party at the forest edge, and everyone's going to be there. It's All Hallows Eve, and it's a big deal in Lunara."

His parents exchanged a knowing glance, and his mom spoke up. "Wyatt, you know you can't go to that party. You have a lot of homework to catch up on, and besides, it's not safe."

Wyatt felt a surge of frustration. This was the third time this month his parents had said no to something with his friends. "Why can't I ever do anything with my friends?" he asked, his voice rising in anger. "You always give me some lame excuse, but you never tell me the real reason."

His parents' expressions turned stern. "Wyatt, we've told you before, there are certain things we don't want you involved in, and this party is one of them," his dad said firmly.

Wyatt's anger boiled over. "You never trust me! You never let me make my own decisions. I'm old enough to take care of myself!"

The argument escalated, with both sides raising their voices. Finally, his parents' faces turned red with anger. "That's it, Wyatt. You're grounded. You're going to go to your room, and you'll go straight to school and back home for the next few days. No parties, no hanging out with friends. Do you understand?"

Wyatt stormed off to his room, slamming the door behind him. He flopped onto his bed, feeling frustrated and trapped. As the night wore on, he lay there fuming, listening to the distant sounds of laughter and music from the party.

Just as he was starting to drift off, he heard a faint tapping on his window. He got up to investigate and saw his friends standing below, throwing tiny pebbles at the glass. "Hey – Wyatt, you coming to the party?" one of them called out softly.

Wyatt hesitated then shook his head. "I'm grounded. My parents won't let me go."

His friends encouraged him to find a way. "Come on, it'll be fun. We'll make sure you're safe. You can't miss out on this. We're going to have a blast!"

As they disappeared into the night, Wyatt's feelings of entrapment started to get the better of him. He sat back on his bed, a plan forming in his mind. He was going to that party, no matter what. He would just have to sneak out.

Wyatt climbed out of his window and dropped down to the ground, his heart pounding with excitement and a hint of fear. He glanced back up at his room, double-checking that he'd left everything as it should be, trying not to arouse suspicion. Satisfied, he took off toward the party, following the edge of the forest until he met up with his friends.

For a while, Wyatt stood around, his nerves getting the better of him. He'd never defied his parents like this before, and the uncertainty of their reaction when he got home weighed heavily on his mind. But before long, his friends spotted him and rushed over, cheering and high-fiving him for showing up.

One of them exclaimed, grinning "Dude, you made it! We knew you'd come through!"

Their enthusiasm was infectious, and Wyatt's anxiety began to fade. The music was loud and pulsating, with people dancing and laughing around the small fire pits that dotted the forest's edge. The older kids kept a watchful eye on the fires, ensuring everyone stayed safe while still having a great time.

As Wyatt let loose and started to enjoy himself, he thought, "Well, I'm in trouble anyway, might as well make the most of it." He let the music and the moment wash over him, feeling a sense of freedom he'd never experienced before. For tonight, at least, he was going to let go of his worries and just have some fun.

As he laughed and joked with his friends, Wyatt noticed a group of older kids gathered near the stage. They seemed to be discussing something in hushed tones, their faces serious. Wyatt's curiosity was piqued, and he wondered what was going on.

Suddenly, the music stopped, and one of the older kids stepped up to the microphone. "Alright everyone, it's time to get started. Tonight's challenge is going to be epic. Are you guys ready?"

The crowd cheered, and Wyatt felt a surge of adrenaline. He had no idea what the challenge entailed, but he was eager to find out. His friends grabbed him, pulling him toward the center of the gathering.

"You in, Wyatt?" one of them asked, grinning.

Wyatt hesitated for a moment, unsure of what they were even asking but the mood in the air was infectious.

He nodded, and his friends cheered, welcoming him to the challenge

The older kids grabbed the microphone, their energies continuing to hype up the crowd. "Are you guys ready for this year's challenge?" one of them asked, pausing for dramatic effect. "Tonight, we're going on a 'Find the Flag' adventure! It's simple: find a blue flag hidden in the forest and bring it back to us. There are five flags out there waiting to be discovered."

The crowd erupted into cheers as the older kids continued, "If you're participating, grab a flashlight from the buckets at the stage and start your search. The five individuals to return with a blue flag will not only win a title for this year, but they'll also secure a spot on tomorrow night's expedition team." Wyatt was new to this tradition so it wasn't a surprise that he asked his friends what the expedition team was.

One of his friends began explaining the stakes of the game. "Every year, a new challenge is announced, and the top five competitors earn a place on the expedition team. On Halloween night, the team heads into the forest to search for the Baraffinx's lair, each of them wearing a camera-equipped headband to record their journey and broadcast it to the rest of us," he concluded.

"Ok guys, let's get started!" the older kid exclaimed, as participants rushed to grab flashlights and head into the forest. Wyatt, now driven to find a flag and earn his spot on the expedition team, joined the throng of kids disappearing into the darkness. The night was steeped in intrigue and mystery, and the challenge was only beginning to unfold.

Wyatt and his friends made their way to the stage, each grabbing a flashlight from the bucket. As they ventured into the forest, they initially stuck together, their flashlights casting eerie shadows on the trees. However, it didn't take long for them to realize that staying in a group would actually hinder their chances of finding a flag. With a nod, they decided to split up, each heading in a different direction.

Wyatt watched as his friends disappeared into the darkness as well as the light from their flashlights. He was now alone. The sounds of the forest began to break its eerie silence that seemed to be there before. As he walked, his initial enthusiasm began to wane, replaced by doubts and uncertainty. What was he doing out here, anyway?

He kicked at the dirt, his footsteps echoing through the stillness. The forest seemed to stretch on forever, with no sign of a flag or any indication of where he was. Wyatt spotted a fallen tree and decided to take a break, sitting down on the damp wood.

As he sat there, he realized that he couldn't hear anyone else. The forest was quiet, except for the distant calls of nocturnal creatures. "How far have I actually traveled?" he wondered, feeling a sense of unease. "I don't even know where I am now?"

Just as he was starting to feel anxious, his flashlight began to flicker. "Great...now the batteries are dying," he muttered, his heart sinking. The light flashed on and off a few more times before shutting off for good.

Wyatt was plunged into darkness, the only light coming from the moon above. He looked up, feeling a sense of vulnerability. Trapped in the dense forest, with no idea which way to go or where he was, Wyatt's situation had just become a lot more complicated.

As Wyatt stood up, the weight of his situation crushed him. He felt lost, not just in the forest, but in life itself. His friends seemed distant, his parents suffocating, and his own luck seemed to be perpetually against him. Tomorrow was his birthday, but the thought of celebrating felt like a cruel joke. He was grounded, lost, and alone.

With a heavy sigh, Wyatt began to walk, the darkness seeming to swallow him whole. The moonlight filtering through the canopy above grew fainter, casting long, ominous shadows on the forest floor. The silence was oppressive, pierced only by the occasional hoot of an owl or the rustle of leaves.

The forest seemed to close in around him, the shadows deepening and the silence growing more deafening. Every step felt like a struggle, as if the trees themselves were trying to slow him down. The moonlight struggled to penetrate the canopy above the further he walked, casting dancing shadows on the ground below.

Wyatt's mind was a jumble of dark thoughts and fears. He felt utterly alone, abandoned by everyone and everything. The thought of not being missed, of disappearing without a ripple, was a bleak and terrifying prospect. He pushed himself to keep moving, driven by a desperate need to find a way out or at least to find something that would give him hope that he could. But with every step, the darkness seemed to press in closer, suffocating him.

As Wyatt continued through the forest, he couldn't shake off the familiar feeling of being watched. It was the same unsettling sensation he'd experienced earlier in the day, first when he was washing his face and saw a figure staring back at him from the window, and then again at school. The sensation sent a shiver down his spine, and he began to wonder if he was walking further into danger.

Convinced that he was heading in the wrong direction, Wyatt decided to alter his course. He hoped to stumble upon another participant or, better yet, find the edge of the forest. He veered off course, his ears straining to pick up any sound that might indicate the presence of others.

The silence continued to follow him like an unwelcome companion. Wyatt walked for what felt like an eternity, his senses on high alert as he scanned his surroundings for any sign of movement or life. The darkness seemed to press in around him, and he couldn't help but wonder if he was truly alone.

As Wyatt trudged through the forest, he suddenly spotted a shimmer in the distance. The knot in his stomach felt a tinge of relief as he called out, hoping to attract the attention of another participant. "Hello? Is anyone there?" he shouted, but his voice was swallowed up by the darkness. Undeterred, he quickened his pace, his eyes fixed on the spot where he'd seen the shimmer.

As he climbed through the thick underbrush, the shimmer seemed to vanish, leaving him staring into the inky blackness. Wyatt's heart sank, and he wondered if he'd just imagined it. But then, out of the corner of his eye, he caught another glimpse of movement. This time, it was right beside him.

He spun around, his heart rate increasing, and that's when he saw it. A pair of glowing eyes stared back at him, belonging to a creature unlike any he'd ever seen. The eyes seemed to bore into his very soul, and Wyatt felt a chill run down his spine. The creature's body was feline in shape, but its coat shimmered and rippled like the moonlight on water.

Wyatt's mind reeled as he tried to process what he was seeing. The creature's eyes seemed to hold a deep wisdom, but there was something unsettling about its gaze. He felt like he was being sized up, evaluated, and unfortunately, didn't quite meet the mark. The creature didn't seem to be moving, but Wyatt could sense its power, its presence radiating an otherworldly energy.

As he stood frozen, Wyatt had no idea that he was staring into the face of the mythical Baraffinx, a creature invisible to the naked eye of most humans. But something about this particular encounter felt—off. Wyatt's instincts screamed at him to run, but his legs seemed rooted to the spot. The Baraffinx's gaze held him captive, and he couldn't look away, even as a sense of primal fear began to build inside him.

Wyatt's eyes were locked onto the Baraffinx's gaze. As the creature began to move closer, its eyes still fixed on him, Wyatt saw the rows of jagged teeth in its open mouth. That was all the motivation he needed to break free from the trance-like state he'd been in. But what Wyatt didn't know was that the Baraffinx was taken aback by his sudden movement. The creature had never encountered a human who could break away from its gaze before, and this unexpected development piqued its interest. For a moment, the Baraffinx was stunned, its eyes narrowing as it watched Wyatt turn and run.

A surge of energy coursed through Wyatt's body, and he felt like he was running faster than he ever had before. He attributed it to adrenaline, but he didn't have time to think about it now. He kept his eyes fixed on the trees ahead, desperate to escape the creature's clutches. The moonlight began to filter through the trees, illuminating his path and casting long shadows behind him.

As he ran, Wyatt caught glimpses of the forest edge up ahead. He poured on the speed, his heart racing with fear. He didn't dare look back, fearing what he might see. The trees blurred together as he sprinted through them, his breath coming in ragged gasps.

Unbeknownst to Wyatt, he had snagged one of the blue flags on his clothing as he fled. It was tangled in his jacket, a trophy he hadn't even realized he'd won in his desperate bid for escape. Wyatt's sole focus was on getting out of the forest alive, and he didn't slow down until he saw the lights of the gathering in the distance.

Wyatt emerged from the forest, gasping for air as he stumbled into the clearing. His friends, noticing his frantic exit, rushed over to him. "Hey, you got a flag!" one of them exclaimed, pointing to the blue cloth tangled in Wyatt's jacket.

Still bent over, trying to catch his breath, Wyatt attempted to explain what had just happened. "Guys, I saw something...in the forest. It was...I don't know what it was, but it was huge and had these eyes...and teeth..." His words trailed off as he struggled to find the right description.

Some of his friends exchanged worried glances, but most of them burst out laughing. "Dude, it was probably just a wild animal," one of them said, chuckling. "The Baraffinx isn't real, Wyatt. It's just a legend."

Wyatt's face fell, but he knew what he had seen. He didn't need anyone else to believe him. Despite his friends' teasing, he couldn't shake off the feeling of being watched. As they tried to persuade him to head back to the party, Wyatt's eyes kept darting back towards the forest.

"Come on, let's just get back to the party," one of his friends said, clapping him on the back. "You need to return the flag anyway."

Wyatt hesitated, his mind still reeling from the encounter. But with his friends surrounding him, he reluctantly agreed to join them. As they walked back towards the party, Wyatt couldn't help but glance over his shoulder, his eyes scanning the forest's edge for any sign of movement. The feeling of being watched lingered, and he wondered if the creature was still out there, waiting for him.

As Wyatt stood by the fire pit, watching the commotion, one of the older kids took the microphone on stage. "It seems we have four of our five blue flags already found," he announced, scanning the crowd. "Who are we missing?"

Wyatt didn't react, his mind still preoccupied with the encounter in the forest but his friends, eager to claim victory, jumped at the opportunity. "Here! He's here!" they shouted, waving their arms wildly.

The kid on stage squinted into the crowd, his eyes locking onto Wyatt. "Ah, Wyatt, it looks like you've got the last flag! Come on up and turn it in!"

Wyatt's friends nudged him forward, urging him to join the celebration. With a sense of resignation, Wyatt trudged towards the stage; the blue flag still tangled in his jacket a tangible reminder of his terrifying encounter. As he climbed the steps, the crowd's cheers and applause washed over him, but he couldn't shake the feeling that he was being watched, that the forest's darkness still lingered just beyond the firelight.

As Wyatt pushed his way through the crowd towards the stage, a tall, imposing figure emerged from the sea of faces, his path intersecting with Wyatt's. The older kid's eyes locked onto Wyatt's, and for a moment, they just stared at each other. The kid's gaze was menacing, and Wyatt felt a shiver run down his spine. There was something familiar about the kid's features, but Wyatt couldn't quite place it. The feeling was unsettling, like a memory from a dream.

The kid brushed past Wyatt, pushing him back slightly as he continued on his way. Wyatt watched him continue moving past him, a sense of unease lingering. Shaking off the feeling, Wyatt handed the blue flag over to one of the girls standing on the stage. "Wyatt is our fifth and final winner, guys!" she announced, and the crowd erupted into a fresh wave of cheers.

Wyatt's eyes scanned the crowd from the stage, and he caught sight of the mysterious kid edging away from the party, bound for the forest. In a final, unnerving glance, the kid turned back locking eyes with Wyatt before vanishing into the darkness.

The older kids' announcement about the next day's search for the Baraffinx fell on deaf ears for Wyatt. After what he'd just experienced in the forest, he had no intention of going back. The party began to break up, and Wyatt made his way home, bracing himself for the punishment he knew was coming from his parents.

As he approached his house, he noticed the side door was already open. "That's weird," he thought, a sense of discomfort creeping in. He stepped inside and called out, "Mom? Dad?" but there was no response. Wyatt made his way down the hallway, calling out again, but still he was met with silence.

He ascended the stairs, wondering if his parents might be waiting for him in his room, ready to dish out his punishment. But as he reached the top floor, he was met with a sight that made his blood run cold. The door to his parents' room was splintered and broken, with giant claw marks on the trim. The door looked like it had been bolted from the inside and then smashed open with incredible force.

"What in the world?" Wyatt whispered, his heart pounding in his ears. He pushed open the door and was met with chaos. The room was in shambles, furniture overturned, clothes scattered everywhere. It looked like a wild animal had torn through the space, searching for something. But where were his parents? Wyatt's mind was jostling with worst-case scenarios as he frantically searched the room for any sign of them.

Wyatt scanned the room, taking in the chaos and destruction. "Where did they go?" he wondered, his thoughts racing with uncomfortable questions. "What happened here?" As he continued to survey the space, his gaze landed on the cedar chest at the foot of his parents' bed. Something caught his eye—a small, hidden compartment on the side seemed to have been shaken loose.

Curiosity piqued, Wyatt walked over to investigate. He pried open the compartment, revealing an intricately carved wooden box adorned with a crescent moon symbol. Alongside the box was an old, handwritten letter, rolled up like a scroll. Wyatt's hands trembled as he unrolled the letter and began to read it aloud.

"To our one and only," he read, his voice steady despite the turmoil inside. "If you're reading this letter, then we have either shared this with you or something tragic has taken place. Wyatt, it's time that you know the truth about some things, about us, about yourself."

As Wyatt read on, the words painted a vivid picture of a night many years ago. His parents had bought this land and built their home, dreaming of raising a family but fate had other plans. Years passed, and they had almost given up hope when a loud commotion at their back door changed everything. It was Hallows Eve, and they had found a woman, half-lying on their porch, battered and bruised. She was holding a tiny child in her arms, trying to keep it wrapped in her tattered clothing.

Wyatt's eyes scanned the page as he read about the woman's injuries—bite marks and bloody gashes covered her body. But it was her appearance that sent shivers down his spine. She had patches of gray fur on her arms, and her eyes seemed to gleam like those of a creature of

the night. Despite her condition, she had pleaded with his
parents to take care of him, to never let him out of their
sight.

The woman had removed a ring from her mangled
hand and given it to them, telling them that one day her
child would need it, and he'd need to know the truth. As
Wyatt read the words, he felt a deep connection to this
mysterious woman. He couldn't help but wonder what
had taken place prior to her showing up, and what had
ultimately become of her.

The letter ended with words of love and devotion
from his parents, who had raised him as their own
despite knowing the secrets surrounding his birth. "We
do not know anything about the ring or anything more
about your mother's message to us," Wyatt read, his voice
cracking. "But we do know that we have always loved you
as our own from that very day." The letter concluded with
a simple heartfelt message, "Love, Mom & Dad."

The words of the letter lingered on the page, but their
impact resonated deep within Wyatt. His gaze fell upon
the ring nestled in the intricately carved wooden box that
he felt an inexplicable bond to. The room around him
dissolved into the background, leaving only the
revelations from the letter and a sea of unanswered
questions. His mind buzzed with queries: What happened
to his parents? Who was the mysterious woman with
wolf-like features who gave him up? Was she his
biological mother? What's the significance of the ring his
father carefully kept safe? The questions grew heavy and
quickly, echoing through his mind like a haunting
melody, refusing to be silenced. A new journey was
dawning for Wyatt, one he never knew existed, and a
transformation was about to take place in more ways
than he could have ever imagined.

Boo

The Land of Lost Souls sprawled out under crimson red skies, illuminated only by flashes of lightning that cast an ethereal glow over the barren wasteland. In the distance, scarlet-tipped mountain peaks bled into deeper hues of eggplant and wine, their rugged silhouettes piercing the dark sky like claws raking at the heavens. Despite its desolate appearance, the Land of Lost Souls was a bustling hub of activity—a shopping district for the monster worlds, where creatures from all realms flocked to browse the eclectic mix of shops and services.

Shops such as "Hexpresso" brewed up steaming potions and enchanted elixirs, serving the monster crowd's cravings in the comforting guise of coffee. Just down the street stood "The Blood Bank"—neither a bank nor a bar, but a peculiar establishment where patrons could deposit and withdraw specimens of blood as casually as others might trade currency. And for those whose interests lay less in consumption and more in culture, the haunting canvases displayed within "The Art Ghoulery" offered a gallery experience unlike any other.

Among the assortment of stores, one stood out as a favorite among the monster crowds: Sweet Screams, a little haunted candy shop that served up sweet treats with a side of spine-tingling fun. The shop quickly became a sensation, attracting monsters from far and wide with its unique blend of worldly goods and spooky charm.

This haunted candy store was more than just a place to satisfy your sweet tooth though – it was really four delights in one. At the entrance lay "The Monster Market," the beating heart of Sweet Screams, where candies, gifts, and eerie apparel tempted every creature from across the monster realms. Beyond that shimmered "Scream Queens," the premier destination for a ghouls' night out, its gowns glowing like moonlight and stitched with hex-tra glamour for prom nights and haunted affairs alike. For those craving adventure, the Virtual Reality Arena offered monsters the chance to step into battles and fantastical quests, born of different worlds, escaping reality one scream at a time. And finally, the Tombstone Theatre invited all realms to gather beneath the stars, its ghostly screen flickering with spooky classics alongside romance, action, and comedies to rattle the bones. Sweet Screams had something for everyone, making it the perfect destination for monsters seeking a chill night out or a screaming good time.

Boo's parents, Wisp and Ember, had acquired Sweet Screams under mysterious circumstances. It had started with an unexpected letter, delivered to their doorstep one morning, offering them the deed to the shop. The letter was cryptic, with no return address and no indication of who the previous owner was. Despite their initial skepticism, Wisp and Ember already had interest in owning their own shop so they couldn't resist the opportunity in checking this one out. They arrived at the building, a sprawling structure with a faded sign creaking in the wind, and were surprised to find it vacant and untouched. The space fit their vision perfectly, and the deed was already in their hands, but it needed far more work before it could become what they dreamed of. As they explored the interior, they discovered a large, floor-length mirror hanging on the wall, in what looked to be a fitting room area. The mirror was dusty with a coffin shaped frame built around it. Despite their initial reservations, the couple decided to leave the mirror in place, using it to add a touch of elegance to the shop's décor.

With tireless devotion, Wisp and Ember poured their hearts and souls into transforming the shop into the beloved Sweet Screams. Their hard work paid off, and the shop quickly became a favorite haunt for monsters of all kinds. At the heart of it all was their young son, Boo, whose infectious enthusiasm and joyful energy drew customers in like a magnet. As a ghost, Boo's abilities

allowed him to float and glide through the shop with
effortless ease, but it was his extraordinary empathetic
gift that truly set him apart. He could sense the emotions
of those around him, tuning in to the subtlest shifts in
mood and atmosphere.

Unbeknownst to the family, the mirror harbored a
secret though, one that would soon be revealed to Boo on
a fateful night. But even before that revelation, Boo had
been inexplicably drawn to—and wary of—the mirror.
Whenever he passed by it, he felt a strange chill settle
over him. The mirror itself was unremarkable, reflecting
the shop's interior with perfect clarity, yet Boo couldn't
shake the feeling that there was more to it than met the
eye. His instincts whispered warnings, hinting that
whatever lay beyond the mirror's surface wasn't
necessarily benign.

One night, Boo caught a glimpse of movement out of
the corner of his eye, his gaze drifting toward the mirror.
As he turned to face it, he was startled to see his own
reflection distort and blur, its features shifting in a
fleeting moment of facial morphing. The image snapped
back into place almost instantly, leaving Boo wondering if
he'd really seen what he thought he saw. Rubbing his
eyes, he chalked it up to fatigue, but the unsettling
memory lingered, refusing to be shaken.

As the night wore on, Boo couldn't shake the feeling
that something was off. He helped his parents close up
the shop, but his mind kept wandering back to the
mirror. He replayed the moment in his head, wondering
if he had really seen his reflection distort or if it was just
his imagination playing tricks on him.

As he said goodnight to his parents and headed to
bed, Boo felt a nagging feeling of curiosity about the
mirror. He tried to focus on sleep, but his thoughts kept
drifting back to the strange occurrence.

The next night, as Boo was helping his parents prep
for closing, he found himself glancing at the mirror more
and more with each pass he'd make. His parents were

busy closing up the shop, and Boo's gaze drifted back to the mirror. That's when he noticed something strange.

The mirror seemed to be rippling, like the surface of a pond disturbed by a tossed stone. Boo felt a sudden jolt of surprise. Suddenly, a low, raspy voice whispered his name. "Boo."

Boo's confusion deepened as he spun around, thinking it was coming from behind him, but there was no one there. The voice seemed to be coming from the mirror itself. He turned back to the glass, and his eyes widened as an odd creature materialized within its silvery surface. The creature was small, with tiny horns on its head and a bluish-purple hue to its skin. A sheepish grin spread across its face, giving it a somewhat endearing and mischievous look. Its tail hung down behind it, ending in a sharp point.

"Hello, Boo," the creature said, its voice still low and menacing as he smiled. I've been waiting for you."

Boo's eyes locked onto the creatures mischievous grin as he stuttered out, "Who...Who are you and what do you want?" he asked, attempting to sound braver than he felt.

The creatures smile grew wider as he replied in his normal, more chipper voice and laughing, "Sorry, I couldn't resist. My name is Flip, and I live here!" Boo's confusion deepened but his anxiety began to subside at least. "Live here?" he repeated. "You mean, in the mirror?"

"Exactly," Flip exclaimed, his eyes sparkling with amusement.

Boo drifted closer to the mirror, his curiosity getting the better of him. "What are you exactly?" he asked, his voice filled with wonder. "I've never seen anything like you before in my entire life."

Flip chuckled. "I'm a demon – well, an imp to be more precise and the one who sent your parents the deed; allowing them to now own this shop."

Boo's brow furrowed in confusion. "Why would you do that?" he asked with uncertainty.

Flip's expression turned somber as he began to tell Boo his story. "The woman who owned this building before your family was a quiet but influential figure, surrounded in mystery. Her name was Samara, and she ran a shop that catered to the demons of The Burning; a fiery under-realm that's home to some of the most malevolent beings in existence. I used to live among them, but I never truly felt like I belonged. I was always an outcast, a gentle soul trapped in a world of darkness. Samara, however, saw something in me that no one else did – potential. She was a wise and powerful woman, with eyes that seemed to see right through to the soul. Her shop was a haven for the creatures of The Burning, a place where they could find solace and supplies. For me though, The Burning was a prison, a constant reminder of the fate that awaited me if I didn't escape but I also knew there really was no true escape from it. So, I begged Samara to help me, and she agreed. She created a special incantation, one that would transport my physical being into the mirror world, where I could live in safety. And this is where I've been ever since, waiting for someone with a caring nature like myself to take over the shop. When I saw your parents looking at the building across the street through the window, I knew they might be the ones. But it wasn't until I saw you, with your playful personality and kind heart, that I knew your family was the perfect fit."

Boo's face began to blush but also lit up with a sense of pride. He was thrilled to have finally found someone to talk to, someone who might actually understand him. But he knew he had to keep this a secret from his parents, just in case they decided to get rid of the mirror. For now, Boo decided to keep his newfound connection with Flip all to himself.

Boo smiled, a smile of joyfulness mixed with just the right amount of relief. "I'll keep your secret, Flip," he whispered. Flip smiled back. "Thanks, Boo. I knew I had a good feeling about you."

With that, Boo and Flip shared a sneaky glance between one another cementing their secret bond in that moment.

Flip's expression turned serious, his voice dropping to a soft whisper. "There's more to my story, Boo. You see, every demon in The Burning has a special gift, a unique ability that sets us apart. Mine is... complicated."

Boo's eyes widened with curiosity. "What do you mean?" he pressed, his brow furrowed in concern.

Flip leaned in closer, his words spilling out like a secret. "I can alter luck and fate, but it's a wild card. To make it work, someone has to place their hand on the mirror, recite a rhyme, and then read an incantation. When they do, my body splits in two—one half of me is kind and benevolent, while the other is dark and twisted."

A quiet gasp slipped from Boo, his eyes tracing Flip's expression for a deeper meaning hidden beneath the surface.

"The catch is, I don't know which half will break free," Flip continued, his voice steady despite the gravity of his words. "The half that escapes will attach itself to the person who summoned me, following them for 24 hours. And here's the kicker—no one can see it, not even the person it's attached to."

Boo's mind began composing question after question but Flip raised a hand forestalling him.

"There are rules to this, Boo. Once the spell is cast, it can't be undone. My body can split multiple times, but only once per person per day. The outcome is always a gamble, but it's my only chance at freedom."

Flip's gaze locked onto Boo's, his eyes burning with intensity. "If you get the good half, you'll be swimming in luck and fortune for 24 hours. But if you get the bad half... well, let's just say chaos and misfortune might be your only companions until the spell wears off."

Boo hesitated, weighing his options. He wanted to help Flip, but the risks seemed daunting. "I...uh...really want to help you out, being my new friend and all...," he said nervously, "...but I'm not entirely sure about all of this."

Flip nodded understandingly, his expression sympathetic. "I get it, Boo. It's a lot to take in. Don't worry; it won't change anything between us if you decide not to do it. You're still my friend, no matter what."

Just then, Boo's parents called out from the back of the shop, their voices growing louder. "Boo, time to close up for the night! Let's go!"

Boo glanced over his shoulder, then back at Flip. "Hey, I have to go for now," he said, "but let's talk more about this tomorrow."

As Boo turned to leave, Flip's smile was a soft goodbye. Boo's thoughts lingered on the mysterious proposal, his mind clouded with uncertainty. Flip watched him disappear into the hallway as his own form dissolved into the mirror's silvery depths, vanishing from sight.

The next day, Boo couldn't shake the memory of his conversation with Flip. He found himself glancing at the mirror more often than usual, wondering if he'd made the right decision. As he worked in the shop, his mind wandered back to the proposal. Good luck and fortune, or chaos and misfortune—the risks seemed high, but the potential rewards were tantalizing.

As the day drew to a close, Boo made his way back to the mirror, his heart beating slightly faster with anticipation. He stood before the glass, his reflection staring back at him. "Flip?" he called out softly.

The mirror's surface rippled, and Flip's form began to take shape. "Hey, Boo," he said, his smile warm. "I wasn't sure if you'd still want to talk to me after everything I explained yesterday."

"Of course I would!" Boo replied and followed with a deep breath, his mind made up. "And I've been thinking," he said, his voice firm. "I'm willing to take the risk. I'll do it."

Flip's eyes sparkled with excitement, but he said nothing, waiting for Boo to continue.

"Ok, I think I'm ready," Boo said with a shaky mix of readiness and doubt written on his face.

Flip's smile grew wider, and he raised an eyebrow, "Ok, but only if you're sure?" Boo nodded silently.

Flip's expression turned serious. "Alright, it's simple. Place your hand on the mirror; recite the rhyme, and then the incantation at the end. That's it."

Boo nodded again, his eyes fixed on the mirror. He reached out and placed his hand on the glass.

With a flick of his wrist, Flip revealed the words on the mirror's surface. Boo hesitated, took a deep breath, and began to read aloud:

"Flip the coin, fate's design,
Heads or tails, fortune's line.
One day's chance, a path to make,
Will yours grant, or will it take?
It's time to let the pendulum sway.
Invoco numisma fati, fortunae meae sorte."

The moment Boo finished speaking the incantation, the lights in the gift shop began to flicker on and off, casting eerie shadows on the walls. Boo's head jerked up, his eyes scanning the ceiling as he watched the lights dance. When they steadied themselves, Boo's gaze returned to the mirror, and his eyes widened in shock.

Flip's body was contorting, twisting and morphing in ways that seemed impossible. Boo's stomach churned with panic as he watched, frozen in place.

Seconds later, a second Flip emerged from the first, identical in appearance yet starkly different in demeanor. One Flip radiated innocence and happiness, his smile warm and genuine. The other Flip, however, was a nightmare incarnate. His smile was a twisted, sinister grin that seemed to darken the air around him. His eyes gleamed with an unearthly intensity, as if they could extinguish the brightest lights.

Boo's fear spiked, and he floated back from the mirror, his mind reeling with the implications of what he'd just witnessed. The two Flips placed their hands on the inside of the mirror, and Boo held his breath. One of them remained behind the glass, while the other disappeared from view.

As the evil Flip's form lingered behind the glass, Boo felt a wave of relief wash over him. The sinister grin still twisted the second Flip's face, but at least it was contained. The other Flip, the one with the warm smile, now stood before Boo, his eyes shining with an aura of good fortune and then as quick as he appeared before him he disappeared once again.

Boo felt it – a shift in the atmosphere, a spark of potential. He couldn't quite explain it, but the air vibrated with promise. With a thrill of anticipation, he sensed that the next twenty-four hours would be filled with delights and possibility. The future felt bright, and Boo couldn't wait to see just what was in store for him.

As the day went on, Boo's luck continued to shine. Monsters strolled into the shop, and to his surprise, they started engaging with him in conversations. They laughed at his jokes, asked about the variety of goodies, and even complimented the decorations. Boo beamed with pride, feeling like he was finally breaking through the ice.

One group of rowdy werewolves left a generous tip, which made Boo's eyes widen in delight. He had never received a tip before, and the gesture made him feel appreciated.

Just when he thought things couldn't get any better, a zombie with a charismatic stage presence walked into the shop. Boo's jaw dropped as he realized it was none other than Havok, the lead singer of his favorite band, Flesh Meat.

Havok flashed Boo a weathered smile, his pale skin and dark eyes giving him a hauntingly cool look. "Hey little friend, I'm looking for an unusual candy that's hard to find and I was told you guys may possibly have it" he said, his voice low and gravelly. Boo stumbled over his words, star struck, but managed to get the details and deliver the treat with a smile.

As Havok reached out to grab the treat, he patted the counter in front of him a few times followed with a, "Thanks, champ." He had scribbled something on a small photo and left it on the counter for Boo. The photo showed Havok in all his undead glory, microphone in hand and it read, "To Boo, keep it fresh in the crypt – Havok." With a nod, Havok turned and shuffled out of the shop, leaving Boo radiating enthusiasm.

As the day drew to a close, Boo's parents called out to him, reminding him to start wrapping things up. Boo began to gather the scraps of trash scattered across the shop floor. When he slid one of the boxes aside, a small piece of paper caught his eye — a torn scrap with writing on it; it sounded like a fortune cookie, "Your crew will grow."

It was an extremely strange thing to stumble across, he thought, especially on a day that had been going so well. Yet he kept circling back to it, wondering if its appearance was intentional — meant for him alone. Could the message mean new staff members were joining the shop? Or maybe it was a sign that he'd finally find friends beyond Flip? The mysterious note seemed to speak directly to him, filling him with an eagerness he was more than ready to embrace.

Before he could ponder further, his parents called out, "Boo, let's go. It's time to close up shop!" Boo hastily finished his tasks and trailed behind his parents, his mind still spinning with the promise of what was to come.

As Boo and his parents entered their house, Boo immediately rushed up to his room to put his new autographed photo of Havok up on his wall. He still couldn't believe he got to meet him. He floated over and laid down on his bed thinking about how wonderful the events of the day had been for him until he finally fell asleep.

The next day at the shop, Boo, still glowing from yesterday, greeted a customer that had just walked. The customer glanced over at Boo with a bit of a snarl look and continued to walk past him. "I guess things are already back to normal," Boo said with a shrug.

Boo made his way over to the mirror in the fitting room and called out for Flip. Flip appeared in the mirror with a smile on his face. "How did things go yesterday?" he asked out of curiosity.

Boo told him about his amazing encounter with Havok, from the candy order to the autographed photo. Flip listened intently, his smile growing wider as Boo spoke.

When Boo finished, Flip's expression turned thoughtful. "You know, Boo, even though I get to partly escape the mirror world for a day when the spell is cast, I never have any recollection of the events that transpire after I leave it."

"Oh...," Boo said, his eyes widening in understanding. "That must be weird." Flip nodded. "It is, but I'm used to it. It's just the way things work between our worlds."

Boo's eyes shone with excitement as he locked glances with Flip. "I'm so tempted to do it all again today," he confessed, still basking in the glow of yesterday's encounter with Havok.

Flip nodded understandingly, but his tone was cautious. "I get it, Boo. But you know how unpredictable things can get. Are you sure you're ready for that?"

Boo's eyes clouded, his voice still low in tone. "I know, Flip, but after this, going back to feeling invisible just feels suffocating. I know I'm a ghost, but I want to be seen. I don't want to be ignored again. I want others to like me for who I am."

Flip's voice was warm and genuine. "I like you for who you are, Boo."

Boo looked down, his voice low and subdued. "Thanks Flip. I like you too. But sometimes it feels like that's not enough. Like, if I vanished, would anyone even notice? I struggle to find my place, and it feels like the world doesn't want me around."

Flip's eyes widened in surprise, "Boo, I had no idea you felt this way. You always seem so cheerful."

Boo's smile faltered, tinged with sadness. "That's because I'm good at pretending, Flip. Keeping up the act is exhausting."

Flip's voice gentled. "I'm sorry you've felt so alone for so long. It's not unusual for someone to try to carry everything by themselves — anyone would, if they thought they had to. Sometimes, though, that weight is too much for one soul to hold alone and you shouldn't feel like you have to do that anymore. I may not be much when it comes to physically being there for you, but I'll always be *here* for you."

Boo wouldn't understand it yet, but those words would settle deep, becoming a quiet strength he'd reach for when the world grew dark.

Flip let a grin slip in. "Well... now that we've established that you've got one truly amazing thing in your life — me — I'd say things are already looking up. I *am* the master of good luck and great fortune, after all."

Boo let out a small chuckle. "You're right." Flip's smile softened, and his voice followed with gentle warmth. "I don't want you thinking you have to cast that spell again just to feel worthy of something. But if you decide you want to... I'm all in."

Boo's eyes brightened a little, and he lifted his head, meeting Flip's gaze with the beginnings of a smile. "Thanks Flip. I really appreciate that. I thought about this all night, and... I just want more days like yesterday. I'm know the risks and I'm willing to accept them. So— I think I'm ready." he said, but just as Flip was about to flick his wrist to expose the spell again, a purplish ball appeared in the shop next to Boo and the mirror.

Boo floated back, unsure what was happening, while Flip watched in amazement from behind the mirror's reflection. The purplish ball began to expand, revealing what looked to be... "A wooden door?" Boo questioned, his voice filled with wonder.

Just as Boo finished speaking, the door creaked open, and out walked a young girl accompanied with a solid black cat companion. Her long, curly autumn-colored hair cascaded down her back, and her bright hazel-colored eyes sparkled with curiosity. The cat, sensing Boo's gaze, turned to face him, its eyes gleaming with the color of envy just like the emerald stone hanging upon its collar.

Boo's eyes widened and his mouth dropped open as he took in the sight of the unexpected arrivals. "Wh...Wh...Who are you?" he asked, bewildered. One thing was certain - the arrival of this young girl and her cat was undeniably magical.

When Fate Comes Knocking

The young girl and her cat companion stepped through the magical doorway, and it shut behind her, collapsing within itself before disappearing into thin air. "What a rush!" the young girl exclaimed.

"Oh gosh, I'm sorry. My name is Winnie, and this is my trusty sidekick, Jynx!" Winnie giggled as Jynx gave her a side-eye expression, clearly unimpressed by the "sidekick" label.

Boo's expression remained stoic, but he managed a polite smile. "Nice to meet the both of you. Where exactly did you come from?"

Winnie's grin faltered for a moment as she considered the question. "Well, that's kind of a long story. I've been practicing with my traveling spell and it opened this door in about twelve different locations, none of which I knew anything about. I wasn't sure where we'd end up."

Winnie's face lit up again. "But I'm not sure where we are now either. So, where are we?"

Boo barely moved his facial expression. "The Land of Lost Souls."

Winnie jumped up and down, her excitement infectious. "Yay! It worked! Well, maybe... but even if it didn't, at least we know where we are this time, Jynx. And if our trip is a total loss, we can still get food while we're here." Jynx purred in agreement, her gaze fixed on Winnie with a hungry gleam at the mention of food.

Boo's curiosity got the better of him. "Where were you trying to go?" he asked his voice a little softer now.

Winnie's face lit up again. "Here! Well, not here, here, but to the shopping district. I wanted to pick up some ingredients for a new spell I'm working on for a special project."

Boo's eyes sparkled with intrigue. "A special project, you say? That sounds fascinating."

Just as Boo was about to ask more questions, he realized he hadn't introduced himself. "I'm sorry; I forgot to tell you who I am! I'm Boo, and this is my friend Flip." Boo pointed to the mirror, but there was no one there.

Winnie glanced at the vacant mirror and whispered to Jynx under her breath, "Great, a ghost with a vanity problem" Jynx nodded her head and raised her brow, completing the confused look.

Just then, Flip formed inside the mirror once more and said, "Hello!" Winnie screamed and jumped back, startled, while Jynx stood on her tiptoes, her back arched and raised fur, hissing at the mirror.

Boo chuckled. "Sorry about that. Flip can be a bit...unpredictable." He smiled apologetically, trying to calm Winnie and Jynx down.

As Winnie's excitement died down, she looked around and noticed they were standing in a colorful candy shop. "Wow, this place is...bright!"

Boo nodded. "Welcome to Sweet Screams. Best sweets in the Land of Lost Souls."

Winnie's eyes widened as she took in the wacky decorations and variety of candies. "I've never seen anything like this! Is this part of the shopping district?"

Boo smiled. "Yes, it is. Sweet Screams is fairly new but it's already become a local favorite."

Winnie's face lit up. "Well, in that case, let's get some goodies! Jynx loves candy." Jynx meowed in agreement once again.

Boo turned to the mirror and said, "Flip, I wish you could join us, but I'll be back soon." Flip smiled understandingly and said, "No problem, I get it." Boo nodded and gestured for Winnie and Jynx to follow him. "Let's get some candy, and you can tell me more about your special project," he said, his eyes sparkling with genuine interest. Winnie agreed enthusiastically, and they headed to the gift shop area.

Behind the counter stood Boo's mom, Ember, with a warm smile as Boo introduced her to his newly acquired acquaintances. "Hey, Mom," Boo said, "this is Winnie and her cat Jynx. They'd love some candy." Ember's eyes lit up as she greeted Winnie, "Wonderful to meet you, Winnie!" Jynx let out a soft grunted snort, and Ember leaned over the counter, apologizing with a chuckle, "Sorry, little one, nice to meet you too!" Jynx perked up, seeming pleased with the acknowledgment.

Boo beamed with pride as he watched his mom work her magic. "My mom's amazing at picking out the perfect flavor of sweet, even without knowing you," he said. Ember chuckled, "That's what they say," her eyes twinkling with amusement.

Winnie's eyes widened as she scanned the colorful array of candy flavors and baked goods. "With so many options, I'm glad someone's picking for me! I wouldn't know where to start," she admitted, feeling a bit overwhelmed. Ember studied Winnie briefly, taking in her enthusiasm and curiosity.

After a moment, Ember decided, "I think 'Black Magic' would be perfect for you, Winnie. It's a delicious red velvet and chocolate fudge" Winnie's eyes lit up in delight. "Yes, please!" she exclaimed, her excitcment being very evident. As Ember began filling Winnie's order, Jynx jumped onto Winnie's shoulder, ensuring she wasn't overlooked. Ember smiled at Jynx and said, "And for you, little one, I think the `Catastrophic Peanut Butter Chews' would be just right." Jynx purred contentedly, rubbing against Winnie's cheek as Ember handed Winnie her treats.

As they moved down the counter, Boo asked Winnie to tell him more about her special project. Winnie took a deep breath and began to share her story. "I'm a new student at Darkspire Academy," she said, "where witches learn to master dark magic."

Boo's eyes widened slightly at the mention of dark magic. "Does that mean you're, like, an evil witch?" he asked, his curiosity getting the better of him. Winnie shook her head emphatically, "No, not at all! I mean, I guess I'm supposed to fit the mold but I just don't feel that way. I've always wanted to use my abilities to help people, not harm them."

Boo's expression softened as he listened to Winnie's words. He felt a sense of kinship with her. "I know exactly what you mean," he said with understanding. "I've never really fit in with the other monsters or ghosts, either."

As Boo spoke, Jynx jumped down from Winnie's shoulder and padded across the counter towards her peanut butter chews, which sat next to Boo. Suddenly, the emerald gem on her collar began to glow brighter, pulsing with some type of supernatural energy. Winnie's eyes widened in surprise, "That's weird — It's never done that before."

Boo's eyes locked onto the gem, intrigued. "Maybe it's reacting to something about me?" he mused, his gaze fixed on the glowing stone. Meanwhile, Jynx was not looking to entertain whatever was going on with her necklace — her mission was to nibble on the treats before her, and she was singularly focused on enjoying every last bite.

The glow of the necklace became steady, and an image appeared within the gemstone. It was an image of Boo, crystal clear and unmistakable. As Winnie stared into the gem, her eyes widened with amazement. Suddenly, it all clicked into place — Boo must be one of the six she required to cast her spell! A thrill ran through her, and she felt a sense of excitement building in her chest.

Winnie stood there, in awe, focused on the gemstone and flooded with questions. How did this happen? The connection between Jynx's collar and finding Boo made no sense to her. She combed through her memories for anything she might have missed, and then a second realization struck her hard — her locator spell. Jynx had been in her satchel when she cast the spell on herself, meaning Jynx must have gotten caught up in the spell as well.

Apparently, the locator spell had lingered in Jynx's collar, remaining dormant until something triggered it.

Reading aloud from the spell book must have been the catalyst that reactivated the spell, connecting it to Boo and now she hoped to the other four as well. The spark of realization lit up her smile as she continued connecting the dots. She felt a surge of happiness and relief wash over her.

Still wearing that huge grin, Winnie chomped into another piece of fudge. With her mouth full, she mumbled through the chew, "I feel like you're gonna be seeing me a whole lot more around here now, buddy!" Boo stared back at her displaying a mix of confusion and curiosity, clearly unsure what to make of Winnie's sudden enthusiasm.

Winnie and Jynx finished their delights, and Winnie began to fill Boo in on her parents' mysterious history. "I enrolled in Darkspire Academy because that's where both of my parents made a name for themselves when they were younger," she said. "But other than that, I really know nothing more about the type of magic they specialized in."

Winnie's eyes sparkled with curiosity. "It wasn't until I un-wrapped my gift from them inside my room that I received the first piece of that puzzle. It was an extremely old book," she said, pulling it out of her satchel to show Boo.

Boo's eyes widened as he took in the book's worn leather cover and its pages with tattered edging. "Winnie, that's a very powerful tome you have there," he said, his voice filled with awe. Winnie looked at him quizzically. "Huh?" she said.

Boo explained, "One of my special abilities is being able to focus on energies around me. I can even see them, and I'm telling you, I've never seen anything emit so much power from it before in all my life." Awestruck, Winnie gazed at her book with fresh eyes, humbled by the realization that she had unknowingly possessed such a potent magical artifact all along.

She opened the book and showed Boo the ancient spell she had run across earlier. "See, right here," she said, pointing to the intricate script. "It says I need a total of six beings, but not just any beings – they have to be beings similar to myself for the spell to work." Boo's face paled as he realized the implications.

Winnie's voice filled with excitement. "Boo, I still don't know much about my family history, but I know this book is a part of it. It looks like it grants the user the ability to manipulate the dream world, also known as The Shadowfel. It's my belief that my ancestors wielded this to terrify and destroy anyone around them from within their dreams. But then it hit me — if they could use dreams to harm, then we could use them to save."

Boo looked terrified. "I'm not a hero, though, Winnie! I'm not even brave! Everything scares me!" Winnie's face lit up with a warm smile. "Do I scare you?" she asked. Boo hesitated before answering, "Well, no... not really you, per se." Winnie chimed in with a triumphant "Well, then see!"

Boo continued, speaking with growing unease, "But your cat kind of does!" Jynx, lying on the counter and licking her paw, glanced over at Boo and gave him a mischievous little smirk. Boo swallowed hard, sensing he was in for a wild ride.

Winnie's face lit up with excitement. "Hey, we can even use this as our headquarters to meet up at!" Boo's expression turned skeptical. "Who's 'we'? And meet up for what exactly?"

Winnie just smiled playfully. "Jynx and I have to go, just for a little bit, but you'll be seeing us again real soon!" Boo watched, still floating at the end of the counter, as the two of them started to leave.

Winnie recited a quick incantation, and the little purple ball popped out again, morphing into the wooden door Boo had seen earlier. The door creaked open, and Winnie turned to Boo with a reassuring smile. "Don't worry, we'll be back!"

With Jynx perched comfortably on her shoulder, Winnie stepped through the doorway. As they disappeared from view, Boo heard Winnie's voice, muffled but still audible, asking Jynx, "Dinosaurs? Jynx, do you remember any dinosaurs back home?" Jynx followed up with a quick but low "Meow" as the door creaked shut, leaving Boo behind to wonder what exactly he had just gotten himself into.

With a soft thud, the wooden door swung shut behind Winnie and Jynx, depositing them back in Winnie's dorm room—eventually. Winnie turned to Jynx, a hint of a grin on her face. "I think I'm starting to get the hang of this traveling thing, Jynx." Jynx gazed up at her, her eyes wide and unblinking.

Winnie began pacing back and forth across the room, her mind buzzing with excitement. As she walked, she started to verbalize her thoughts, ticking off points on her fingers. "Okay, Jynx, let's break it down. Here's what we know so far."

"One, the locator spell somehow linked itself to your collar, and reading from the book triggered it, allowing us to find one of the five people we need for the spell." Winnie's eyes sparkled with excitement as she continued.

"Two, we've found Boo. He's...not exactly what I expected, but I suppose beggars can't be choosers, right?" She chuckled softly to herself.

"Three, Boo thinks my magic book is incredibly powerful – more so than I realized. We'll need to figure out how to tap into its full potential, Jynx." Winnie's gaze fell upon the book, now sitting on her desk, its leather cover seeming to glow with an unknown arcane energy.

"And four, we have a headquarters! Sweet Screams is perfect – it's one of the few places where monsters from different worlds overlap, and we don't know who we're looking for yet." Winnie's pacing slowed, her thoughts racing ahead to all the what-ifs and possibilities. She stopped in front of Jynx, looking down at her cat with a determined glint in her eye. "This is going to be an adventure, Jynx. Are you ready?"

Jynx let out a reassuring meow, as if affirming Winnie's entire analysis. Winnie scooped up Jynx and gently placed her on the desk, saying, "Okay, now we just need to figure out how to use this collar of yours to find another one." Jynx tilted her head, her whiskers twitching, suggesting she was just as clueless as Winnie.

Winnie picked up her spell book, her eyes scanning the pages. "Maybe there's something in here that can help us trigger it again." Jynx's eyes grew wide, and she darted off the desk, scurrying under the bed. Winnie chuckled. "Jynx, you're safe with me!"

Jynx slowly poked her head out from under the bed, her ears perked up. Winnie continued, "I would never do anything to hurt you..." Jynx slid out from under the bed, but Winnie's finishing phrase, "...on purpose, at least," sent her scurrying back under the bed with a startled jump.

Winnie crouched down, her voice softening. "I can't do this without you, Jynx." Jynx remained stubbornly under the bed, unmoved by Winnie's plea. Winnie tried again, "If you help me, I know there's going to be a lot more candy in it for you!" Jynx's ears perked up at the mention of candy, and she cautiously emerged from under the bed, rubbing against Winnie's side with a purr.

Winnie smiled. "I had a feeling you'd be happy to hear that." She turned her attention back to the book, flipping through the pages with growing urgency. Just as she was about to give up, she stumbled upon a spell midway through the book – "Potentia Cresco."

"Let's try this one Jynx." Winnie exclaimed. "We need to increase the amulet's power to help us find the other four, and from what I can gather, that's exactly what this spell does – I think." She placed Jynx back on the desk and began preparing the candles required for the spell.

Winnie instructed, "Okay, Jynx, I just need you to sit really still," as she began lighting the candles and arranging them around Jynx. With the setup complete, Winnie ran her hand across the page, reading the incantation:

"By candles' glow, in circle bright,
Powers surge, with magic's might.
Infuse this form, with strength so grand,
Empowered now, by magic's hand."

The flames from the candles shot up, swirling around Jynx in a mesmerizing dance. Jynx, seeming to sense that remaining calm was the best course of action, lay down and covered her face with her paws. The flames circled her for a few moments before suddenly sucking back into the candles wicks, extinguishing the flames.

Jynx peeked out from behind her paw, checking to see if she'd survived the ordeal. Winnie was just standing there smiling, "Well, I guess now we just have to see if it worked!"

Winnie gently set her spell book aside and leaned in closer to Jynx, her eyes fixed intently on the collar. Jynx sat back up, her tail twitching slightly as Winnie began to examine the emerald gemstone. "Hmm, everything looks the same," Winnie muttered, trying to figure out how to activate it again. She snapped her fingers, flicked the gemstone, and even whispered a few words of encouragement, but nothing seemed to work.

Jynx, attempting to remain patient despite Winnie's enthusiastic but slightly rough handling, let out a vibrating "Meow." To Winnie's surprise, the collar suddenly began to glow again, its emerald gemstone pulsing with a soft, green light. Winnie couldn't believe what was happening before her very own eyes. "Jynx, look – It's working again!"

As she watched, a tiny image began to take shape within the emerald – a vampire, sitting amidst crumbling tombstones in a dimly lit cemetery. Winnie's grip on the collar tightened, her enthusiasm getting the better of her. "A vampire!" she exclaimed, forgetting that Jynx was still attached to the collar.

The sudden tug on the collar sent Jynx tumbling off the desk, slipping free from the golden strap. Jynx landed on the floor with a soft thud, looking somewhat

82

disheveled as she let out a defeated "Meow." Winnie, already refocusing on her task, didn't notice. "No time to waste, Jynx!" she called out. Jynx lay on her back, watching Winnie pick back up her spell book and push unnecessary items off the desk to make room for the work she was about to begin.

Winnie glanced over at Jynx, who was sprawled out on the floor, looking rather unimpressed. "It's no time for a nap, Jynx," Winnie said, trying to rouse her feline companion. "We have serious work to do!" Jynx let out a disgruntled snort as she sat back up.

Jynx hopped up onto the desk, where Winnie was flipping through the spell book in search of the perfect incantation. Winnie's eyes displayed a sense of confusion as she looked over at Jynx. "Why aren't you wearing your collar, silly?" she asked, gently fastening it back around Jynx's neck. Jynx shot her a withering look, her eyes narrowing into a slight death stare.

"Okay, to find a vampire," Winnie muttered, her eyes scanning the pages of the spell book. Her gaze drifted to the crystal ball sitting on the corner of a nearby shelf. "Let's try using this for the next part," she said, a hint of intrigue creeping into her voice.

As she continued to flip through the book, Winnie stumbled upon a spell called "Lumen Arcanum." She looked up at Jynx, her face lighting up with hope. "This one looks promising. It requires an object for looking – and I already have that," she said, patting the crystal ball.

Winnie's eyes scanned the spell's requirements, best she could. "I just have to place my hand on the object and repeat the spell – I think. That seems simple enough." Winnie placed her hand on top of the crystal ball and began to recite the incantation that appeared on the page:

"Shadows part and secrets gleam,
Truth awakens from the dream.
Fog dissolves in silver light,
Allow this spell to grant mindful sight."

As soon as the words left her lips, an ominous purplish-gray cloud began to swirl inside the crystal ball, filling it with a thick, misty smoke. Winnie's voice was steady as she spoke directly to the crystal ball. "Show me where to find the vampire."

The smoke swirled and circled within the glass, and then, like a television tuning into a clear channel, an image began to take shape. Winnie's eyes widened as she took in the details – a sign that read "The Silent Sanctum."

"There – That's where we'll find the next member of the group, Jynx!" Winnie exclaimed, her excitement growing the longer she watched. She threw her satchel over her shoulder and carefully placed Jynx inside. "Maybe this time we'll get the travel part right on the first try, even?" Jynx's eyes grew wide, and she tried to scramble out of the satchel but Winnie was too quick, gently but firmly holding her in place.

"Oh, stop, it's not that bad," Winnie said, trying to soothe Jynx's ruffled feathers. With a wave of her hand and a whispered incantation, the wooden door materialized once more. Winnie stepped through it, Jynx secure in her satchel, ready for their next adventure.

Some Fang's Not Right Here

Meanwhile, back in The Midnight Sector, Vaughn had grown close to Auri, their friendship blossoming over countless nightly meetings at the crumbling wall where they first met. The two would often sneak across the wall to spend time together, their bond strengthening with each passing day.

However, unbeknownst to Vaughn, his defiance had not gone unnoticed. Several elder vampires had caught wind of his unconventional friendship and were determined to put an end to it. They had assigned two of Vaughn's peers, the siblings Jace and Mina, to monitor his activities and eliminate him if he was found to be a traitor to their kind.

As the sun dipped below the horizon, Vaughn made his way to the mausoleum, waiting for the perfect moment to meet Auri at the wall. Jace and Mina, in their bat forms, shadowed him from a distance, their eyes fixed on Vaughn as they observed his every move.

As the night wore on, Vaughn bid Auri farewell, promising to catch up again soon. Alone now, he made his way back through the alleys, unaware of the danger lurking in the shadows. As he walked toward the wall, Jace dropped down from a nearby roof rafter, transforming back into his vampire form right in front of Vaughn. Vaughn's eyes widened in surprise as Jace's figure materialized before him.

Meanwhile, Mina transformed back into her vampire form behind Vaughn, her presence now looming as she closed in. "Well, I guess the rumors are indeed true," Jace sneered, his eyes gleaming with malice. Vaughn's stare intensified in panic as he realized he'd been caught. Vaughn spun around, his eyes locking onto Mina's figure behind him. He was now trapped with Jace in front of him and Mina closing in from behind.

Mina stepped forward, her voice dripping with sarcasm. "I have to hand it to you, Vaughn. I never thought you'd be brave enough to enter the city, let alone befriend it."

Vaughn was pivoting in position, his eyes darting between Jace and Mina as they continued to creep towards him. Desperate to escape, he shut his eyes, gritted his teeth, and clenched his fists, hoping to transform. But nothing happened.

Jace chuckled, his voice mocking. "I don't know if that's adorable or sad, Mina. Little Vaughny here's trying to transform to escape from us. Don't leave now, buddy – the fun's just about to begin!" Mina chimed in, her voice equally sinister. "See, we've been given orders to follow you tonight, and if we didn't like what we see... well, let's just say we were asked to handle it."

Vaughn's heart began to beat at a rapid pace, his panic growing with each passing moment. Desperate to escape, he attempted to transform once more, only this time a purple ball of light quickly appeared just behind him. For a fleeting instant, Jace and Mina's eyes widened in alarm, their faces pale in the moonlight. They exchanged a fearful glance believing that Vaughn was finally manifesting some kind of a powerful transformation – one that could potentially give him the upper hand in this battle.

But before they could react further, the brilliant purple ball of light erupted, illuminating the dark alleyway. Jace and Mina stumbled backward, their initial fear giving way to confusion and surprise as they realized the light wasn't emanating from Vaughn himself. The siblings' eyes locked onto the spectacle, their faces twisted in a mixture of shock and uncertainty.

As the purple light dissipated, a wooden door materialized behind Vaughn, opening with a soft creak. Winnie and Jynx stepped out of the doorway, Winnie's expression beamed with eagerness while Jynx's ears perked up in alertness. They had landed awkwardly, with Winnie stumbling slightly and Jynx darting out of the satchel to take in their surroundings. Before they could regain their footing, they found themselves standing directly behind Vaughn, who was still frozen in panic between Jace and Mina. The mood was thick with tension as the three vampires turned to face the unexpected newcomers, with two of them narrowing their eyes in unison.

Mina's voice pierced the night air, her shout echoing off the alleyway walls. "It's a witch!?" Jace's eyes narrowed, his gaze fixed on Winnie. "What's a witch doing in The Midnight Sector?"

Winnie, still disoriented from her sudden arrival, didn't seem to notice the tension. Her eyes landed on Vaughn, and a bright smile spread across her face. "Jynx, it's the vampire! We found him!" she blurted out.

Jynx, however, seemed to sense the danger that they had just walked into. She arched her back, her fur standing on end, and let out a low, warning growl. Her eyes fixed intently on Jace and Mina, as if daring them to make a move.

Vaughn, distracted by Winnie and Jynx's arrival, didn't notice Jace's subtle shift in stance. Jace's eyes gleamed with a sinister light as he summoned his Phantom Grasp. His body tensed, legs shoulder-width apart, hands hanging loose by his sides, and his head tilted up toward the sky.

Two purplish-gray misty hands erupted from Jace's aura, grasping Vaughn and slamming him into the side of a building. Vaughn's body pinned against the wall, his eyes wide with pain and fear.

Mina, meanwhile, transformed into her bat form, her body now glowing a bright crimson red. She split into several smaller, crimson colored bats, each one darting through the air with deadly precision. Vaughn managed to yell out a warning, "Watch out!"

One of the crimson bats zeroed in on Winnie, its fangs and claws extended. But before it could strike, Jynx sprang into action. With lightning-fast reflexes, she leaped up and snatched the bat out of the air, her jaws closing around it with a swift crunch. The bat dissolved into a puff of red smoke, and Jynx dropped back down, her eyes still fixed intently on the remaining bats fluttering in the air around her.

Winnie let out a startled shriek as she dashed behind a pile of wood next to a nearby building, her heart racing with fear. Jynx stood tall, her eyes focused on the crimson bats that were diving through the air. She was a picture of alertness, poised to strike at any moment.

Vaughn, still pinned to the wall, let out a pained groan as the spectral hands tightened their grip. Winnie, meanwhile, frantically flipped through her spell book, her mind racing with uncertainty. She knew she had to act fast, but she wasn't sure if she was equipped to handle the situation.

As Winnie searched for a solution, Jynx leaped from crumbling stone pillars to the sides of buildings, swatting at the bats with deadly precision. Her agility and quick reflexes kept the bats at bay, giving Winnie precious time to find a spell.

Winnie's eyes scanned the pages, one after another. Her fingers traced the words of each spell until she had finally found one that caught her attention; transforming the ancient text over to its English version – "Clarus Ruptura." She stood up, her voice steady as she recited the incantation,

> *"From shadow's grip, I call the flame,*
> *A blinding surge, no dark shall tame.*
> *Let brilliance rise and skies ignite,*
> *Erupting truth in sacred light."*

A brilliant dome of light burst forth from Winnie's position, illuminating the night sky. The Midnight Sector was bathed in an intense, blinding radiance that seemed to rival the sun itself. The crimson bats fell from the sky, landing with a soft thud on the ground, and Mina was forced to transform back into her human-like form.

Jace stumbled forward, his concentration broken, and Vaughn was released from the spectral grip. Both vampires fell to their knees, temporarily blinded by the light. Vaughn stumbled forward, trying to clear his vision, and made his way over to Winnie.

"Thank you!" he exclaimed, grabbing Winnie's arm. "Quick, follow me!" He pulled her toward the opening in the wall, and they slipped through it, Jynx darting ahead.

As they emerged on the other side, Vaughn led them up the mountainside toward the mausoleum. The sign carved into the stone read "The Silent Sanctum". Winnie's excitement flared up all over again. "I knew we'd find you."

Vaughn turned to her, his eyes curious. "Find me? Why were you even looking for me?"

The three of them climbed to the highest point in the mausoleum, Vaughn's favorite lookout. From this vantage point, they could see the city below, and even spot Jace and Mina still struggling to regain their composure.

As they watched, the siblings transformed back into bats and flew off into the night. Vaughn's expression turned serious. "They'll report back to the elders," he said. "Thank you again for helping me though. You saved my life tonight."

Winnie smiled, "You're welcome. I'm just glad I was able to help. I've never been in a fight before, let alone a magical one. It was terrifying and somewhat thrilling all at once."

Vaughn chuckled, his eyes crinkling at the corners. "I'm Vaughn, by the way. And those two were Jace and Mina – two of the worst siblings you'll probably ever meet."

Winnie laughed, extending her hand, "Nice to meet you, Vaughn. I'm Winnie, and this is my friend and companion Jynx."

Vaughn smiled, scratching Jynx behind the ears. "Thank you, Jynx. You definitely played a part in tonight's rescue." Jynx purred with a warm rumble, her eyes closing in bliss as she leaned into her newly acquired massage.

As they sat on the mausoleum's highest point, Winnie's curiosity got the better of her. "Why were those two after you, anyway?"

Vaughn's expression turned somber. "It's a long story, but the short version is that I defied the rules of the vampires." Winnie's eyes widened with intrigue. "Oh...," she breathed.

Vaughn's gaze drifted toward the city below as he pointed. "See that city down there?" Winnie nodded following the direction of his gesture

"The creatures that live inside that city are called The Abandoned," Vaughn continued. "The vampires of this world not only feed off of them physically but also emotionally, instilling fear throughout." Winnie's face twisted in disgust. "That's terrible!" she exclaimed.

Vaughn nodded in agreement. "I know. I've recently gotten to know one of the creatures a lot better, and she's really nice. Her name is Auri. They haven't done anything wrong, and they just want to live their lives in peace. But the vampires will never allow that to happen. They view them as worthless and prey upon them day and night. I'm supposed to be doing the same thing, but I don't want to."

Winnie's eyes gleamed with understanding as her tears formed in the moonlight. "So, that's why Jace and Mina were after you?"

Vaughn nodded. "They'll report back to the elders that I've escaped and that you helped me. They're going to be out looking for both of us now. It's not safe for you to be here anymore."

Winnie's expression grew certain. "You won't be safe here either though."

Vaughn's smile curved into a small smirk. "I know, but I don't have anywhere else to go. You do."

Winnie's face lit up with a solution, a spark catching in her eyes. "Then you'll come back with me!" she exclaimed. "I'm working on a special project, and I was led to find you here for a reason. You can just stay with me until we figure everything out." A warm smile spread across her face, reassuring Vaughn that she had a plan.

With a gentle wave of her hand, Winnie recited the traveling spell, and the wooden door materialized once more, its intricate carvings seeming to shimmer in the fading light. As the door swung open, Winnie turned to Vaughn, her eyes shining with anticipation. "Well...are you coming?" she asked in a subtle but sweet tone.

Vaughn hesitated for a moment, his eyes narrowing as he weighed his options. His curiosity got the better of him, "What kind of special project?" he asked as he slid off the top of the mausoleum. He found himself to be both intrigued and cautious, revealing his uncertainty about trusting this stranger – no matter how kind she seemed.

As Vaughn's question drifted between them, Winnie's smile grew wider, and she beckoned him to follow. With a deep breath, Vaughn stepped through the doorway, Jynx padded ahead, taking the lead. The wooden door creaked shut, leaving a world of despair behind them, while a world full of hope beckoned ahead.

The Stitching Hour

As the wooden door creaked open, Winnie, Jynx, and Vaughn stepped into the cozy confines of her dorm room back at Darkspire Academy. The sudden transition from the unknown to the familiar surroundings was a welcome relief. Winnie turned to Vaughn, her voice quiet and steady. "You'll need to keep a low profile in my room for now, until we figure out the details of your... situation. I'm not supposed to have anyone in here, especially not a boy – and definitely not a vampire boy." Vaughn nodded in understanding, his response soft and measured. "No problem."

Winnie smiled slightly. "I'll run down to the school café and grab us something to eat. Err... you do eat, don't you?" Vaughn's lips curled into a teasing smile as he replied, "Of course I eat! Any small animal will do." Winnie's eyes widened in alarm, and Jynx's eyes grew even larger, her fur standing on end. Vaughn chuckled, his fangs glinting in the dim light. "I'm kidding! I'll just have whatever you're having." Winnie let out a soft sigh of relief, her expression stern but her eyes crinkling at the corners. "That's not funny," she said, though a giggle slipped out despite her best efforts to suppress it.

"Okay, I'll be right back," Winnie continued, "and then we need to tackle another problem that's just occurred to me. Remember, not a peep while I'm gone!" Vaughn's fingers mimicked the motion of zipping his lips shut, a silent promise to keep quiet. As Winnie turned to leave, she glanced at Jynx, who had already curled up on the bed, looking like she had no intention of moving. "Want to come with me, Jynx?" Winnie asked, though the answer was clear. She chuckled, shaking her head. "I guess not. I'll bring you back something too, then." With a gentle smile, Winnie closed the door behind her, leaving Vaughn and Jynx in the quiet of her room.

When Winnie returned she pushed open the door, expecting a quiet, orderly room. Instead, she was met with chaos. The space was in disarray, her belongings scattered everywhere. Vaughn and Jynx sat in the midst of the mess, looking remarkably calm. Vaughn was holding what looked to be a small make up bag, while Jynx sat beside him, a sock draped comically over half her face and head.

Winnie's eyes widened in dismay as she nearly dropped the food. "I've only been gone fifteen minutes! How did you two manage to make such a mess in such a short time?" Vaughn's eyes sparkled with mischief as he chimed in, "We were having a staring contest."

Winnie raised an eyebrow, unimpressed. "That doesn't even begin to explain this," she said, gesturing to the mess, before laughter bubbled up from her chest. "Come on, let's eat," she said, setting down the food. "We can worry about cleaning up this disaster afterwards." As she spoke, she couldn't help but smile at the absurdity of it all.

As they sat amidst the chaos, the three of them devoured the food Winnie had brought back. With mouths full, Vaughn and Jynx looked up at Winnie as she spoke, her brow furrowed in thought. "Okay, there's something I need to figure out," she said, her eyes darting between the pair. "Once I find the rest of you, we'll need a way to communicate with each other. I don't know where everyone is, and traveling all over the monster worlds to pick everyone up isn't exactly efficient."

Vaughn popped another meatball into his mouth, while Jynx slurped up a spaghetti noodle, her eyes fixed on Winnie. "I see it's still going to be just me figuring this out, huh?" Winnie chuckled, shaking her head. Vaughn swallowed his food and suggested, "What if we had some sort of device, like a walkie-talkie or a transponder?" Winnie's face lit up. "Hey, that's not a bad idea!"

She stood up, grabbing her spell book, and began flipping through its pages. "This book has been handy, but it's a real challenge to follow. It's all written in a different language, and it only translates when I pass my hand over the words and even then sometimes they're not in English." Vaughn nodded, burping softly. "Sorry," he said, earning a quiet laugh from Winnie.

As she thumbed through the book, Winnie's eyes landed on another spell that caught her attention. "Well, it's not what I was looking for, but we could definitely use the help," she said, raising her hand. "Ordinare Domum," she spoke aloud followed by reciting the rhyme:

"Dust and clutter, fade from sight,
Let every corner gleam with light.
Books and baubles find their place,
Restore this room with gentle grace."

As the rhyme was completed, the room began to transform before their eyes. Books flew onto bookshelves, clothes hung themselves in the closet, and the bedcovers smoothed out. The room was tidy once more, and Winnie looked amazed. "Wow," she muttered under her breath, "...definitely gonna bookmark that page for later use."

Vaughn and Jynx exchanged pleased glances, relieved that their mess had been so easily fixed. Winnie continued to flip through the book, searching for a solution to her bigger problem. Hours passed, and the daylight outside gave way to night. Vaughn and Jynx lay on the bed, playing chess, with Jynx dominating the game. Winnie sat at her desk, still poring over the book.

Suddenly, she rose up out of her chair, a look of excitement on her face. "I found it!" she exclaimed. "Vocare Via," she read aloud, her hand tracing the words on the page. "The spell requires specific ingredients: a centered candle, carved with the destination, surrounded by a ring of colored candles, each different and each bearing the name of one of the companions. I'll explain more about it all when we're ready to do it," Winnie added, seeing the confusion on their faces.

Winnie explained the rest of the spell's requirements, her words met with confusion from Vaughn and Jynx.

Without missing a beat, Jynx swatted down Vaughn's king on the chessboard with her tail, her expression unmoved.

Winnie's eyes locked onto Jynx's collar, her hands reaching out to grasp it once more. Jynx hesitated, recalling the rough handling from their previous attempt, but ultimately allowed Winnie to take hold of the collar. As soon as Winnie's hands made contact, Jynx let out a short "Meow," and the collar sprang to life once again. A soft green glow emanated from it, illuminating a sweet-looking monster stitched together from various pieces.

Winnie's eyes widened in wonder "I've never seen a monster like that," she said, her voice filled with curiosity. "I don't even know how to ask my crystal ball to find it." She pondered for a moment before a thought struck her. "Maybe I can just try to draw it and go from there?"

Winnie pulled out a piece of paper and sat it on her desk next to the crystal ball. She attempted to sketch the monster, her pencil moving swiftly across the page. "Well, here goes nothing," she murmured, placing her hand on both the crystal ball and the drawing. With a clear voice, she spoke the words, "Show me the monster."

The crystal ball began to fill with swirling smoke, and shortly after, the monster's image appeared once more. "It worked!" Winnie exclaimed. Vaughn and Jynx leaned in, their eyes fixed on the crystal ball.

As they watched, the monster moved through the scene, and soon a sign came into view. "Brindlemire Tailoring," Winnie read aloud "Ah ha!" she exclaimed. "Guys, we're going to Brindlemire!"

Back in Brindlemire, Freddy and his father, Ethan, had been spending quality time together, trying to recreate old memories while making new ones. Despite Freddy's hazy recollections, Ethan cherished every moment with his child. Weeks had passed since Ethan had brought Freddy back to life, and he'd almost forgotten about the old, gnarled woman who had given him the power to do so.

That evening, as the sun dipped below the horizon, a knock on the door broke the tranquility. Ethan's eyes widened in surprise as he opened it to find the old woman standing before him, "I know you remember me," she said, her voice low and mysterious. Ethan nodded, gratitude etched on his face. "You gave me not one but two lives back; my child and my own. Thank you!"

The old woman's expression remained serene as she replied, "Your debt is now due." Ethan's brow furrowed in concern. "What kind of debt are you referring to exactly?" As he spoke, Freddy walked into view, carrying his teddy bear, and the old woman's gaze fell upon him. She pointed at the child, and Ethan's heart sank. "I don't understand – Freddy? You want to take away the very thing you helped me get back??"

The old woman's nod sent a chill down Ethan's spine. "My dear man, the child you have is still not your own; he never was," she said, her words piercing Ethan's heart. "I gifted you the power to bring him back, but that was only because the spell required an undying love for the one in question. I knew that could not be me, so I placed the spell upon the toy I gave you, knowing you'd follow through with what I could not."

Ethan's face contorted in anguish as he shouted, "You will never take my son from me. I won't let you!" He tried to slam the door shut, but the old woman's foot blocked it. "You will give me the child, or I will take him on my own," she declared, her voice cold and menacing.

As Ethan held the old woman back, he shouted to Freddy, "Freddy – run!" But Freddy, hearing his name, had started walking towards him, only to see the confrontation unfolding between his father and the old woman. Ethan's voice grew more urgent as he shouted again, "Freddy – run!" Freddy's eyes widened as he took in the scene and he turned to flee but it was too late. The old woman broke free from Ethan's grasp, crossed her hands in an X pattern, and released them with a swift motion. In an instant, Freddy vanished without a trace.

Ethan collapsed to his knees, overcome with grief, pulling at the old woman's cloak. "Please, give me back my son!" he begged. The old woman's expression turned sinister as she looked down at him, "Worry not. Your boy is well kept. He's joined my collection, and the life you granted him will soon be put to better use." With a final tug, she pulled her cloak free and walked away, leaving Ethan in a state of utter despair.

As Ethan sat crying in the doorway, the old woman walked down the path, her figure fading away into nothingness. Ethan was beside himself, unsure of what to do or how to get his son back. He didn't know who the old woman was, where she lived, or what she planned to do with Freddy and that uncertainty was suffocating.

Just as Ethan's despair seemed to deepen, a purplish ball of light materialized outside the cottage door. The ball morphed into a wooden door, and Winnie, Vaughn, and Jynx emerged from it. Ethan's eyes widened, still brimming with tears, as he looked at the trio. "Who are you?" he asked, his voice still shaking.

Winnie stepped forward, introducing herself and her companions. "Hi! I'm Winnie and this is my friend Vaughn, and my companion Jynx." She asked, "Are you okay, mister?" Ethan's response was laced with sorrow. "My son was just taken from me." Vaughn's expression turned sympathetic. "That's terrible! Is there anything we can do to help?" Ethan forced a weak smile. "I don't think so, but thank you."

Winnie's gaze fell upon the wooden sign hanging from the cottage wall, reading "Brindlemire Tailoring." Her eyes met Vaughn's, and she whispered, "Guys, look, it's the sign from earlier." Ethan, still lost in grief, stood up and stumbled back into his home. Vaughn called out to him, "Mister, we've come looking for a young boy. He's probably around our height. Umm...I know this may sound a bit odd but he looked like he had a yellowy-green skin and was stitched together in different pieces. Have you maybe seen someone like that around here?"

Ethan's expression changed from despair to surprise. "That's my Freddy. How do you know about my boy?" Winnie's eyes lit up with intrigue. "He's your child? Is he the one that was just taken?" Ethan nodded, and Winnie turned to Vaughn. "Vaughn, we have to help get Freddy back. For one, he's the reason we're here, but most importantly, look how upset his dad is." Vaughn nodded in agreement.

Winnie turned back to Ethan, her voice filled with conviction. "Sir, we came in search of your son, Freddy and we'd like to help you find a way to get him back!" Ethan's eyes narrowed slightly. "What are you wanting with my son?" Winnie's response was reassuring. "If you'll allow us to come in and talk to you, I think I can explain everything, and maybe you can help us figure out some kind of clue that will lead to this old woman you're talking about." With little else to lose, Ethan invited them in, hoping that together; they might find a way to bring Freddy back home.

As the conversation flowed, Winnie explained everything to Ethan about her spell, her project, Vaughn, and the rest. However, the focus quickly shifted to finding and rescuing Freddy. Ethan's eyes clouded over as he recounted the story of how he lost his son the first time due to illness and how that was the first time he met the mysterious woman. He knew nothing about her, except that she had appeared twice, with devastating consequences.

Winnie leaned forward, her voice hopeful, "Do you think you could draw her?" Ethan hesitated, unsure of his artistic abilities. "I'm an artist in my craft, but not like that," he replied. Winnie's expression remained encouraging. "I don't think that truly matters. Do you think you could draw her well enough to distinguish certain features?" Ethan nodded, and Winnie handed him a piece of paper and a pencil.

As Ethan worked on the sketch, Winnie pulled out her crystal ball from her satchel. Once the drawing was complete, she placed her hand on both the drawing and

the crystal ball, commanding, "Show me the old woman."
But to their surprise, nothing happened. Vaughn's eyes lit
up with a thought. "It worked in your room earlier, but
you were looking for Freddy, not the old woman."

Vaughn spotted an older family photo on the desk
and brought it over to Winnie. "Here, try it again with
this one," he suggested. Winnie took hold of the photo
and said, "Show me Freddy." The crystal ball began to
swirl with the gray mist of smoke, and shortly after, a
clear image of Freddy appeared within the glass. He was
locked in a cage, crying and hugging his teddy bear.

The group gasped in unison, their reactions a mix of
shock and concern. Ethan's eyes welled up with tears as
he saw his little boy trapped and scared. "Freddy," he
cried, his voice cracking with emotion. "Stay strong. I'm
going to find you. I'm going to get you back."

Winnie's voice was a calm contrast to Ethan's
anguish. "Well, we found him, and we didn't. We still
don't know exactly where he's at, but at least we know
he's still safe." Vaughn's voice dropped as he added the
words, "For now, at least." The group continued to watch
the crystal ball, hoping to catch a glimpse of something
that would reveal Freddy's location.

As they stared into the mist, they saw Freddy sitting
in the corner of the cage, his eyes red from crying. The
cage itself was made of dark, rusty bars, and the
surroundings were dimly lit. After a few moments,
Freddy stood up and began to move around, his
movements restless.

As he walked, the view in the crystal ball shifted,
revealing more of his surroundings. The group saw an
intricately carved wooden door with symbols etched into
it. Winnie's eyes widened as she recognized one of the
symbols from her spell book. She quickly began to flip
through the pages, her fingers moving swiftly as she
searched for more information.

After a few moments, she stopped on a page and her
eyes scanned the text. "I think I can use this symbol to
our advantage," she said, her voice filled with thought.

"The symbol on the door is also in my book. If I can link these two symbols, I might be able to create a beacon that will allow us to travel to Freddy's location."

Winnie's eyes lit up with a plan. "I'll draw the symbol on the floor, and use it as a grounding beacon. If I can match the symbol's energy to the one on the door, we might be able to create a stable portal." Vaughn and Ethan watched as Winnie carefully drew the symbol on the floor, her hands moving with precision. "This could work," she said, her voice infused with confidence. "Let's prepare for the spell, and hope it takes us to Freddy."

As the four of them gathered around the symbol, Winnie's expression turned thoughtful. "Wait a minute, before we do this, let's consider a few things," she said. Vaughn raised an eyebrow. "Like what?" Winnie's eyes narrowed. "We should think about what we might be walking into. Remember when Jynx and I stumbled upon you? We need to be prepared for unexpected situations and have a backup plan." Vaughn nodded in agreement, and the group began to discuss their strategy, determined to rescue Freddy safely.

With a deep breath, Winnie asked, "Is everyone ready? Does everyone know what they're supposed to do?" The group nodded in unison. Winnie raised her hand and began to recite the words of her traveling spell, the familiar incantation echoing through the air. As she finished, the traveling door materialized before them.

Winnie quickly sketched the symbol on the door, and as she finished, both symbols – the one on the floor and the one on the door – burst into a brilliant pale blue glow. The light faded, leaving behind a soft hum of energy. "I think we're linked now," Winnie said. "Everyone follow in line, remember the plan, and stay as quiet as possible when we arrive." With a nod, the group prepared to step through the doorway.

As the door closed behind them, it swung open once more, revealing a cavernous dwelling that seemed to swallow the light around them. The air was thick with darkness, and the sound of dripping water echoed off the cold stone walls. The four of them stepped out of the doorway, their eyes adjusting slowly to the dim light.

The only illumination came from a fire crackling in a nearby fireplace, casting flickering shadows across the room. Freddy's eyes locked onto his father, and he shouted "Daddy!" but was quickly silenced by the group's urgent gestures for quiet. As they approached the rusty cage, Freddy reached out through the bars and grasped his father tightly. Ethan whispered, "I wasn't about to lose you again. We have to hurry and get you out of here."

Vaughn's gaze fell upon the massive lock on the cage, and he whispered, "We need a key." Winnie's eyes scanned the room, and she urged, "Quick, everyone spread out and see if they can find it." But Freddy's voice was laced with worry as he said, "It's not in here, she keeps it with her." His words were followed by a more ominous revelation: "...and this room is being watched."

The group's nervous whispers echoed the word "Watched?" Freddy's response sent a chill through them: "Yes, that door over there is set on some kind of a magical timer. Every time it opens, this big black panther comes in to patrol the room." Vaughn's grip on Winnie's arm tightened as he whispered, "Now what do we do? None of us rehearsed having to fight a panther." Winnie, trying to sound sure, responded "We'll just have to wing it. Let's just focus on getting Freddy out of the cage before that door opens. If we can do that, we might not have to worry about the panther at all." Now more determined than they were before, the group set to work, their eyes fixed on the task ahead.

Ethan's desperation grew as he grasped a nearby rock, attempting to smash the lock open. The sound of metal clanging against stone echoed through the cavern, but the lock held firm, refusing to yield. Meanwhile, Winnie flipped through her spell book, searching for the unlock spell she'd found earlier, the one she'd picked out before they even stepped through the traveling door. She whispered the incantation and flicked her fingers toward the lock, but the magic fizzled out before it touched the metal. Her stomach tightened. The woman had anticipated this — a counter-spell wrapped around the lock, smothering any magic she tried to use.

Vaughn was about to try his hand at picking the lock when the symbols on the door began to glow. One by one they began casting an ominous light across the cavernous room. Freddy, still trying to stay quiet, tried to warn the others, "It's opening again. You've got to find a place to hide!" The group swiftly scanned their surroundings, but the cavern offered very few hiding spots. The fire pit and nearby shadows were their only hope, but would it be enough? The sound of the door creaking open seemed to grow louder, and the group's hearts sank in unison.

Jynx's small frame allowed her to slip into a narrow opening in the cavern wall, disappearing from view. The others scrambled to find hiding spots, scattering across the floor in search of cover. The cavern's landscape offered some hope, with stalagmites jutting out from the ground like jagged teeth.

Ethan managed to tuck himself behind the fire pit, its stone structure towering above the rest of the room. Winnie found a stalagmite that provided decent cover, but Vaughn's hiding spot was less ideal. His stalagmite was too small, leaving parts of him exposed. As he cowered behind the stone, he muttered a comical thought to himself, "Already deal with a black cat at home, now there's one at work too?" The darkness of the room might conceal him, but he knew it was a slim chance. The sound of paws padding against stone echoed through the cavern, growing louder with each passing moment.

Vaughn's panic escalated with each step the panther took, its slow and deliberate movements sending his heart racing. He'd occasionally peek out from behind the stalagmite, watching in horror as the beast glided its head from side to side, sniffing the air. Desperate for a plan, Vaughn scrambled through his options. He could try to fly — though that usually ended with him kissing the ground or flailing like someone in a bathroom emergency. His other idea was to bite the panther but even he knew that was basically asking the world's angriest house cat to just bite back harder.

As the panther drew closer, Vaughn's breathing grew heavier, his fear threatening to overwhelm him. He risked another glance and his blood ran cold – if that were even possible. The panther's face was mere inches from his, its eyes locked onto his. Vaughn froze, staring back into the ferocious gaze as his hand crept upward beside him — slowly, stupidly, reckless in thought. Before his brain could stop him, he leaned in and whispered, "Boop," tapping the panther's nose.

The panther unleashed a roar so powerful it blasted Vaughn's hair straight back and left his cheeks flapping like a windsock in a hurricane.

Vaughn let out an "Ah!" the sound rattling through the cavern as he whipped around and ran off in the opposite direction with zero hesitation and even less of a plan.

Freddy tried to divert the panther's attention, but it was too focused on Vaughn, ignoring Freddy's attempts entirely. Vaughn, backed into a corner, raised his hands in a desperate bid to defend himself, though he knew it was a futile effort. Just as the situation seemed hopeless, Winnie and Ethan leapt into action, shouting loudly and hurling rocks at the panther.

The rocks whizzed through the air, striking the cavern walls with loud thuds and the panther's ears folded back in annoyance. It let out a low, rumbling growl, clearly irritated by the sudden barrage. The panther's eyes flashed with anger as it spun, its tail whipping through the air with a sharp crack like a whip. For a moment, Vaughn was forgotten as the panther's attention shifted to the new threats, its gaze zeroing in on Winnie and Ethan.

Seizing the opportunity, Vaughn sprinted towards the cage. Winnie tried to grab her spell book, but the panther swiped her satchel away; knocking it to the opposite side of the room. Ethan grabbed a flaming log from the fireplace, waving it back and forth as the panther advanced.

Freddy watched his father desperately swinging the burning log, trying to keep the panther away from him and Winnie. Fear surged through him — his father was going to get hurt. Without understanding the strength building inside him, Freddy ran to the edge of the cage and grabbed the bars, his small hands clamping around the cold metal.

Driven by pure desperation, he pulled. What he expected to be impossible happened with startling ease — the bars snapped clean in half with a sharp metallic crack. Freddy stared at the broken pieces in his hands, confusion and awe flooding his face. He tossed the bars to the ground and stepped through the opening, hardly believing the cage he once thought unbreakable had never been strong enough to hold him.

Hearing the metal bars clatter to the floor snapped the panther's attention back to Freddy; its mission had never changed — keep the boy contained. With a low, furious growl, it lunged toward the cage, claws scraping against the stone as it charged. Without even thinking about it, Vaughn instinctively threw himself between them and yelled "Stop!" To everyone's utter surprise, the panther began to slow its charge, its powerful legs decelerating from a full-on sprint to a gradual halt. Its eyes locked onto Vaughn's, and it seemed to become entranced, its fierce demeanor melting away. The panther's muscles relaxed and it sank to the ground, eventually sitting down in front of Vaughn with an almost docile demeanor, as if awaiting further instructions. In a moment of unexpected power, Vaughn's presence seemed to captivate the creature, rendering it motionless and transfixed by his gaze.

Winnie whispered, "It's like he's put it to sleep or something." Freddy added, "Yeah, but its eyes are still open." Ethan's insight, "I think he's hypnotized it," sent a wave of wonder through the group.

As the panther sat before him, Vaughn's words took on a commanding tone. "Leave us alone. Return to your post." The panther's response was immediate and obedient, rising to its feet and padding silently out of the room. As the door clicked shut, Vaughn stood there, stunned but blinking. "That was amazing... how did I do that?" he whispered to himself. Winnie's urgent voice broke the spell. "We need to leave, now. Before it comes back or whatever you did wears off."

With swift efficiency, Winnie scooped up her satchel, calling out to Jynx, who obligingly jumped inside. Vaughn was still catching his breath, staring at the now-closed door as if expecting the panther to burst back through it. Winnie didn't give him the chance. She recited the familiar words of the traveling spell, magic crackling faintly in the air as the wooden door shimmered into existence once more. "Go, go," she urged, ushering them forward. The group stepped through the doorway, re-emerging back at the tailor's cottage leaving the chaos of the cavern snapping shut behind them.

Winnie, being slightly prepared for the moment of their return, had researched a way to temporarily shield the cottage from the old woman's magic. She quickly briefed Freddy on his role in the spell, and the four of them, including Jynx, took their positions around the cottage. Freddy stood at the northern side, Ethan at the southern side, Vaughn at the eastern, and Winnie and Jynx stood at the western side.

Each member spoke their side as part of the spell: Freddy called out "North," Ethan declared "South," Vaughn proclaimed "East," and Winnie completed the spell with her part "and West..." followed by the remainder of the incantation:

Veil this truth in shadow's crest,
where prying spells shall find no rest."

As she spoke the final words, a large black dome appeared, enveloping the cottage, before vanishing as suddenly as it had formed. "I think it worked!" Winnie exclaimed, and the group erupted into cheers.

As they celebrated, Vaughn, Winnie, and Jynx were finally officially introduced to Freddy, and Ethan expressed his heartfelt gratitude to the trio. Winnie glanced at the clock, noting the late hour. "It's past midnight," she said, her voice tinged with reluctance. "We should probably head back."

Even Vaughn, accustomed to being a creature of the night, felt the weight of exhaustion letting a small yawn slip out. Winnie erased the previous symbol from the floor and indicated she was drawing a new, unique symbol. With a smile, she began to draw the new symbol, explaining that it would allow them to return under the dome's protection if needed. With a wave of her hand, she summoned the traveling door once more.

Vaughn entered first, followed by Jynx. As Winnie prepared to follow, she turned to Ethan and Freddy, her eyes warm with concern. "I'm glad you're okay, Freddy," she said, and Freddy's face lit up with a smile as he hugged his teddy bear tightly. With a final glance, Winnie said "We'll see you again soon," and stepped through the doorway, disappearing into the night, bound for her dorm room.

As they stepped out of the doorway and back into Winnie's dorm room, the familiar surroundings felt like a welcome break from the night's adventures. "Man, what a night!" Winnie exclaimed. Vaughn chuckled, shaking his head. "Yeah no kidding, I almost became a steak dinner tonight – and I don't really care for stakes." The grim pun sent all three of them into fits of laughter as the tension of the night slowly seeped out of their bodies.

As soon as they had composed themselves, Winnie's expression turned thoughtful. "It was definitely a close call, but I think we handled it all pretty well. We reunited a dad and his son, made a new friend, and — well, you discovered a special power you didn't even know you had," she teased. Vaughn's excitement flared, his voice lifting with a giddy edge. "A really cool one too!" The three of them chuckled again as the excitement and wonder of Vaughn's newfound ability played out in their minds once again.

As the laughter faded, Winnie yawned, stretching her arms above her head. "I don't know about you two, but I'm ready for bed. We've got two more teammates to find, and who knows what those adventures will bring. Let's leave that for tomorrow's problem though, tonight —let's just sleep." Her words were met with nods of agreement, and the three of them began to settle in for a well-deserved night's rest. Winnie snuggled under the covers. Jynx curled up beside her at the pillow; the little creature's gentle purring a soothing accompaniment to Winnie's own tired sighs. Vaughn stretched out across the foot of the bed, his cape wrapped around him like a blanket, a contented smile still playing on his lips. As the soft glow of the room's lamps began to dim, the three friends let out a collective sigh; their eyelids growing heavy as the night's exhaustion finally caught up with them. Soon, the room was filled with the soft sounds of sleep with the night's adventure temporarily forgotten.

Mummy's Cell Service

As morning dawned, the warm light streaming through the blinds cast a golden glow over the dorm room, awakening the three friends. Winnie was the first to stir into action, hurrying down to the school cafe to fetch breakfast for the group. She returned with a tray laden with food, and the enticing aromas filled the room, teasing Vaughn and Jynx awake. Winnie's excitement was practically written all over her face as she devoured her meal with a zealous enthusiasm. "Okay, let's get started!" she exclaimed, her voice bubbling with driven tone.

Jynx, who had been lounging on the bed, suddenly sat up straight, her fur mussed and breakfast crumbs scattered across her face; her expression depicting a response of, "Already?" Winnie chuckled and gently wiped Jynx's face clean with a cloth napkin. "You always make the biggest mess," she teased, shaking her head in amusement. Vaughn, afraid of being called out for the same thing, seeing his face was also covered in food, began wiping his own face clean.

With everyone ready, Winnie held on to the emerald, and Jynx summoned the collar's power with a soft "Meow." The gemstone began to glow with a bright green light, and as it faded, an image took shape behind its façade – a small mummy wrapped in tattered bandages. "It's a mummy!" Winnie exclaimed. Vaughn's response was immediate. "Who's mommy?" he asked, his brow furrowed in confusion. Winnie playfully rolled her eyes. "Not a mommy, silly – a mummy!" Vaughn grinned, his eyes sparkling with mischief. "Oh, sorry – my bat!" he said, chuckling at his own pun. Jynx shot him a look that seemed to say, "Really?" but Vaughn just laughed, enjoying his own joke.

Winnie chuckled, shaking her head at Vaughn's antics, and then made her way over to her desk, where her crystal ball sat waiting. She held out her hand and placed it gently on top of the orb. Closing her eyes, she focused her thoughts, and in a solemn voice, said, "Show me the mummy." But before she could fully concentrate, Vaughn burst out laughing, his infectious chuckles disrupting Winnie's moment of focus. "Now what?" Winnie asked, as her forehead creased in frustration. Vaughn managed to gasp out between laughs, "You sound like a game show host!" Jynx couldn't help but join in, and soon all three of them were laughing together. Winnie couldn't resist the absurdity of the situation, and her serious demeanor melted away, replaced by the joy of sharing a lighthearted moment with her friends.

Winnie's expression turned stoic as she placed her hand back on the crystal ball. "Okay, we have to be serious now. Maybe turn around while I try and do this part," she said, attempting to compose herself. She quickly opened one eye to glance at Vaughn and Jynx, who were sitting on the bed with their backs to her. Although their bodies were shaking with suppressed laughter, they seemed to be trying their best to cooperate. Winnie closed her eye again, focusing on the task at hand. "Show me the mummy," she stated firmly.

The crystal ball began to fill with gray smoke, swirling around inside like a small vortex. As the smoke filled the orb, a small mummy appeared within its depths, standing within the walls of a castle. Winnie's eyes narrowed as she took in the details of the scene. She leaned in closer, her eyes fixed intently on the crystal ball. "I see a flag – it's waving over an army," she muttered. The wind seemed to be blowing fiercely, making it hard to discern the details. But then, for a brief moment, the wind died down, and Winnie's expression filled with excitement. "There... Aridia!" she exclaimed. "That's the fastest one we've discovered yet. You guys think you're up for another adventure?"

Vaughn and Jynx, who had been quietly observing from the bed, stood up and nodded in unison. Vaughn snapped to attention, throwing a hand to his forehead in

a sharp, soldier-like salute, his face suddenly blank.
"Ready!" Jynx, meanwhile, climbed into the satchel,
ready to be picked up. Winnie slung the satchel over her
shoulder. "Well ok then...Aridia, here we come!" she
declared, waving her hand and reciting the traveling
spell.

As the wooden door materialized before them, the
three friends stepped through it, ready to face whatever
lay on the other side. Just as the door began to close
behind them, Vaughn's voice could be heard echoing
back, mimicking Winnie's earlier words: "Show me the
mummy!" The sound of his laughter faded away, leaving
only the anticipation of the adventure still to come.

As the wooden door closed behind them, the three
friends found themselves transported to a vast, sandy
expanse. The sun beat down upon them, casting long
shadows across the dunes. Winnie squinted, scanning the
horizon for any sign of...well, anything, to be honest. The
endless dunes stretched out before them, seemingly
without end.

"Well, we're here," Vaughn said, not sounding
entirely convinced. As the group scoured their
surroundings, Vaughn threw out another thought. "Looks
like your litter box just got a major upgrade, Jynx." Jynx,
who was peeking out of the satchel, gave Vaughn a
disdainful look and swatted at his leg. Vaughn chuckled
and dodged her paw. "Now what?" he asked, looking over
at Winnie for guidance.

Winnie's eyes continued to scan their surroundings
as she stammered, trying to find the words for a plan that
wasn't quite forming in her mind. "Uh... we find the
mummy!" she said finally, her voice reaching for
confidence, though it came out more clueless than
convincing

Vaughn raised an eyebrow. "Well, we already know
that part of the plan. What do we do now, though?
There's nothing out here! I thought we were going to a
castle or something?"

Winnie's gaze remained fixed on the horizon, blocking the sun from her eyes with her hand. "We are! We're just not there yet."

Just then, Jynx poked her head out of the satchel again, her ears perked up as she sniffed the air. She meowed softly and began to squirm out of the satchel, as if eager to lead the way. Winnie's expression brightened with curiosity. "Jynx, do you know which way we need to go?"

Jynx turned her head around, meowed again, and continued walking in the direction she had started in. Winnie smiled, and the three friends set off across the dunes, their footsteps sinking into the sand.

As they walked, the sun beat down relentlessly, making every step feel like a chore. Although only an hour had passed, the trek across the desert already felt like an eternity. Finally, they caught sight of the castle wall in the distance, its stone facade rising up from the sand like a monolith.

As they approached the castle, Winnie and Vaughn began to catch a whiff of decay. Vaughn wrinkled his nose. "Well, I guess we know now how Jynx knew which way to go," he said, trying to cover his nose with his shirt.

Winnie nodded, her eyes watering slightly from the smell. "I guess it does make sense. Everything in this city is already dead, and this heat sure isn't helping it." Jynx, seemingly unaffected by the odor, continued to pad across the sand, leading the way toward the castle.

As they approached the castle, two guards stood on either side of the tall, iron gate, their stern expressions a warning to anyone who dared to approach. "State your names and reason for being here," one guard demanded.

Winnie took a step forward, her confidence unwavering. "My name is Winnie; this is Vaughn, and my companion Jynx. We've come in search of a young mummy." She launched into a lengthy explanation of the circumstances that had led them to this place, but before she could finish, the second guard interrupted her.

"You have no rightful standing to be presented to the prince," he said brusquely. "Move along."

Vaughn's eyes dropped in confusion as he shot Winnie a side-eye, then turned toward her and whispered, "Prince?"

Winnie shrugged, her shoulders barely rising off her back. This was news to her as well.

Undeterred, Winnie tried to explain the importance of her seeing the prince to the two guards, but they were unmoved. "You've been told to move along," one guard repeated. "So either move along or we'll do it for you."

Winnie's face fell and she let out a pouty hmph." "Fine," she said in frustration. "Let's go, guys."

The three of them began to walk away from the city gate, but Winnie's determination didn't waver. "Where are we going?" Vaughn asked, falling into step beside her.

"I don't know exactly," Winnie replied, "but I'm sure if we look hard enough, we can find another way into the city. We didn't come all this way to just turn around and go home, did we?"

Jynx, who had been walking beside them, tilted her head to one side, her expression seeming to say that going home didn't sound like a bad idea to her.

As they walked along the city walls, they seemed to stretch on forever, with no visible openings or weaknesses. The walls were in pristine condition, with no cracks, breaks, or openings of any kind that would allow them to sneak in.

"I'm at a loss, guys," Winnie admitted, frustration etched on her face. "I don't have a clue as to how to get inside. Why is this wall the only part of this city that's not falling apart?"

Vaughn thought for a moment before speaking up. "If I could transform into a bat, I could get over..."

".... but that wouldn't really help the two of you get over, I suppose," Vaughn added tapping his lips with his finger.

As they continued to brainstorm, Jynx wandered off to a quiet spot next to the city wall and began to dig in the sand. Vaughn happened to glance over and chuckled. "See, I told you she'd end up using it as a litter box."

Jynx's head popped out of the hole she was digging, and she gave Vaughn a withering look of death before ducking back down into the hole to continue digging. Sand began to fly out of the hole at an alarming rate, and before long, a small tunnel had appeared, leading right into the city itself.

Winnie and Vaughn exchanged a look of excitement. Both of them were thoroughly impressed with Jynx's plan, which she'd not only conceived but also executed completely on her own. With no other options in sight, they prepared to follow the tunnel into the city, uncertain of just where it would lead.

As the three crawled through the narrow tunnel, they finally emerged into a bustling bazaar, the vibrant colors and lively chatter a stark contrast to the darkness they'd just left behind.

On the other side of the wall, however, two guards just happened to be standing near the spot where the tunnel was being dug. They stood and watched, awaiting the arrival of what or whoever was digging from the other side. As they stood watching the sand pour into the hole, the guards crossed their arms and traded smug looks, clearly waiting to greet the trespassers. When the last of the sand tumbled down, Vaughn and Winnie's heads popped up out of the hole and into view.

With a quick motion, one of the guards grasped Vaughn, as he flailed his arms wildly, trying to land a punch. "Put me down!" Vaughn shouted, his feet kicking futilely at the air. The other guard scooped up Winnie in one arm, while snatching her satchel with his other hand. Unlike Vaughn, Winnie knew she was no match for the guard, and the realization settled over her face and body as she crossed her arms.

"Seems we have ourselves a couple of intruders," the first guard sneered to the other. The other guard chuckled, his voice dripping with malice. "I don't know where you thought you were going, but I know where you're going now!"

As the guards carried Vaughn and Winnie away, Jynx peered out of the tunnel, watching her friends disappear into the crowd. Her eyes widened with worry, and she knew she had to act fast. With a determined glint in her eye, Jynx set off in pursuit, trying to stay hidden as she followed the guards from a distance.

As she moved stealthily through the alleys, Jynx's heart pounded with anxiety. She had to rescue her friends but for now, she had to keep a low profile and follow the guards, hoping to find an opportunity to strike. The weight of Vaughn and Winnie's fate rested solely on Jynx's shoulders, and she knew she was their only hope for rescue.

Jynx darted between the shadows, her eyes fixed on the two guards as they carried Vaughn and Winnie through the winding alleys. She followed them closely, careful not to be seen, until they finally stopped in front of a sturdy wooden door with a small window of iron bars set into a stone wall.

The guard, holding Vaughn, produced a ring of keys and unlocked the door, pushing it open with a creak. Both guards stepped inside, carrying their prisoners with them and the door swung shut behind them, echoing through the alleyway. Jynx's ears perked up as the sound of the lock clicking into place rang out.

Without hesitation, Jynx sprang into action, leaping up from the ground and squeezing through the iron bars of the door with ease. She found herself in a dimly lit passageway while the smell of damp stone followed. The guards were nowhere to be seen, but a downward staircase beckoned, and Jynx's instincts told her to head downward.

She descended the stairs, her footsteps quiet on the cold stone. At the bottom, she peeked around the corner, her eyes scanning the hallway. The two guards had just thrown Vaughn and Winnie into an empty jail cell at the far end of the corridor. A third guard, seated at a desk just before the entrance to the jail area, looked up as the others approached. The guard who had been carrying Winnie dropped her satchel onto the desk and the third guard nodded in acknowledgment.

Her gaze fell upon the satchel that had been dropped upon the desk and she began to scan the area, her eyes and mind working in tandem with one another to devise a plan to retrieve it. For now though, she had to focus on getting Vaughn and Winnie out of their cell. She watched as the guards locked the cell door, their movements confident and routine. She knew she had to be careful or she'd find herself captured and thrown in a cell of her own.

Jynx moved stealthily down the hallway, her body pressed against the cold stone wall as she inched closer to the desk. The guard seated there seemed absorbed in his writing, his gaze occasionally flicking up to scan the dark passageway. Jynx froze, holding her breath, whenever his eyes swept in her direction.

As she drew nearer, she realized that even the slightest movement would give her away. Just as she was contemplating her next move, Winnie's eyes met hers, and Jynx knew she had been spotted. Winnie discreetly motioned to Vaughn, and together they began to create a distracting clatter, beating small rocks against the bars of their cell.

The guard, though not particularly concerned about their escape, was nonetheless pulled away from his writing. He stood up, grumbling, and began to make his way towards the cell. "Stop all that clanging back there, I can't think up here," he called out, his footsteps echoing down the hallway.

Jynx took advantage of the distraction, creeping silently behind the guard as he approached the cell. Winnie whispered to Vaughn, "Hey, why don't you hypnotize him and make him open the gate?" Vaughn's reply was slightly muffled from the clanging, "I would, but I don't even know how I did it the last time. I guess I could try, though?" The guard continued to advance, unaware of the silent conversation taking place mere feet away, with Jynx following closely behind.

As the guard approached the cell, Vaughn pressed his face against the bars, his eyes locked intensely on the guard's. "What's he doing?" the guard asked, his voice expressing concern rather than fear. Winnie whispered urgently to Vaughn, "Keep going." Vaughn contorted his face, his cheeks rising to partially cover his eyes, but the guard's expression only grew more puzzled.

The guard's brow furrowed in concern as he asked, "Is your little friend having some kind of fit?" His gaze was fixed on Vaughn's distorted features. Winnie's face scrunched up in a mixture of worry and embarrassment as she watched Vaughn's face keep rearranging in different poses. "I'm starting to wonder that myself," she admitted.

Vaughn pushed away from the bars, his face smoothing out into a mask of incredulous annoyance as he turned to Winnie. "You're the one who told me to do this, and now you're acting like I've lost my mind?" he whispered angrily.

Winnie's eyes darted towards the guard, ensuring he wasn't paying attention, before she replied in a hushed tone, "I know but you kind of looked like you had lost your mind."

The guard's expression turned stern. "Listen; stop making things worse for yourselves. Just sit tight until we have time to sort out all the details, and then we can start figuring out what to do with the both of you." With that, he turned and headed back to the desk area, unaware that Jynx had slipped into the cell behind him.

As soon as the guard was gone, Winnie scooped up Jynx and showered her with affection, squeezing her tightly. "Oh Jynx, I was afraid something terrible was going to happen to you. I missed you so much, I was afraid I'd never see you again!" Vaughn intervened, gently prying Winnie's arms from around Jynx's neck. "It's been like 10 minutes," he said, allowing Jynx to drop back down to the floor, gasping for air.

Once Jynx had recovered, Vaughn said, "Now that Jynx is here and we know she can get in and out of the cell, I think we should try to formulate a plan of escape." Winnie's eyes lit upon an idea. "My spell book could help...but it's in my satchel...and it's on the desk." She frowned, knowing the limitations. "I know Jynx can't carry it in her mouth. Plus the satchel is going to be too heavy for her to drag and even if she could, the guard would notice."

Vaughn asked, "Don't you know any magic of your own, though?" Winnie shook her head. "Well, we were learning how to cast a shadow in class the other day." Vaughn's expression turned slightly hopeful. "Okay, do that then!" But Winnie hesitated. "But I was never able to do it. It's much easier to cast the spell when I can just read it out of the book. I'm just not that great of a spell caster yet."

Vaughn's expression turned desperate. "Well, we have to try something." Winnie nodded reluctantly and began to attempt the spell, but her efforts were in vain. "I'm sorry, I told you I wasn't any good," she said with disappointment.

Vaughn placed a reassuring hand on her shoulder. "It's okay, I'm sure you'll get the hang of it soon enough. You're just like me and my own powers. We just haven't quite figured them out yet, but we will one day." His words brought a small measure of comfort to Winnie, and they continued to brainstorm, determined to find a way out of their predicament.

Vaughn and Winnie paced back and forth inside their cell, their thoughts running just as restlessly as they searched for any new escape plan. Suddenly, Winnie believed she had a miraculous idea and whispered excitedly, "The Prince!" Vaughn's gaze snapped towards her, "Where?" But Winnie's enthusiasm wasn't about spotting their royal friend; it was about using him to their advantage. "No, we just need to get to the prince," she clarified.

Vaughn raised an eyebrow, sarcasm dripping from his words. "I don't know if you've noticed the same things I have lately, but..." He swept a hand around the room in a presenting gesture. "...I'm pretty sure that's how we ended up in here in the first place." Winnie's gentle smile and soft chuckle diffused Vaughn's skepticism. "No, silly," she said. "I mean, we know Jynx can get in and out of the cell, right? Well...she can get to the prince."

Vaughn's confusion deepened, but Winnie's explanation was forthcoming. "It's simple, really. See the window up there?" She pointed to the narrow opening high above their heads. Vaughn nodded, and Winnie continued, "If I stand on your shoulders, and Jynx stands on mine, I think we can get her up to the window. And if she can reach the window, she should be able to slip between the bars."

Vaughn's eyes widened as understanding dawned. "Ah, now I get it!" Winnie turned to Jynx, who had been watching their exchange with interest. "Well, Jynx, think you can handle a big mission on your own?" Jynx meowed confidently, and Winnie smiled.

Vaughn urged them to hurry, his voice low and insistent. "We need to move, before the guards come back and find Jynx with us then." With a swift motion, he positioned himself under the window, his back flat against the cold stone wall. He laced his fingers together, creating a makeshift stirrup for Winnie. She placed a foot into his clasped hands, and with a gentle heave, Vaughn lifted her upwards. Winnie stepped onto his shoulders, her jacket cascading down around his face like a veil. "Okay Jynx, your turn." she whispered.

Jynx sprang into action, jumping from the creaky mattress to Winnie's arms. Winnie lifted her up towards the window, and Jynx peered out into the night. To her surprise, the window was ground-level with the street outside. With a nimble leap, Jynx climbed from Winnie's hands onto the bazaar's stone-paved streets once more.

Jynx's eyes scanned the bustling bazaar, her gaze darting between the crowded stalls and winding streets.

To get her bearings, she sought a higher vantage point and spotted a majestic fruit-bearing tree nearby. She scampered up the trunk, her agile body weaving between the branches, until she reached the highest limb that would support her weight.

From this lofty perch, Jynx surveyed the cityscape, her eyes tracing the jumble of rooftops until one structure stood out: the palace. Its walls towered above the surrounding buildings, a majestic silhouette against the night sky. With a clear direction in mind, Jynx descended the tree and set off through the winding streets and alleys, dodging pedestrians and carts with ease.

Within minutes, she stood before the heavily guarded palace walls. Though the barriers still seemed, somewhat formidable, Jynx's small size proved an advantage. She could squeeze through the iron bars that adorned the walls, but first, she needed to find a less-guarded spot.

After a quick scan, Jynx spotted a section of the wall with fewer guards. She darted towards it, slipping between the bars with ease. As she landed on the palace grounds, she began to make her way towards the entrance. However, the grounds were patrolled by guards, and Jynx knew she was going to have to time her movements just right.

She watched the guards' rhythmic patrols, waiting for a brief moment when their attention was diverted. Seizing the opportunity, Jynx took off in a sprint towards the front door. But just as she was about to reach it, one of the guards turned the corner unexpectedly, forcing Jynx to abort her run. She veered sharply to the side, dashing towards a fenced off area that offered temporary cover. With a burst of speed and agility, Jynx scaled the fence unknowing of what was even on the other side.

As Jynx landed on the other side of the fence, she found herself in a small, enclosed courtyard filled with old crates and discarded furniture. But her relief was short-lived, as she soon realized that now she was trapped. The fence was too high for her to climb back over, and the only exit was a small door that led back into the palace—directly into the path of the guard she had just evaded.

Undeterred, Jynx searched the courtyard for an alternative escape route. That's when she spotted a narrow gap between two crates, just large enough for her to squeeze through. She darted towards the gap and managed to wriggle free to the other side of them.

Breathless, Jynx peered around the corner, checking to see if the coast was clear. As she did, she overheard a conversation between two groups of guards. One guard, stationed near the palace wall, was speaking to a group of his colleagues.

"The king and queen have me on Prince Patrol," he said with a sigh. "Again?" one of the other guards asked, chuckling. "Yeah—again," the first guard replied. "He's locked in his room again to keep him out of trouble but that never seems to keep him out of trouble, you know. So, I just patrol the grounds below his room, and every so often I have to go up and peek through the keyhole to make sure he's still in there."

Jynx's ears perked up at the mention of the prince, and she listened very carefully. The palace was too vast an area to just go trailing off on a scavenger hunt. She knew following the guard, on prince patrol, was going to be her fastest option in finding the prince but actually getting to him was going to be something else entirely.

Jynx followed the guard discreetly, her eyes fixed on his uniform as he moved through the palace's corridor. She darted between shadows, using her small size and agility to stay out of sight. The guard's route was fairly predictable, and Jynx soon realized he was following a set path, pausing at regular intervals to peer through a specific door's keyhole.

After several passes, the guard's routine became clear. He would patrol the corridor, check on the prince, and then take his leave, descending to the grounds below. Jynx waited for her moment, her eyes locked on the guard as he began to walk away. Sure enough, he started down the corridor, his footsteps echoing off the stone walls as he made his way down the steps to the outside courtyard beneath the prince's room. As the sound of his footsteps faded, Jynx knew her chance had arrived.

Jynx crept towards the door. She listened carefully for any sound from the other side, and after a moment of silence, she lightly scratched on the door in an attempt to get the prince's attention.

The scratching sound seemed to have an effect, and Jynx stooped down to peer under the door, trying to get a glimpse of the prince's room. As she looked, she saw a pair of eyes staring back at her—the prince had also stooped down to look under the door.

Their eyes met, and Jynx felt a spark of connection. The prince whispered, "Hello? Who's there?" Jynx meowed softly, and the prince's eyes grew happy. "A cat?" he muttered "Where'd you come from?" Jynx meowed again, and the prince's face broke into a smile.

As they looked at each other, Jynx's agile mind began to work out a plan. She noticed the layout of the rooms and the windows above. She realized that if she could get into the adjacent room, she might be able to crawl along the ledge to reach the prince's window.

The prince's eyes followed hers as she stood up and moved away from the door. He whispered, "Wait...don't go!" But Jynx was already thinking several steps ahead as she quietly pranced away towards the room next door.

Jynx slipped into the adjacent room, her eyes scanning the space for the window. She spotted it and made her way over, her tail flicking back and forth with excitement. She peered out, taking in the view of the palace grounds below.

From this vantage point, Jynx could see the prince's window was just a short distance away. She measured the gap between the two windows, her whiskers twitching as she calculated the jump. It was doable; she just needed to be careful.

Jynx took a deep breath, preparing herself for the leap. She crouched low; her muscles tensed, and then sprang up onto the windowsill. She carefully balanced, her paws gripping the stone. From there, she inched her way along the narrow ledge, her eyes fixated on the prince's window.

As she approached the window the prince's eyes locked onto Jynx's, and he mouthed a question, "What are you doing out there?" Jynx examined the window; her whiskers began to fidget up and down as she searched for a weakness in the window's design. She spotted the hinges and noticed that the pins holding them together were slightly loose.

With a delicate touch, Jynx began to work on the pins, her claws digging gently into the metal. She carefully pried out the pins, pushing them upward until she could grasp the top with her mouth then she'd drop it, letting it clatter to the ground below. The sound echoed through the air, but Jynx didn't hesitate, repeating the process until all the pins were removed from each hinge.

As the last pin fell to the ground with a metallic clang, the window casing shifted slightly, and the prince was able to pull the window inside his room. He swung his leg over the sill, and Jynx helped guide him as he climbed out onto the ledge. "Wow, I don't know how you found me but I'm sure glad you did," he whispered, his voice filled with gratitude. "Now, let's figure out how to get down from here."

Jynx had just helped the prince climb out of his window and onto the narrow sill. He pressed his back flat against the stone, refusing to look down as he edged along behind her. When they reached the end of the first ledge, Jynx leapt easily to the next one. The prince froze— there was no way he could make that jump. Thinking fast, he unwound several of his bandages and knotted them together into a makeshift lasso. With a shaky breath, he tossed it toward one of the protruding stones jutting from the castle wall and managed to hook it, using the line to swing himself across to the second ledge.

As they reached the final window ledge, Jynx slipped back into the castle, with the prince following closely.

They crept through the corridors, trying to avoid detection. The prince was still tangled in his makeshift lasso and he tried to untie the knot as they moved.

Suddenly, they heard the sound of footsteps approaching from the opposite direction. The prince's eyes widened and he turned to run back the way they came but then he heard another guard approaching from that direction as well. They were trapped.

The prince looked around frantically and spotted the balcony overlooking the interior courtyard. He rushed towards it with an idea in mind.

The prince hooked his bandages around the banister, trying to lower himself and Jynx to the balcony below. But as he shifted his weight to balance them both, his foot slipped. Instead of descending, they lurched forward and swung off the upper balcony in a sudden arc. They swung down between two guards on the lower level—guards who had just crossed paths and somehow failed to notice two upside-down fugitives drifting past like a badly trained security team.

The guards continued walking, none the wiser, as the prince let go of the lasso and reached out to grab a nearby torch bracket. His fingers closed around it, and he held tight, stabilizing their swing.

Jynx, who had been clutched tightly in his arms, let out a small meow, seemingly unharmed. The prince held his breath, his eyes fixed on the guards as they disappeared around the corners of the corridor. When they were out of sight, he let out a sigh of relief and gently lowered himself and Jynx to the floor. "Next time, let's stick to the stairs," he whispered, staring blankly ahead with a tone of disbelief.

Jynx and the prince moved stealthily along the palace walls, using statues and large floor vases as cover as they dodged in and out of the guards' patrol routes. They timed their movements carefully, waiting for the guards to pass before darting to the next hiding spot.

As they neared the palace gates, the prince's heart quickened. The guards were more frequent here, and the risk of detection higher. Jynx seemed to sense his tension, staying close as they crept behind a row of bushes.

The prince peeked through the leaves, watching as a pair of guards passed by, chatting idly. He nodded to Jynx, and they sprinted across the open space, reaching the gates just as the guards turned a corner, out of sight.

They slipped through a narrow service entrance, used by palace staff to fetch supplies from the nearby market. The prince recognized the route, having used it himself on occasion. Once outside the palace walls, they found themselves standing inside the bustling bazaar.

The prince stooped down, petting Jynx on the head. "Thanks for helping me escape, little one. I won't forget it." Jynx relaxed into the gentle massage, beginning to purr. "You be careful out there, ok?" the prince said, standing up to leave.

As the prince began to walk away, Jynx sprang into action, weaving between his legs, tripping him up.

Stumbling as Jynx wound between his legs, the prince caught himself and muttered, "Whoa, easy there! Listen; I appreciate the help, but you can't come with me. Don't you have a home to get back to?" Jynx's ears folded back in annoyance. She grasped the prince's loose bandage in her mouth, tugging gently.

The prince chuckled, trying to pry his bandage free, "Hey, let go of those!" but Jynx held tight, pulling him along like a reluctant sled. The prince's eyes met hers, and he raised an eyebrow. "You want me to follow you?" Jynx released the bandage and meowed softly. The prince smiled a curious smile. "Alright then, you helped me; I'll help you. Lead the way."

Jynx led the way, navigating the crowded bazaar with ease. The prince followed, intrigued by her purposeful stride. They arrived at a familiar window, and Jynx popped her head inside, meowing softly. Winnie, pacing anxiously, and Vaughn, bouncing pebbles off the wall, looked up in unison, their faces a glow with happiness at the sight of their friends face.

"Jynx!" they whispered in tandem, their eyes darting to the prince standing behind her. The prince leaned in, peeking into the window. "She did it!" Vaughn exclaimed, a grin spreading across his face. "She actually brought the prince back!"

The prince offered a brief hello, his gaze shifting to Jynx as he asked, "So, this was why you needed my help? Looks like I wasn't the only one in a prisoner situation today, huh?" with a hint of amusement in his voice.

Winnie's gentle voice spoke up. "We were caught sneaking in, trying to find you, Your Highness." The prince shook his head, a dry smile on his face. "Just call me Wraps, okay? I'm a bit past formalities right now."

Wraps thought for a moment before continuing. "Jynx here helped me earlier, and now I'm going to repay that debt. I'm going to help get you two out of there. Just hang tight, okay?" Winnie and Vaughn exchanged a hopeful glance, their voices overlapping in a heartfelt "Thank you!"

Wraps stepped back, his eyes scanning the window's framework. "If I could remove these bars somehow..." he muttered to himself, lost in thought.

Wraps' eyes scanned the iron bars, searching for a weak point. He noticed a spot where the metal was slightly worn and corroded, a potential vulnerability. A plan formed in his mind. "Let's see if this works," he muttered, unwinding his bandage.

He looped the bandage around the bar, tying it off securely. "Okay, Jynx, I need you to help me with this," he said, handing her the end of the bandage. Jynx took the bandage in her mouth, her eyes locked on Wraps. Together, they began to pull, Wraps using his weight and strength, Jynx digging her paws into the ground and tugging with all her might.

For a moment, it seemed like the bar might budge. But then, the bandage suddenly snapped, sending both Wraps and Jynx tumbling backwards. They landed with a rustling crash in a nearby pile of trash. Wraps groaned, sitting up amidst the stench, and Jynx popped up out of the pile, unamused, with a banana peel stuck to her head.

Wraps couldn't help but laugh at the sight. Jynx gave him a withering look, her upper lip snarled at the laughter as she quickly shook the banana peel from her head. Wraps' laughter slowly died down, and he stood up, brushing himself off. "Okay, let's try something else," he said, his eyes scanning the area for a new plan. Jynx pulled herself to the top of the trash heap and trailed Wraps as he continued his search.

Wraps rummaged through the stalls, his eyes scanning for anything that might help him. He gathered a few items: a small pouch of sulfur powder, a vial of acidic liquid from a perfumer's stand, and a handful of saltpeter crystals he'd spotted in a spice merchant's stall. Jynx watched with interest as Wraps carefully mixed the ingredients in a small ceramic bowl.

The air around them filled with the pungent smell of sulfur as Wraps stirred the mixture, creating a potent corrosive paste. He applied the paste to the iron bars, carefully spreading it over the metal. Jynx sat back, her ears perked up, as they waited for the mixture to take effect.

At first, nothing seemed to happen. But then, tiny bubbles began to form on the surface of the bars, and the metal started to hiss and crackle. Wraps smiled, satisfied, as the corrosive paste ate away at the iron. The bars began to weaken, their surface pitting and flaking.

The bars finally dissolved, allowing an easy access point to be revealed. Wraps stuck his head through the new opening of the previously barred window. "You're just moments away from freedom guys!" He continued with his plan of action, "Okay, I'm going to lower my bandages for you guys to use as a makeshift rope. One at a time, make your way up the bandages to the window."

Vaughn gestured for Winnie to go first, and he cupped his hands to give her a boost onto his shoulders. From this new vantage point, Winnie was able to grasp the bandages as Wraps lowered them through the window. With minimal effort, she ascended the makeshift rope and reached the sill, where she pulled herself up and through the opening.

As Winnie emerged into the bazaar, she swept Jynx into a warm hug, showering her with praise and gratitude for her crucial role in their rescue. "Now it's your friend's turn," Wraps said with a smile, lowering the bandages back down into the cell. Vaughn secured the bandage around his foot, forming a makeshift stirrup, and grasped the fabric. "I'm ready," he called out and Winnie, Wraps, and even Jynx lent their strength to the effort, pulling Vaughn up until he could grasp the window ledge and haul himself to safety.

Once Vaughn stood beside them, he thanked Wraps for his ingenuity and bravery. "One good deed deserves another," Wraps replied, his eyes crinkling at the corners as he patted Jynx on the head once more.

As Vaughn and Winnie stood in the moonlit bazaar, they finally had a chance to introduce themselves to Wraps, their rescuer. Winnie's eyes sparkled with gratitude as she explained their quest to find him, and the reason behind it – the urgent need for his expertise in deciphering an ancient spell.

Wraps listened intently, his interest piqued by the mention of spell casting. "I'd be happy to help you with your mission," he said, a hint of excitement in his voice. But just as they were about to discuss the details, Winnie's face fell.

"My satchel!" she exclaimed. "It's still inside the jail with the guard. I completely forgot about it." Wraps' eyes narrowed, and he tapped his chin thoughtfully.

"I've got an idea," he said after a moment, "but it's going to require Jynx to take the lead again." Jynx, who had been watching the conversation with interest, nodded and let out a confident meow, as if to say, "I'm game."

Wraps smiled, a plan already forming in his mind. "Ok, here's what we're going to do," he began, his voice low and conspiratorial. The four of them huddled together, their heads bent in a tight circle as they worked out the details of their next move. Jynx's ears perked up, and she let out a series of soft meows, as if offering her own suggestions.

As they finalized their strategy, a sense of anticipation built among them. They knew that retrieving Winnie's satchel wouldn't be easy, but with Jynx's cunning and Wraps' quick thinking; they might just have a chance to succeed. With a nod, they set off into the night, ready to put their plan into action. It would need to be quick and precise in order to pull it off.

The four of them crept back to the bolted door, their plan already set in motion. "Everyone remembers what to do, right?" Wraps asked, his eyes scanning the group. The other three nodded in unison, their faces displaying a sense of driven energy.

With a silent leap, Jynx sprang up through the iron bars, squeezing through the narrow opening with ease just as she had before. She dropped to the floor below, her eyes adjusting to the dim light. Wraps unwrapped his bandages, forming a makeshift lasso once again that he slid through the bars. Jynx grasped the rope, her agile body moving swiftly as she positioned it around the heavy bolt that locked the door from inside.

Winnie and Vaughn joined Wraps in pulling the rusted bolt from its latch, their combined strength finally yielding to the metal's stubborn resistance. The door creaked open, and the four of them descended the musty staircase, this time by choice.

At the bottom, Wraps, Winnie, and Vaughn hung back, hiding in the shadows as Jynx padded silently down the corridor. She approached the guard's desk, where he sat hunched over paperwork. With a fluid motion, Jynx leapt onto the table, her tail twitching as she tilted her head and meowed, her eyes locked on the guard.

The guard, startled, dropped his pen and reached out to pet Jynx, his face softening. "Where'd you come from, little kitty?" he cooed, oblivious to the danger lurking in his midst. Jynx rubbed against his hand, purring, as she expertly snagged the keys from his belt loop.

The guard's expression changed from affection to alarm as he realized what was happening. "No, no little kitty. You can't have those. Give them back to me, please." Jynx let out a warning hiss, her claws extended, as she jumped to the floor, keys clutched tightly in her jaws. The guard lunged after her, but Jynx was too quick, darting into the jail cells with the guard hot on her heels.

As Jynx disappeared around the corner, Winnie, Vaughn, and Wraps moved swiftly to the guard's station. Winnie snatched her satchel, rummaging through it to ensure everything was still there. "Thank you again, Wraps," she whispered, her voice low and urgent. "We'll be back soon, you can count on it."

Wraps nodded, his face set in a serious expression. "Take care of yourselves, and I look forward to our next meeting." Wraps knew he couldn't be seen helping the prisoners escape so with a quick nod, he turned and made his way back to the stairwell, leaving Winnie and Vaughn to await Jynx's return.

Winnie turned to Vaughn, a confident look crossing her face, "Ready or not, it's now or never." She waved her hand, conjuring the traveling door once more. The wooden door materialized, its surface etched with intricate carvings.

As they waited, Vaughn's brow furrowed with concern. "You don't think he caught her, do you?" Winnie's expression remained calm. "She's got this." She muttered under her breath, "Come on, Jynx, I know you can do this."

Just then, a blur of black fur came racing around the corner, Jynx's eyes fixed intently on the magical doorway. Winnie and Vaughn cheered, relief washing over them. Without slowing, Jynx leapt into Winnie's arms, and together they stepped through the doorway, disappearing into the mystical world as the door closed behind them.

As they stepped back through the magical door, it materialized once again in the cozy confines of Winnie's dorm room. The three of them breathed a collective sigh of relief, their exhaustion evident after the day's ordeal. Vaughn gazed around the room, his eyes settling on Winnie as she began to ready herself for bed.

"Why does it seem that each one of these gets harder and harder?" Vaughn asked, a wry smile playing on his lips. Winnie chuckled, her hands moving deftly as she prepared for a well-deserved rest. "We only have one more to find, so let's just say a prayer that the last one isn't like that," she replied, her voice mixed with a bit of humor and concern.

As Winnie settled in for the night, Jynx had already claimed her favorite spot on the bed, curling up in a happy ball of fur. Vaughn lingered by the window, his gaze drawn to the night sky. "I'll head to bed in just a moment," he said, his voice in a contemplative state. "I just want to sit here and look at the sky for a bit."

Intrigued by Vaughn's introspective mood, Winnie walked over to him, and together they stared out of the window, their eyes meeting in a shared moment of self reflection. The moon's cast was a silver glow that covered the grounds of Darkspire, illuminating the darkness, and somehow, its gentle light seemed to seep into their hearts, softening the shadows that today's adventure had left behind.

Vaughn's words came softly, his voice filled with a newfound appreciation. "Today taught me that we take too much for granted in our everyday lives – our choices, our freedom. I just want to savor it for a bit longer."

As they stood there, side by side, the night sky stretched out before them like an endless canvas of wonder. The stars twinkled like diamonds, and the moon's gentle light cast a serene ambiance on the landscape. In that moment, the world felt huge and full of possibility and while Vaughn and Winnie might have felt small, they couldn't help but feel like they were also a part of something bigger.

Howl You Doin'?

s the morning sun streamed through the curtains, illuminating the cozy room, Winnie, Vaughn, and Jynx gathered around the breakfast spread Winnie had brought in. The familiar routine of sharing a meal and conversation was a comforting start to the day. Vaughn, however, was curious about something that had been on his mind. "Hey, I have a question," he said, his eyes locking onto Winnie's as she looked up from her food.

"Aren't we, like, in a school or something?" he asked, doing his best to speak around a mouthful of muffin. Winnie, amused by the sight in front of her, smiled, nodded, and answered with a simple, "Yeah."

Vaughn's curiosity grew deeper from her reply. "Well, how come you don't go to classes, then? I mean, every day we've been traveling to somewhere different. Aren't you going to get into trouble?"

Winnie let out a small giggle, her lips curling into a smile. "Oh, well, that's because school here at Darkspire runs a little differently than it does in most schools," she explained. "I don't have classes every day. In fact, we have very few classes each academic quarter, so we can not only practice but supposedly perfect our skills. It varies with each class quarter, but right now, I only attend every couple of weeks for each class."

Vaughn's eyes widened as he listened. "So, what's the catch?" he asked.

Winnie's expression turned serious. "The idea is to give us the basics we need to start our training, and then it's up to us to develop them. When I show up to class, I'm supposed to already show improvement from the weeks before. If I don't, I could be kicked from the list."

Vaughn's curiosity slowly became understanding. "Oh, so shouldn't you be studying, then?" he asked.

Winnie, in a somewhat unconvincing tone, "I mean, I kind of am, aren't I? Besides, there's still plenty of time for me to learn how to conjure a shadow before I go back to class. Right now, learning about this book seems much more important. This book could finally help me discover more about my family's history and who I really am or meant to be."

Vaughn's words brought a smile to Winnie's face. "You know I'm going to help you finish what we started here and when it's time for you to study, I'll help you with that too." he said, his voice filled with a confirming certainty. Winnie's eyes shone with gratitude as she threw her arms around him. "Thank you!"

She stepped back, still smiling. "Now, how about we take on one more adventure to find that last connection for the spell?"

Vaughn's eyes lit up as he nodded in agreement. He took another rather large bite of muffin and replied, "Sounds like a plan," sending tiny crumbs flying as he talked. Jynx, who had been quietly observing the exchange, slowly stood up from her early morning cat nap, as she knew what was to come.

"I've been studying over the ancient texts," Winnie said "and I think I've found a lead." She pulled the spell book out from her satchel, flipping through the pages until she found the right passage. "The last connection is hidden in a place where shadows dance and moonlight whispers secrets," she read, her eyes scanning the words.

"I think I know where this may be already," she said, looking up at Vaughn and Jynx, "but we'll still use the spell on Jynx's collar to help us pinpoint a more precise location."

"One last time," Winnie said to Jynx, her hands closing around the collar. Jynx responded with a soft "meow," and the emerald began to glow with a bright, pulsing light. As the intensity faded, the gemstone settled into a pale green hue, revealing an image of a young boy walking.

Winnie's brow raised in curiosity. "Huh—that's odd," she murmured. Vaughn's eyes snapped to hers, his interest piqued. "What is?" he asked.

Winnie's gaze remained fixed on the image. "This one isn't a monster, it's a boy," she said with a hint of surprise in her voice. A mischievous grin spread across her face, and she giggled, her cheeks flushing slightly. "A rather cute boy, at that," she added.

Vaughn rolled his eyes good-naturedly. "Girls," he muttered, earning a snort of disapproval from Jynx for his comment.

Winnie ignored the teasing, her focus returning to the task at hand. "My parents told me stories of a place called Lunara when I was growing up," she said. "There were a lot of strange folktales surrounding it, and I just always found it fascinating. That's where I think we're going, but we'll soon know for sure!"

Winnie approached the crystal ball and placed her hand on its surface. "Show me where the boy lives," she said in a commanding voice. The crystal ball responded, swirling with purplish-gray smoke that obscured the image. As the smoke cleared, the trio watched as the young boy walked through a home, his movements quiet and somber.

Their eyes followed the boy as he straightened up a room that looked like it had been robbed, his movements methodical and careful. He found a small box and a letter and as he began to read, his face crumpled, and tears streamed down his cheeks.

Winnie's expression softened, her eyes filled with compassion. "This is so terribly sad," she whispered. "I wonder what could be wrong." Vaughn's response was more pragmatic. "I don't know, but I just know there's going to be more trouble attached to it, whatever it is."

As Winnie, Vaughn, and Jynx continued to watch the young boy through the crystal ball, Winnie's gaze swept the room, searching for any hint of his precise whereabouts. Her eyes landed on a wall adorned with family photos, some smashed and still clinging to their frames, others hanging lopsided to the point of nearly falling to the floor. Amidst the chaos, one photo caught her attention: a school portrait of the boy, his smile faltering despite the forced cheer. The frame read "Wyatt Douglas" in bold letters and Winnie's eyes lingered on the name. Her gaze drifted to the school's logo stamped on the photo's corner – a cartoon chipmunk in a backpack, with the words "Crestwood Pines" etched in bold font beneath it. Winnie's face contorted in distaste. "Oh – that's unfortunate," she muttered, her eyes narrowing as she committed the logo to memory. Vaughn and Jynx exchanged a weighted glance, Jynx's head tilting slightly to one side as Vaughn's shoulders lifted in a silent shrug. "I'm fairly certain I know how we can find him," Winnie said as she began removing her hand from the top of the crystal ball.

As the smoke within the crystal ball dissipated, Winnie strode across the room. She reached the foot of the bed and grasped the worn leather satchel, its familiar weight a comfort in her hands. Jynx, ready for yet another adventure, hopped into the satchel, settling in with the air of a queen claiming her throne. Vaughn, meanwhile, finished tying his shoe and jumped down from the bed, his eyes locked onto Winnie's expression.

"Alright, guys," Winnie began, "we have a plan. We know the boy's name is Wyatt Douglas, and he goes to Crestwood Pines. With any luck, we should be able to track him down fairly quickly." Her words were met with a soft murmur of excitement from Jynx and a nod from Vaughn.

Unbeknownst to Winnie, however, their conversation was not as private as they thought. In the hallway outside, Ravyn and her familiar, Midnight, were passing by Winnie's door. Ravyn's curiosity was piqued as she caught snippets of Winnie's pep talk, and she pressed her ear against the door in an attempt to hear more of what was going on. "Who do you think she's talking to?" Ravyn whispered to Midnight as her eyes grew annoyed yet interested.

Midnight fluttered her wings silently, her gaze fixed on Ravyn's face. Ravyn knelt down, her eyes peering through the keyhole but the angle was wrong, "I can't see anything," she muttered. "Quick, fly around to the window and see what's going on and hurry!"

Midnight took to the skies, swooping down the hallway and out into the courtyard before rising up to Winnie's window. But as she reached the sill, she saw only a flash of Winnie's form stepping through a shimmering portal, the traveling door spell already activated. The room was empty, devoid of any signs of life. Midnight winged her way back to Ravyn, landing softly on her shoulder and emitting a soft "Caw, Caw."

Ravyn's eyes narrowed as she interpreted the bird's call. "A door?" she whispered in confusion. "So, little miss incompetent can't summon a shadow, but she can summon a traveling spell? Something seems off about all of this, and we're going to figure out just what it is, Midnight."

With the room now empty, Ravyn stepped back from the door, her gaze pivoting to both sides of the corridor to ensure they were alone. Satisfied, she began to whisper the words of a spell. As she spoke, her form began to shift, dissolving into a shadowy mist that seeped beneath the door and rematerialized on the other side. Ravyn's eyes gleamed with determination as she took solid form once more. She began scanning the room for any clues that might reveal Winnie's secrets and was determined to find a way to get rid of her once and for all.

Ravyn's eyes scanned the room, her gaze lingering on every inch of Winnie's space. Midnight perched on her shoulder, watching with equal intensity as they searched for any hint of what Winnie might be hiding. But despite their thorough search, they found nothing out of the ordinary – no hidden journals, no mysterious artifacts, no cryptic messages. Ravyn's frustration simmered just below the surface.

"There's nothing here, Midnight," she muttered, her voice low and irritated. "Dang it!" She paced across the room, her footsteps silent on the soft carpet. Midnight watched her, her head cocked to one side.

But Ravyn's determination didn't waver. "Well, no matter," she said, her voice cold and calculated. "We know she's up to something now, and you and I will figure it out soon enough." Her eyes locked onto Midnight's as she ran her hand down the side of her wing, and she continued, "I'm putting you on watch for the next few days. We'll know the moment she returns, and then we'll see just how fast she's able to travel away from what I'm about to bring down upon her."

Midnight let out a soft "Caw, Caw," her eyes blinking with understanding. With that silent agreement between them, Ravyn and Midnight slipped out of the room, careful not to leave a trace of their presence. Ravyn moved through the dorm building with practiced ease, stepping back out into the cool air outside. Midnight, perched on her shoulder, hopped down to Ravyn's hand. Ravyn met the bird's stare, giving a quiet, deliberate command. Midnight took flight, gliding up to Winnie's window sill, where she settled into her perch to wait for her return; her feathers ruffled slightly, as if already anticipating the challenge ahead. Ravyn's smile was methodical and malicious and her eyes became void of depth or color. The game was on, and Winnie had just become the target.

Meanwhile, the portal's door reappeared inside a beautiful grassy knoll set between an overtly dense forest and the three of them – Winnie, Vaughn, and Jynx – stepped out into what they now believed was Lunara. "Oh man, are we gonna have to walk for hours again?" Vaughn asked, his eyes scanning the surroundings. Winnie replied, "I sure hope not," her gaze drifting over the peaceful landscape. "But if we do, at least it's not as hot here."

Jynx slowly emerged from her catnap inside Winnie's satchel, stretching her tiny body and arching her back in a languid yawn. She settled into a sitting position, her eyes following the fluttering dance of butterflies as they flitted past. "It's so beautiful here," Winnie declared, her voice filled with wonder.

Vaughn, however, was distracted, smacking at his neck with a muttered irritation. "Is it? I haven't had time to notice because I keep getting attacked by mosquitoes - stupid little bloodsuckers." Winnie and Jynx exchanged a knowing glance, their faces breaking into subtle smiles as they savored the irony of Vaughn's complaint.

Winnie's expression quickly returned to a practical one, however, as she gazed out at the forest. "We should probably start walking," she said. "We don't know exactly where we are or how long it's going to take us to get out of here so we should probably figure that out before night falls." With a shared nod, the trio set off, their footsteps quiet on the forest floor as they ventured through the tall grassy knoll and into the forest before them.

As they ventured deeper into the forest, the sounds of nature enveloped them – the melodic croaks of frogs, the soft rustle of leaves, and the gentle flapping of birds' wings above. Winnie's eyes sparkled with a mix of wonder and unease. "Kind of spooky isn't it?" she asked.

Vaughn hoisted himself over a fallen tree, a chuckle rising from his throat. "Spooky? Please, I've endured Jace's shower concerts at school – this forest is nothing compared to that." The mental image was too much for Winnie and Jynx, and they burst out laughing.

Winnie's curiosity was piqued as she asked Vaughn, "So you guys have school too?" Vaughn's expression turned thoughtful as he replied, "Well, yes, but not in the traditional sense. It's more like a group home, actually. Vampire life is far from typical, even though each of us falls into a different lineage; we still come together like one big family."

Winnie found Vaughn's description confusing. "Huh?" she said, prompting Vaughn to elaborate. "Okay, so when you're a young vampire, you're not raised by an individual family. Instead, we have something called a colony. The young ones are usually left with the elders, who shape the new generation of vampires."

Winnie's eyes widened as she processed this information. "So... Jace and Mina are like your brother and sister, then?" she asked, her curiosity getting the better of her. Vaughn shrugged, as a hint of displeasure struck his face. "I guess you could say it that way, yeah."

Winnie's interest was now thoroughly piqued, and she bombarded Vaughn with question after question as they ventured deeper into the woods. Vaughn answered each one patiently, sharing stories about his life in the colony and the unique dynamics of vampire family structures. Jynx listened in as the sun began to set, casting a warm orange glow over the forest, the trio continued on their way, their conversation flowing easily as they continued walking.

As they ventured deeper into the woods, Winnie's questions continued to flow, but just as she was about to ask another, the sound of voices carried through the trees. "Hey, do you hear that?" Vaughn whispered, his eyes scanning the surroundings. Winnie's head cocked to the side. "Yeah, what is that?" she replied softly. "Maybe we're getting close to the edge of the forest near a town or something?" she suggested.

Vaughn's response was low and cautious. "Maybe, but wouldn't we see lights or something from the town if that were the case?" Before he could say more, Jynx's head shot up out of the satchel, her ears perked up like a satellite dish receiving a signal. "Everyone stay low and try to stay quiet," Vaughn whispered, motioning for Winnie to follow him behind a nearby fallen tree.

As they crouched down, Winnie's eyes widened in horror. "Oh no!" she gasped. "It's a man and a woman tied up, and they look really hurt. We've got to untie them!" She made a move to stand, but Vaughn's grip on her arm stopped her. "Wait! Something's not right here," he warned.

Winnie's confusion was evident. "What do you mean?" Vaughn's gaze swept the area, his eyes narrowing. "This whole situation doesn't add up. Why would someone leave two people tied up in the woods, beaten and bloody, with no one else around?"

Winnie took heed and began pondering Vaughn's words. "You'd think they'd try to escape or... or someone would be guarding them though," she whispered, her eyes fixed on the bound couple. Vaughn nodded in agreement. "Exactly – there's got to be someone else nearby. Let's just sit tight and observe for a bit, see what's really going on before we get mixed up in this. They could also be the bad guys for all we know."

As Vaughn continued to watch from behind the tree, Winnie pulled out her spell book, her fingers tracing the pages as she searched for something that might help them in the impending trouble. She could feel it – something was about to go down, and this time, she wanted to be ready.

The minutes ticked by with an oppressive slowness, the only sound the distant hooting of an owl and the soft rustle of leaves. The bound couple lay motionless on the ground, their labored breathing the only indication they were still alive. Vaughn's gaze swept the area, his eyes scanning the trees and underbrush for any sign of movement. Winnie, meanwhile, pored over her spell book, her eyes strained in concentration as she searched for a spell that might help them in this volatile situation.

Suddenly, Jynx's head popped up out of the satchel, her eyes fixed intently on something in the distance. Her head moved slowly, tracking the movement, and she let out a soft hiss that only Vaughn and Winnie could hear. "What's wrong, Jynx?" Vaughn whispered, his eyes narrowing as he followed Jynx's gaze.

Winnie leaned forward, her eyes scanning the area. "I don't see anything," she whispered, but Jynx's gaze remained fixed on something only she could see.

Vaughn's eyes locked onto Jynx's, his expression questioning, but Jynx's attention remained riveted on the invisible threat.

As they watched, the air seemed to ripple and distort, and a figure materialized in the clearing. The Baraffinx stood tall, its camouflage appearance dissolving as it gazed down at the bound couple. Its eyes seemed to gleam with an otherworldly intelligence, and Winnie felt a shiver run down her spine as she realized they were staring at something truly malevolent. Vaughn's grip on her arm tightened as he whispered "You know, we seem to have a lot of bad luck when it comes to cats" keeping his eyes locked on the creature. They all held their breath, waiting to see what the creature would do next.

The Baraffinx loomed over the couple, its imposing figure casting a dark shadow on the forest floor. With an unsettling gentleness, it lifted them both to their knees, their bound wrists still secured. Taking a step back, it spoke in a voice that was strong and grounded with a quiet force behind each word. "Where is the moonstone?" it asked, the words edged with a desperation that didn't match its powerful presence.

The man's head lifted slowly, his battered face a testament to the brutal treatment he had already endured. His eye was swollen, his cheek slashed and bleeding, yet he managed a defiant glint in his eye. "What are you talking about?" he rasped, barely getting the words out.

The Baraffinx's grip was swift and merciless. It seized the man by the neck, lifting him off the ground as he choked for air. "Don't play games with me, mortal," it hissed, its voice coated with ill intent. "We know you have it, and you will hand it over."

The Baraffinx dropped the man from mid-air, and he crashed to the ground, falling limp to his side. The woman's anguished cry pierced the night air as she threw herself across his battered body. "Henry!" she sobbed, her voice shaking with desperation. "We don't know anything about a moonstone... please, just let us go."

Winnie's eyes met Vaughn's, and she whispered urgently, "Vaughn, we have to do something." Vaughn's face was tense, his eyes darting back and forth as he searched for an opening. "I know – I know – I'm thinking – I'm thinking!"

The Baraffinx turned to leave. "I'm very disappointed in the outcome of our meeting today. I had truly hoped that you would have seen that this moonstone wasn't worth your life or the life of your sons – but so be it."

The man's anger flared, despite his weakened state. "If you so much as lay a hand on my son, I'll—" But the Baraffinx cut him off, its voice cold and menacing. "You'll what? Your presence is weak before my own. You don't even know what it is you possess and only those of descendant blood can even use it. So, I'll ask you one last time, for the sake of your family's life... Where is the moonstone?"

Vaughn turned back to Winnie, "We're running out of time, and I haven't come up with a plan yet. We've got to do something, and fast." Winnie's eyes widened in panic as her anxiety began to settle in.

The bound couple remained silent, and the Baraffinx's expression twisted in contempt, "Such brave yet stupid mortals. No matter, with or without your help, we'll find that stone and when we do, know now that your son will endure a worse death than your own."

The Baraffinx raised its claw, poised to strike, but just as it began to swing downward, a blur of black fur hurtled toward it. Jynx had burst from the satchel, her eyes blazing with fury. She launched herself at the creature, delivering a powerful side kick that sent the Baraffinx stumbling back. Landing with a fierce grace, she arched her back and turned to face the creature, her eyes flashing with defiance.

"Jynx!" Winnie and Vaughn gasped in unison. Vaughn's voice was tight with urgency. "Well, now we really are out of time. Do something – anything!"

Winnie's hands trembled as she flipped through the pages of her spell book, her eyes scanning the words in desperation. Without hesitation, she began to read aloud, the words tumbling from her lips in a frantic rush. She didn't know what spell she was casting, but she knew she had to act – and fast.

Winnie stood up, her voice ringing out as she recited the words of the spell, Pulchra Metamorphosis:

By shimmered hue and mirrored light,
Let form distort in gleaming flight.
Unleash the charm of chaos dressed,
And turn the world to well-groomed mess!

As she spoke the final words, a flurry of magical activity erupted around the Baraffinx. Bubble brushes materialized out of thin air, scrubbing the creature's body with frantic intensity. Buckets of water poured down on it, drenching its fur and leaving it dripping wet. Vaughn's eyes widened in surprise as he turned to Winnie, "You're giving him a makeover?" he asked in disbelief.

Winnie's face was flushed with embarrassment. "I just read the words on the page! I didn't know what they did!?" Vaughn grabbed her arm, his purpose urgent. "Come on, we've got to get Jynx and the couple." Together, they sprinted out from behind the fallen tree, racing towards the magical chaos.

As they approached, the brushes and buckets vanished, leaving the Baraffinx confused and enraged. It took a step forward, its claws extended, but before it could strike, a group of magical hair dryers appeared, blasting it with high-speed air from all sides. The creature stumbled back, its fur standing on end, and was knocked into a chair that had suddenly materialized behind it. The chair's arms strapped the Baraffinx down, holding it in place.

Vaughn helped the couple to their feet, quickly untying their bonds. Winnie scooped up Jynx, cradling her in her arms. "That was very brave of you, and also very stupid," she whispered, her voice filled with relief. "You could have been hurt. Come on, we've got to get out of here. This thing wasn't happy before and it's definitely not happy now."

As they began to run past the strapped-down Baraffinx, a magical hand appeared, holding a bottle of bright pink nail polish. The hand began to paint the creature's claws, and Winnie couldn't resist stopping for a brief moment as she was running past it. "Oooo... that's a pretty color," she said, her eyes growing with affection.

Vaughn quickly back tracked to grab Winnie by the arm and began pulling her along. "Are you serious right now? Come on!" he urged. Together, the group sprinted through the forest, the sound of the Baraffinx's enraged roars echoing behind them.

Vaughn led the group through the forest, his pace swift and purposeful. The injured man leaned heavily on the woman, his arm wrapped around her neck as they stumbled along, trying to keep up. Winnie had tucked Jynx back into her satchel, and now clutched her spell book, flipping through the pages as she ran. The sound of the Baraffinx's enraged roar echoed through the trees, growing louder with every step.

As they fled, Vaughn turned to Winnie, his eyes scanning the pages of her book. "He's loose! You got anything else in that book of yours that could help us? Maybe we could throw him a birthday party or even a wedding reception, perhaps?" Winnie shot him a playful glare, sticking out her tongue. "I told you already, I don't know what any of this says until I start reading it!" she shouted back, her breath coming in ragged gasps.

Vaughn's expression turned serious. "Well, start reading something, because he's closing in on us again!" he warned in urgency. Winnie's eyes darted back to the pages, her fingers flying as she searched for a spell that might help them escape the Baraffinx's clutches. The sound of crashing branches and snapping twigs grew louder, and Winnie knew they were running out of time.

Winnie's fingers flew through the pages of her spell book, stopping randomly on a spell that seemed to leap off the page. She began to recite the words aloud, her voice carrying through the forest as she ran – Naturea Clamor:

"Nature weeps in wind and thorn,
Her voice a hiss where swarms are born.
From leaf and root, the call takes flight,
A thousand wings blot out the light."

As she spoke the final words, the sky around them began to darken, as if day was turning to night. The group looked up to see thousands of tiny insects swarming towards them, their sheer numbers blocking out the light. The sky was thick with the buzzing of wings and the group stumbled, their visibility reduced to almost zero. Vaughn's voice came out of the chaos. "I feel like a windshield," he said, trying to keep bugs out of his mouth.

The group pushed on, their footsteps faltering as they tried to navigate the thicket of insects. But luckily, Winnie's magic wasn't strong enough to sustain the spell, and the swarm began to dissipate, leaving them gasping for air. Vaughn glanced back, seeing the Baraffinx closing in on them. "Try again!" he shouted.

Winnie's fingers flew through the pages once more, stopping on a new spell. She began to recite the words, her voice ringing out through the forest – Arcana Displosio.

"Thread the weave and twist the core,
Let silence crack what came before.
A shimmer builds, the air turns thin –
Then magic bursts from deep within."

As she finished the final words, the ground beneath them began to rumble and quake. The group stumbled, forced to stop running as the seismic forces shook the earth. For a moment, there was silence. Vaughn's voice was nonchalant as he spoke up. "Well, that one wasn't so bad."

But before he could finish, the ground began to crack open in random areas throughout the forest, the sound of thunder booming through the trees. Vaughn froze, his eyes darting to the side as the ground cracked open around them. His expression changed in an instant, and he muttered, "...and there it is."

With the Baraffinx closing in and the ground no longer shaking, the group picked up their pace, desperate to escape the forest. The air was filled with the sound of explosions and the ground splitting open, releasing pulsing blasts of white and purple energy. The once peaceful forest had transformed into a battlefield, with blasts erupting all around them. They dodged and weaved through the pockets of energy but the Baraffinx was relentless, adapting its pursuit to their movements.

As the seams in the earth began to close, Winnie's powers fading once again, the Baraffinx drew closer, its rage and fury obvious. "It's gaining on us! We're not going to make it!" Vaughn shouted in panic.

Winnie frantically flipped through the pages of her spell book, her eyes scanning the words as she searched for a solution. Her fingers stopped on a page, and she began to read aloud, her voice steady and clear – Cavea Temporis.

> *"Freeze the pulse and lock the air,*
> *Suspend the world with quiet care.*
> *No motion now, no sound, no age –*
> *All held fast in moment's cage."*

As she spoke the final words, Winnie ran around a tree that had laid fallen, losing sight of the others that had once been beside her. When she turned to look, she saw that the spell had worked. Everything was frozen in time – the Baraffinx, the trees, and the couple. The Baraffinx was poised to attack, its claws outstretched, mere inches from the couple's backs.

Winnie knew her magic wouldn't last forever, she had to act fast. She rushed over to the couple, grabbing them and pulling them towards her. As she touched them, they sprang back to life, stumbling forward as they regained their momentum. "Keep going!" Winnie urged.

She repeated the process with Vaughn, grabbing his arm and pulling him towards her. Vaughn stumbled, his eyes wide with confusion. "What in the world?" he muttered, but Winnie just shook her head. "No time, just run."

Together, the group made their way to the edge of the forest, the silence and stillness a welcome relief from the chaos they had just faced. As they emerged into the open, they slowed their pace, gasping for breath.

The woman turned to Winnie and Vaughn, her eyes shining with gratitude. "Thank you...for everything. I don't know who or what you are or even where you came from, but we're truly grateful."

Vaughn's expression was grim. "You're welcome, but I don't feel like we're out of the woods just because we're out of the woods."

The woman nodded in agreement. "I feel you're right. We must get back to the house. We have to get to Wyatt."

Winnie dragged in a breath and looked up at the woman. "Wyatt... Wyatt Douglas?"

The woman's eyes showed caution, "Yes, do you know my son?"

Vaughn interrupted, "I'm sorry but could we possibly finish escaping while you guys catch up?"

The group quickly composed themselves and started making their way back into town as fast as they could. Winnie and Vaughn filled the couple in on their story, explaining that Winnie was searching for five others like her in order to perform a magical spell that would unlock the secrets of the spell book she held. The couple listened intently, their faces etched with both concern and curiosity.

As they walked, the couple began to share their own story. "Years ago, a woman showed up at our doorstep, holding a small baby," the woman explained, her voice filled with emotion. "She was slashed and bleeding, but she was doing everything she could to protect the child from the cold. She handed the baby to us and begged us

146

to take care of him, to always protect him. She told us his name was Wyatt."

The woman's eyes seemed to glaze over as she recounted the story, reliving the memories. "She looked human, but her eyes...they shone like a wolf's. And there were patches of gray fur still clinging to her human form. We didn't know much about her, but she passed away soon after giving us the baby. Before she died, however, she also gave us a ring and told us to protect it and Wyatt at all costs."

The man took over, his voice filled with a sense of importance. "We've taken care of Wyatt all these years, and we've always felt like there was something special about him. The woman who brought him to us didn't leave any instructions about what to do if danger came looking for Wyatt, so we wrote a letter to him, explaining everything we knew about his past and the woman who brought him to us. We tucked it away in a safe place, hoping it would never be needed."

The couple shared every detail they could remember, from the woman's appearance to the ring and the letter. As they spoke, Winnie and Vaughn exchanged a look of growing unease. It was clear that the couple's story was connected to the supernatural events they had been experiencing and that Wyatt's safety was definitely in peril – maybe even more than they had initially thought.

Winnie's eyes met Vaughn's, and she spoke in a hushed tone. "When Wyatt showed up on the crystal ball, we saw him crying and reading a letter. I bet that's the letter he was reading, the one his parents had written." Vaughn's expression turned grim as he nodded in agreement. "I bet you're right. He's in some serious danger and doesn't even know it. He's nowhere prepared to deal with whatever it was we just went through back there in the woods. We have to find him and fast."

Winnie nodded. As they entered the town, Mrs. Douglas quickly unlocked the car and ushered everyone in. "We were out searching for Wyatt last night when we were attacked and dragged off," she explained. The five of

147

them, including Jynx, flooded into the Douglas's car, and with a pressing weight upon them, they sped off towards their house.

The sun was beginning to set, casting a golden glow over the landscape. Unbeknownst to them, the fading light would soon grant the Baraffinx freedom to roam beyond the forest's edge, unleashing a new wave of terror upon them. The group drove in silence, their anxiety growing with every passing moment. They knew they had to find Wyatt before it was too late with hopes that it wasn't already.

As the car pulled up to the family home, relief washed over the group, only to be quickly replaced by a sense of immediacy. The five of them piled out of the vehicle and quickly made their way towards the front porch, Mrs. Douglas still supporting her husband's weight. Just as they reached the steps, Wyatt burst out of the front door, his eyes fixed on his parents' battered faces. The letter and ring box clutched in his hand trembled as he rushed towards them.

"Mom, Dad—what happened?" Wyatt demanded, fear tightening his voice. As he reached his parents, a flurry of questions tumbled out. "Who did this to you? Are you okay? We need to get you to a hospital! Who are these guys?" But his mother cut him off, her voice firm and commanding. "Wyatt, there's plenty of time to go over all of this later. Right now, we need to get some things and get out of here."

Wyatt's face shifted into a look of confusion. "Get out of here? What do you mean? What's going on?" But his mother's expression left no room for argument. "Wyatt, not now – I need you to get in the house and pack a bag. We've got to go!" The tone in her voice was unmistakable, and Wyatt quickly sprang into action, helping his mother support his father's weight as they entered the house.

As they helped Henry onto a lounge chair, the chaos erupted around them. Mrs. Douglas rushed to gather medical supplies, while Vaughn, Winnie, and Jynx kept watch, their eyes scanning the windows for any sign of the creature. Wyatt dropped the letter onto the coffee table, the paper fluttering to a stop, and slipped the ring box into his pocket.

"Veronica," Henry grunted, his voice strained. His wife rushed back into the room, iodine, cotton balls, and gauze bandages in hand. "I'm here, honey!" she said, quickly setting to work on his wounds. Vaughn turned from the window, his expression grim. "We need to hurry." The sun was setting, casting long shadows across the room, and the daylight was fading fast. As the last rays of sunlight disappeared behind the treetops, the forest outside seemed to grow darker, more menacing.

Just then, Jynx's head jerked towards the back of the house, her ears perked up in alert. She hopped down from Winnie's shoulder and let out a low, menacing meow as she slowly crept towards the side door. Winnie's eyes followed her, squinting to focus on any sign of movement. "What is it, girl?" she whispered, but Jynx's agitation only grew.

The wind outside began to pick up, causing the door to slam open and shut with increasing force. The lights in the house flickered, their eyes darting towards the ceiling causing the group to exchange nervous glances. Wyatt, who had been descending the stairs, froze, his eyes fixed on something behind them.

"Look out!" he shouted.

The group turned to see the Baraffinx standing in the room, its massive frame seeming to fill the space. Winnie and Vaughn huddled together, Jynx positioned protectively in front of them, her fur standing on end as she hissed at the creature. Henry struggled to shield his wife, who was screaming at the top of her lungs, "Leave us alone!"

The Baraffinx began to stalk towards them, its eyes fixed on its prey. "I want that moonstone," it growled, its voice like thunder. "And I'm not leaving here again without it."

Vaughn, trying to distract the creature, picked up a heavy object from the nearby desk and hurled it at the

Baraffinx's head. "Would you settle for a paperweight?" he quipped in a sarcastic tone.

The creature grunted as it struck, causing the Baraffinx to reveal its rows of teeth. Vaughn whispered to Winnie, "I may have made a terrible mistake here," as he grabbed her arm tighter and tried to slide in behind her, crouching down. He then slowly rose back up behind Winnie and whispered in her ear, "And that is NOT a pretty nail color by the way."

Vaughn had been successful in attracting the Baraffinx's attention but then it suddenly redirected its attention to Wyatt, who stood frozen on the stairs. "You!" it growled. "You have it! I can feel its power from here. Give it to me, or watch your parents die in front of you."

"Wyatt, run!" his mother screamed but Wyatt was frozen on the stairs, paralyzed by fear and confusion. "The what?" he stammered. "I don't even know what that is?" He tossed the bag he was carrying down the steps, sending it sliding across the floor towards the creature. "Here! Whatever it is, take it. Just leave my parents alone!"

The creature's eyes lit up as it followed the bag, its claws ripping through the fabric as it searched for the moonstone. The group took advantage of the distraction, hastily gathering together and making their way up the stairs. They barricaded themselves in the parents' bedroom, the door creaking under the pressure as it still hadn't been fixed from before.

"This won't hold him for long," Winnie warned. "We're going to have to get out of here." Suddenly, an idea struck her, and she began to recite the words of a spell, her hands weaving intricate patterns in the air. The air shimmered and a portal of light appeared before them.

The creature's roar of frustration echoed through the hallway as it clawed at the barricaded door. Winnie drew a symbol on the door and it glowed with a bright blue light, illuminating the portal. "Quickly, everyone inside!"

she urged, and the group stepped through the doorway, disappearing into the light.

As the doorway vanished, the Baraffinx burst through the barricade, its eyes scanning the empty room. Realizing the moonstone was gone yet again, it let out a deafening screech that echoed through the night.

On the other side of the portal, the group stumbled out into a familiar living room. Vaughn's eyes widened as he took in the surroundings. "Hey, you brought us back to Freddy's house!" he exclaimed.

Winnie nodded, a small smile playing on her lips. "I remembered we cast a cloaking spell on the house. I figured it would be the safest place to hide the Douglas's... at least for now."

Freddy and Ethan burst into the room, their faces etched with concern. "Winnie – Vaughn – Jynx," Freddy shouted, rushing to hug his friends.

Winnie quickly explained the situation, and Mr. Sutorre's face softened with gratitude. "You can stay as long as you need to," he said, his voice warm. "We'll take care of the Douglas's."

Winnie made her way over to Wyatt, who still looked dazed. "I know you have a lot of questions," she said gently. "And honestly, I wish I had more time to answer them but I need to get back to school. Take some time, sit down and talk with your parents. I think you all have a lot to talk about" She hugged Wyatt, who stood there, still looking baffled and said "These are some friends of ours and they're going to look after you guys for a bit and keep you safe." Wyatt, not even knowing who this girl was, watched as she, Vaughn, and Jynx slipped through the summoned door once again, leaving him alone with unfamiliar faces in an unfamiliar place — and more questions than he knew what to do with.

What are you Ravyn About?

The darkness had long since settled over Darkspire Academy, casting a somber silence over the grounds. Midnight, Ravyn's faithful familiar, stood vigilant on Winnie's windowsill, her piercing gaze fixed on the night. She had been stationed there for hours, watching and waiting. Suddenly, a soft hum of magic filled the air, and a wooden door materialized within the room. Midnight's eyes widened as she watched, her feathers ruffled by the sudden burst of energy.

As the door swung open, Winnie stepped out, pulling her satchel off from around her neck and setting it on the bed. Midnight let out a soft squawk and took to the skies, flying swiftly across campus to deliver her message. As she disappeared into the night, Vaughn emerged from the doorway behind Winnie, none the wiser to Midnight's swift departure, nor was she of his arrival.

Moments later, Midnight landed on Ravyn's windowsill, her beak tapping insistently against the glass. Ravyn, who had been sitting at her vanity, rose to her feet, a knowing glint in her eye. "So, the troublemaker's back is she?" she murmured, a sly smile spreading across her face as she opened the window to admit Midnight.

The raven let out a series of sharp caws, and Ravyn's laughter echoed through the night air. "Well, classes start back in the morning, and Professor Silvermist has already warned us that there will be consequences if we don't improve. What do you say we give little Miss Know-It-All some additional help during tomorrow's performance, Midnight?" The raven responded with a series of caws, as if mimicking Ravyn's laughter and the two of them shared a moment of amusement at Winnie's expense.

The morning routine unfolded with practiced ease. Winnie descended upon the school cafe, returning with a tray laden with bowls of cereal and milk. As she set the breakfast before Vaughn and Jynx, she gazed at Vaughn with a concerned expression. "I've got a few classes today, so I'll be a little while before coming back. Will you be okay here all alone for a few hours?" Vaughn, his face buried in his cereal bowl, murmured a distracted "M'hmm."

Winnie's eyes lingered on him, unsure if he'd even registered her question. "Uh-huh... well, I'll get back as soon as I can, and we can discuss the next part of the plan," she said, standing up to finish getting ready. As she grabbed her satchel, she called out to Jynx. "Jynx, are you ready to go?"

As she turned back to the breakfast area, she was met with a sight that made her face cringe. Vaughn was lowering his bowl, a wide grin spreading across his face, his mouth and chin smeared with milk and cereal. Beside him, Jynx lifted her head out of her bowl, her fur matted with cereal pieces and milk dripping from her whiskers.

Winnie's eyes rolled heavenward, "Really guys? You two act like a bunch of animals sometimes." Vaughn wiped his mouth with his sleeve, his gaze meeting Jynx's, and the two of them exchanged a mischievous glance.

"I don't see any animals in here, do you, Jynx?" Vaughn asked in amusement. Jynx shook her head, sending milk and cereal flying in all directions. Vaughn followed up with a rather impressive burp and the two of them dissolved into a fit of silent laughter.

As they finished their antics, they turned back to Winnie, who stood frozen in the doorway, a complex mixture of anger, disgust, and disapproval etched on her face. With pieces of cereal and splashes of milk now dripping from her hair and face, "Get in the bag," she said to Jynx, her voice icy calm, her face immobile.

With a swift motion, Winnie brushed off the cereal and milk splashes from her clothes and hair, her eyes still flashing with a mix of annoyance and amusement. Meanwhile, Jynx had begun to clean herself up, licking her paws and smoothing her fur. Satisfied with her cleanliness, she hopped into the satchel, settling in with a soft rustle.

"Okay, Vaughn, we're heading out," Winnie said..
"Remember to be quiet in here. No one can know you're
in here and there are some snacks on the desk for you to
munch on later. Oh, and don't forget to lock the door
behind us."

Vaughn, still riding the high of his mischievous
breakfast escapade, sprang to his feet and saluted Winnie
with a grin, his eyes sparkling with amusement. Winnie's
expression remained stern but a hint of a smile played on
her lips as she closed the door behind her.

As the door clicked shut, Vaughn's smile broadened
and he sauntered over to the door to turn the lock, the
soft click of the mechanism engaging a satisfying sound.
With his task complete, he flung himself onto the bed,
letting out a comfortable sigh as he sank into the pillows.
A post-breakfast nap was just what he needed, and he
closed his eyes, drifting off into a peaceful slumber.

As Winnie and Jynx took their seats in Dark Arts 101,
Professor Black's monotonous drone threatened to lull
them into a deep slumber themselves. The lecture was a
familiar routine, one that required minimal attention and
maximum restraint to stay awake. Winnie's eyes drooped,
her chin dipping toward her chest as Jynx shifted
uncomfortably beside her.

Meanwhile, in the dorm room, Vaughn was enjoying
a peaceful nap, oblivious to the dangers that lurked
outside. His slumber was short-lived; however, as the
sound of voices outside the door pierced the silence. A
girl's voice, low and methodical, spoke just outside the
room. "Okay Midnight, fly down the end of the hall and
keep an eye out for me."

Vaughn's eyes snapped open as the doorknob began
to turn. Panic set in as he realized someone was trying to
enter the room and it wasn't Winnie. He darted back and
forth across the room, his mind racing with desperation.
In a moment of absurdity, he grabbed the lampshade and
placed it over his head, only to realize how ridiculous he
must look. He quickly discarded the idea and dropped to
the floor, attempting to slide under the bed. However, the

space was cluttered with boxes, making it impossible for him to fit.

With his heart racing and his ideas running low, Vaughn leapt to his feet and dove into a pile of stuffed animals in the corner of the room. He buried himself under a mountain of fluffy bodies, trying to remain still and silent. Just as he thought he'd managed to conceal himself, a black smoke began to billow into the room. Vaughn's mind flashed with visions of fire and destruction, and he thought to himself, "Great, I'm going to die under a rhinoceros." But as he felt the soft plush of the stuffed animal above him, he second-guessed himself, "or is that a dragon?" The absurdity of the situation wasn't lost on him, even in his panicked state.

The smoke continued to swirl, and Vaughn's thoughts were replaced by a growing sense of unease. The smoke began to fuse into a stunning young woman, her eyes scanning the room with an air of confidence. Vaughn's eyes widened as he took in her ethereal beauty, his fear of being discovered momentarily forgotten. The girl moved with a confident air, her eyes darting across the room as if she knew it intimately. Vaughn watched, transfixed, as she glided across the floor. Who was she, and what did she want? And how had she managed to just... appear like that?

As Vaughn lay hidden beneath the pile of stuffed animals, he watched in growing unease as the girl continued to search the room. She moved with a quiet purpose, her eyes scanning the space as if searching for something specific. Her lips moved in a whispered chant, "Something to use, something to use," as she examined the room's contents. Vaughn's confusion deepened; what was she looking for?

The girl's eyes narrowed and she stood in the center of the room, her hands on her hips. She spun slowly, her gaze sweeping the space as she murmured, "Something personal, what could it be?" Her eyes seemed to lock onto the pile of stuffed animals, and Vaughn felt a jolt of fear as he thought she was looking directly at him. He froze, holding his breath as she held his gaze for a moment longer.

But then she took a step closer, and Vaughn's panic spiked. He squeezed his eyes shut, bracing for the worst as he felt her presence looming over him. He felt the pile of stuffed animals shift, and his heart sank. He was caught.

"Perfect," the girl's voice declared in a soft yet vile tone and Vaughn's eyes remained clamped shut, waiting for the inevitable.

But instead of being grabbed or exposed, he heard the girl's voice continue, "Now to teach that stupid little witch and her feline beast a thing or two about putting their noses and claws where they don't belong. This little trinket is all I need for my little spell to work."

Vaughn's eyes snapped open and he saw the girl standing nearby dangling a small object in her hand. Her eyes gleamed with malice as she stood there looking at the trinket. Vaughn suddenly realized that she was after Winnie and Jynx.

The girl's head jerked towards the door, her ears perked up as she caught the faint sound of Midnight's warning calls echoing down the hallway. With a swift movement, she turned and glided towards the door, her dark form silhouetted against the dim light of the room. As she reached the threshold, she raised her hands, and the familiar words of the magic spell spilled from her lips once more. The air around her began to shimmer and distort, and she dissolved into a mist of black smoke, slipping effortlessly under the door to vanish into the hallway beyond. The room was left silent; the only sign of her presence was the faint whisper of darkness that fell back with Vaughn's secret encounter.

Vaughn knew in that moment that he was going to have to find a way to warn Winnie about what just took place, but how? He was a trespasser, not even supposed to be in the realm of GrimWood, let alone in the school. The weight of his situation settled upon him and he knew he had to act fast. The girl's malevolent intentions were clear, and Vaughn couldn't just lie there and do nothing. But what could he do?

Vaughn's eyes darted frantically around the room as he tried to form a plan in the rapidly shrinking window he had. He needed to act fast, to find a way to warn Winnie before it was too late. But how could a vampire possibly navigate the halls of a witch's school without being detected? That's when it hit him - a marvelous idea; a disguise. He suddenly knew exactly what he needed to do. However, as he realized the specifics of his plan, he already hated the idea of having to do it.

With worry steadily growing, Vaughn began to gather the items he needed. He shed his cape and outer layers, replacing them with Winnie's witch's hat, which sat awkwardly on his head. Next, the wig — a riotous tangle of fur pilfered from one of the stuffed animals in the corner of the room. Winnie wasn't going to be thrilled about owning a bald pony now, but time was of the essence. A cream-colored turtleneck followed, pulled up over his mouth to conceal his fangs. The long gray skirt seemed to swirl around his ankles as he stepped into it. Winnie was a tad taller than him so everything seemed to fit just a little on the larger side of things. And then, he slipped his feet into a pair of heels that fit him perfectly — finally, a lucky find, but also a blow to his ego all at the same time.

Vaughn surveyed his reflection, or rather, the lack thereof. As a vampire, he didn't cast an image in the mirror but he could sense the absurdity of his situation. The floating clothes seemed to mock him, the hat askew, the wig a tangled mess. He felt like a fool but he pushed the thought aside. He had a role to play and play it he would.

Vaughn grasped the doorknob, nausea quickly hitting his stomach. "It's now or never," he thought, taking a deep breath before turning the handle and stepping into the hallway. The empty corridor stretched out before him, a welcomed relief. "So far, so good," he muttered, his heels clicking on the floor as he made his way down the hall. He winced with each step, struggling to walk in the unfamiliar shoes.

As he navigated the unfamiliar surroundings, Vaughn's mind turned to remembering Winnie's schedule. "Dark Arts 101, that's right. And then...come on, think!" he muttered to himself, trying to recall the details of her class schedule.

Just as he was starting to get his bearings, a soft voice spoke up behind him. "Hi there – Are you lost?" Horror flashed in Vaughn's eyes, the kind that made him feel like he could've died all over again — as he turned to face the young student witch. He forced a smile onto his face, adopting a higher-pitched tone. "Oh, yes! Maybe you can help me. I'm looking for my...uh...cousin. She's in class right now and I'm not sure where to find her. There's been a family emergency and I need to speak with her right away."

The young witch's expression turned sympathetic. "Oh, that's just dreadful! Is it serious?" Vaughn's high-pitched voice trembled slightly as he launched into an absurd tale he'd concocted on the fly. "Oh my, yes! It's quite horrible. It seems Grand ma-ma took a sneezing fit during one of her spells and took out a door-to-door broom salesman."

The young witch looked taken aback, her eyes wide with surprise. Vaughn couldn't resist adding another detail, his nervousness getting the better of him. "Yes, it seems the poor lad had no sooner said 'half off' than...well, that's exactly what happened – Right after...half off." The young witch stared at him, her expression a mixture of confusion and horror.

Vaughn's heart sank, realizing he'd gone too far. But then, to his surprise, the young witch nodded briskly. "Why don't we just get you to where you need to go."

Vaughn's eyes crinkled at the corners as he smiled under the turtleneck, though the young witch could only see him squint slightly. "Ok," he replied in a higher-pitched voice, trying to maintain the facade.

The young witch nodded and asked, "So, where is it that you do need to go?" Vaughn hesitated, unsure of Winnie's exact schedule. "You know, I'm not quite sure actually," he admitted, hoping his awkwardness wouldn't arouse suspicion. "I'm not too familiar with her schedule, but I know she's a first year and taking Dark Arts 101."

Rosanna's face lit up with a bright smile. "Oh, ok! I can take you there. It's just around the corner. I think Professor Black is still teaching, even." Vaughn's face contorted into a giddy expression, though it was muffled by the turtleneck. "Wonderful!" he exclaimed.

As they walked down the corridor, Rosanna turned to him and said, "I'm Rosanna, by the way. What's your name?" Vaughn's mind went blank, and before he could think, he blurted out his real name. "Oh, I'm Vaughn...da...Vonda," he stuttered, hastily adding the feminine suffix to his name.

Rosanna didn't seem to notice his slip-up, smiling warmly instead. "It's nice to meet you, Vonda. Well, here's the class. Would you like for me to knock and ask for your cousin?" Vaughn's eyes locked onto the classroom door, his nerves starting to get the better of him. "Would you please?" he replied, trying to sound grateful rather than anxious.

Rosanna nodded and stepped forward, raising her hand to knock on the door. Vaughn held his breath, wondering what would happen next.

A hum drum voice answered to Rosanna's knock "Yes?" Rosanna pushed the door open and poked her head inside. "I'm sorry to intrude, Professor Black, but I'm looking for one of your students. It seems there's been a family emergency."

Professor Black's expression turned serious. "Oh? And who exactly is it that you're looking for?" Rosanna turned to the disheveled figure standing behind her, a questioning look on her face. "Who was your cousin again?" she asked.

Vaughn, trying to maintain his disguise, replied in a higher-pitched tone, "Her name is Winnie; very sweet girl. Has a black cat with her, she's not as sweet." Rosanna's expression turned odd but she nodded and turned back to the professor. "I'm looking for Winnie."

Winnie's head snapped up in her seat, her eyes widening in surprise. Jynx, sitting beside her, mirrored her expression, both of them caught off guard. Professor Black began to speak, addressing Winnie before allowing her to leave. "Winnie, you'll need to review three and complete the accompanying exercises. Next lesson, we'll be discussing advanced shadow magic."

Winnie nodded, her eyes fixed on the doorway as she made her way out of the classroom. As she emerged into the hallway, her gaze landed on Vaughn and her eyes went wide with shock. Jynx followed suit, her eyes widening in surprise as she took in Vaughn's ridiculous outfit. Then, her face cracked, and she burst into a fit of laughter, quickly stifled as Winnie pushed her head into her satchel and closed the flap. Vaughn grabbed Winnie's arm, his eyes locked on Rosanna. "Thank you so much for your help," he said, gratitude softening his expression even more.

Rosanna smiled and nodded. "You're very welcome! I hope everything works out for your grandmother." Vaughn's eyes crinkled at the corners as he smiled; still trying to maintain his disguise. "Oh, I'm sure it will. She didn't need a new broom anyway. Thanks again! Come, Winnie, we can't keep Grand ma-ma waiting!" With that, he tugged Winnie down the hallway, his ankles twisting and teetering in her shoes. On occasion he'd nearly take Winnie down with him as he tried to walk upright in them as the two quietly bantered back and forth trying to make it down the hall.

As they disappeared around the corner, Rosanna watched them with a puzzled expression. "I don't think that's the only emergency in that family" she muttered to herself before turning and heading in the opposite direction.

As they turned the corner, Winnie's grip on Vaughn's arm tightened and she spun him around, her eyes

160

horrified at the site she had just witnessed, for more reasons than one. "What are you doing?" she asked sharply.

Vaughn's response was muffled by the turtleneck, but his words were heavy with desperation. "I had to find you and I didn't know of any other way to do it!" he whispered anxiously.

Winnie's gaze narrowed. "Why? You could have been found out. What was so urgent that it couldn't have waited until I got back to the room later tonight?" Her voice now mixed with frustration and fear.

Vaughn quickly recounted what he had witnessed in the room, his words tumbling out in a hushed, urgent tone. Winnie's eyes widened as she listened and she let out a sharp gasp. "Ravyn!" she exclaimed, causing Jynx to pop her head out of the satchel once more, this time with a distasteful look in her eyes.

Winnie's expression turned determined. "Ok, go back to the dorm room, I'll meet you there in a moment," she instructed Vaughn, her voice firm. As she turned to dismiss him, a spark ignited within her eyes. "Two can play at this game," she said, her voice steady and resolute.

Vaughn's footsteps echoed down the hallway, the click-clack of his heels fading into the distance as Winnie watched him with a mixture of embarrassment and gratitude. She turned her attention to the satchel at her side, where Jynx sat patiently. "We don't have much time, Jynx," Winnie whispered urgently. " Spell-Casting class will begin soon, and we have to figure out a way to stop whatever Ravyn's plan is."

Jynx nodded in agreement, and Winnie pulled out her spell book, thumbing through its pages with a look of frustration. "I really wish this thing was easier to read, Jynx," she muttered, flipping page after page. She flipped back to the front of the book, where the table of contents was written in a language she couldn't decipher. She ran her fingers over the page, and the words began to reveal themselves as she moved. "Potions, Charms, Hexes, Spell crafting...Let's take a look at charms, Jynx."

As she flipped to the charms section, Winnie's eyes scanned the pages, her fingers moving quickly over the text. "Luck, Sleep, Warding, Counter, Mood...Oh Jynx, I wish I knew what she was planning. I don't have a clue where to begin, really? We could try to ward off her magic?" Jynx nodded, and Winnie continued to deliberate. "Or should we attack back with a counter spell? That could get us in some major trouble though and would probably make her even angrier with us on top of it all."

Jynx took her paw and tapped the book on the page of warding and Winnie nodded in agreement. "I think you're right, Jynx. Warding is our safer bet." She ran her hand over the page and the directions and incantation for the spell revealed themselves. Winnie's eyes scanned the text. The bell would be ringing soon and the halls would be filled with students again. There was little time to waste.

Winnie's fingers slid across the pages of her spell book, the words and symbols revealing themselves as she moved. She was searching for a warding spell that could help her and Jynx counter Ravyn's plans. As she scanned the pages, one spell in particular caught her eye. She read the passage aloud but softly, as her fingers continued to guide her through the text. "The spell needs an item that can be a grounding point, Jynx. I guess that's the charm."

Winnie rummaged through her satchel, her eyes scanning the contents as she searched for anything that might work. "Well, we have an eraser and a piece of candy," she told Jynx, holding up the two items. Jynx's eyes fixed on the candy, snatched it from her hand with lightning-fast speed and swallowed it whole. Winnie chuckled and shook her head. "Eraser it is, then."

With the eraser selected, Winnie held out her hand, palm up, and placed the small object in the center. She took a deep breath, her eyes focusing on the eraser as she began to recite the spell. Her voice was steady and clear, the words flowing from her lips like a gentle stream.

"Magia Obsto," she whispered, the words seeming to take on a life of their own.

"By mystic words, I seal this charm,
To stop all magic, keep safe from harm,
For the one who holds this token true,
Magic stops, but only with you."

As she spoke the final words, the eraser began to project a soft glow, filling Winnie's palm with a warm, gentle light. She felt a surge of energy flow through her, and she knew that the spell had taken hold. The eraser, now imbued with magical power, should protect her from any magic that might come her way. Winnie smiled, feeling a sense of confidence wash over her. She now felt ready to take on whatever Ravyn had to throw at her.

Winnie placed the eraser back into her satchel and looked at Jynx. "Okay, Jynx, I think we're ready." She smiled, and together they made their way to Professor Silvermist's class.

As they entered the classroom, Professor Silvermist clapped her hands, her voice ringing out across the room. "Okay class, settle down...settle down now. We have a lot to get done today and very little time to do it in. The first half of the class we'll be reviewing and towards the end we'll begin our demonstrations once again." She surveyed the room, her eyes meeting the eager faces of her students. "As you probably remember, the last time we were together, we were trying to work on the most basic of spells – conjuring a shadow. Some of you had success, others not as much. Today, we'll be re-examining that task and seeing how much you've learned and how you've improved since last time."

Ravyn sat on the other side of the class, giggling with some of the other girls. She seemed confident, almost smug and Winnie couldn't help but wonder what she was planning. As the class continued on Professor Silvermist eventually began asking for volunteers to demonstrate the spell and Ravyn's hand shot up, the only one in the room.

"Very well, Ravyn, you may proceed to the front of the class," Professor Silvermist instructed.

Ravyn made her way to the front of the class, a self-assured smile spreading across her face. She stood behind the cauldron, her eyes closed and her hands rose in a parallel formation above it. With a few quick gestures and muttered words, a tiny shadow began to take shape inside the cauldron. It grew larger and larger, spilling out of the container and into the air, enveloping the room. The students gasped in amazement, including Winnie, who hadn't expected Ravyn to conjure such an extended version of the spell.

"Very impressive, Ravyn," Professor Silvermist said, her voice filled with admiration. "I see you're already a very accomplished young witch with the powers of darkness."

Ravyn smiled, her eyes glinting with pride. "Thank you, Professor Silvermist."

The professor turned to the class. "Now, who would like to go next?"

Ravyn's voice cut through the room, her tone thick with deceit. "Why don't you give it another go, Winnie?"

Winnie's head turned towards Ravyn allowing a questioning "huh" escape her lips. Some of the girls around Ravyn began to snicker and Winnie felt an immediate surge of nervousness. She reached into her satchel and grasped the eraser, feeling a sense of reassurance with it in her pocket.

"Uh, yeah...okay," Winnie mumbled, making her way to the front of the room.

As she stood behind the cauldron, several of the girls surrounding Ravyn began whispering and laughing in her direction. "Get her Ravyn." "Teach her a lesson." Winnie noticed Ravyn had begun muttering something under her breath, dangling what looked to be a charm bracelet in her hand. Winnie felt a surge of anxiety but she tried not to let it get the better of her. She raised her hands and her eyes met Ravyn's, who was watching her with a smug expression.

Ravyn pressed on with the spell, frustration beginning to set in. Around her the girls began whispering in confusion, "What's wrong?" "Why isn't it working?" Seconds continued to pass but still nothing happened. The magic seemed to be blocked and Winnie realized that her charm had worked – perhaps a bit too well though. She was not only blocking Ravyn's magic but she had blocked her own as well.

Professor Silvermist's voice cut through the tension. "Girls, enough – proceed when you're ready, Winnie." The classroom fell silent with all eyes on Winnie once again

Winnie took a deep breath and began the summoning spell, her voice steady. As she spoke the incantation a dark mass began to rise from the cauldron. It was an oddly shaped shadow and it quickly faltered, falling back into the cauldron almost as fast as it had originated.

"Thank you, Winnie," Professor Silvermist said, her voice warm with approval. "That was very good; a definite improvement from last time."

The bell rang as the professor was about to call the next student, signaling the end of the class and the students began to file out of the room. Winnie let out a sigh of relief as she gathered her things. When she stepped out into the hallway, Ravyn was waiting for her by the door.

"You know, Winnie, I know you're up to something," Ravyn said, her voice darkening in suspicion. Winnie played clueless denying her accusation but Ravyn just smiled. "I'm not sure what it is just yet but I will and when I do, I'll use it to get rid of you and that flea biting carpet of yours."

With that, she turned and walked away, leaving Winnie feeling both relieved and uneasy. As she watched Ravyn disappear into the crowd, she couldn't shake the feeling that this war between them was just beginning and far from over.

When the classroom was officially empty, Winnie pushed open the door and slipped back inside. At the sound of the door, a tiny black head popped out of the cauldron. It was Jynx. She had taken the opportunity to jump in when everyone's attention was focused on Ravyn.

"Thanks, Jynx," Winnie whispered, smiling. "I didn't know what I was going to do up there. You really saved me today."

As Winnie massaged Jynx's head in gratitude, Jynx purred and nuzzled her hand. With a loving sigh, Jynx settled back into the satchel, already dozing off and ready to move on to the next part of their day.

The evening sun had long since dipped below the horizon, casting a golden hue over the dorm room. Vaughn was already there, patiently waiting for their return. As soon as Winnie and Jynx walked in, he asked, "So, how did it go?"

Winnie flopped down onto the bed, Jynx still cat-napping inside the satchel. "It was a long day," Winnie began, launching into a detailed account of the events that had transpired in Professor Silvermist's class. Vaughn listened intently, his expression shifting from curiosity to amusement as Winnie recounted Ravyn's failed attempt to sabotage her.

As Winnie finished her story, her eyes welled up with gratitude. "I have two amazing friends right here in this room with me," she said, her voice filled with emotion. "Jynx probably saved me from being kicked out of class today and Vaughn, you risked your own freedom just to save me from a brief moment of embarrassment. I don't know what I'd do without you guys."

Vaughn's face softened, a warm smile spreading across his face. "You're forgetting that you already saved me once before, Winnie," he said sincerely. "And mine was going to be a lot more than just embarrassment. We're not just friends, Winnie – we're a team. I'll always have your back."

Winnie's heart swelled with affection as she threw her arms around Vaughn, pulling him into a tight hug.

"Thank you, Vaughn," she whispered, her voice muffled against his shoulder.

As they pulled away from one another, Winnie's face lit up with a sly grin. "I wanted to show my appreciation to both of you, so I stopped by the cafe on my way back up and picked us up some chocolate cake," she said, holding up a box filled with the decadent treat.

Jynx, who had been napping in her satchel, suddenly shot out like a cannonball, her eyes, fixed intently on the box. Winnie and Vaughn burst out laughing at the sight.

As they sat down to enjoy the cake, Winnie's expression turned excited yet uncertain. "Classes are over for a while, so tomorrow when we get up, a new adventure begins for us. We're finally going to get everyone together and figure out just what all of this means."

Those words resonated deeply within each of them. They sat in comfortable silence for a moment, savoring the sweetness of the cake, the warmth of the moment, and the promise of the adventures yet to come. As they lingered over their dessert, the night stretched out before them like a blank canvas, waiting to be filled with laughter, friendship, and possibility.

Gate Expectations

The morning sun streamed through the window, casting a warm glow over the dorm room. For Winnie, it brought a sense of purpose, a sense of anticipation that was more than noticeable. Today marked the beginning of a new in her life, one that would hopefully bring her closer to uncovering the secrets of the Dream Diary and her family's mysterious past.

Winnie sprang out of bed, her enthusiasm infectious, if not slightly premature. "Come on, guys!" she whispered loudly, already dressed and ready to go. Vaughn groggily sat up on the bottom of the bed, rubbing the sleep from his eyes. Jynx, who had been lounging beside him, lifted her head, blinking slowly. Both looked like they were still half asleep, and Winnie's exuberance only seemed to make them more sluggish.

"I'll go grab breakfast," Winnie said, barely containing her excitement. "Be up and ready by the time I get back, okay?" She slipped out of the room, closing the door behind her.

The moment the door shut, Vaughn fell back onto the bed, and Jynx laid her head back down, both of them closing their eyes in a futile attempt to snag a few more minutes of sleep. The sound of Winnie's footsteps faded into the distance, leaving them to their morning slumber.

Several minutes later, the door creaked open, and Vaughn's eyes snapped toward the sound. His instincts kicked in, and he reacted on pure reflex, reliving the moment Ravyn had snuck into the room. He shot up from the bed, grabbing Jynx and holding her protectively in front of him like a shield. Jynx, caught off guard, let out a startled hiss, her claws extending as she arched her back.

Winnie walked into the room, a bemused expression on her face, carrying containers of breakfast. Her eyes widened as she took in the scene before her: Vaughn, frozen in a defensive stance, holding a furious Jynx with claws out and teeth bared.

"I'm not even asking," Winnie said. She casually walked over to the bed and set the containers down, seemingly unfazed by the sight of her vampire friend cowering behind a hissing cat.

Vaughn quickly threw Jynx back onto the bed, trying to diffuse the image Winnie had just seen. He strolled over to the containers of breakfast Winnie had brought in as if nothing had even happened; his eyes scanning the contents as they sat down to eat. Just as they were settling in, a piece of paper slid under the door, catching their attention.

"What's that?" Vaughn asked.

"I don't know," Winnie replied, getting up to retrieve the paper.

As she unfolded it, her eyes scanned the contents before beginning to read aloud. "Darkspire Academy cordially invites any and all first year witch or warlock, plus their familiars, to this year's annual Obsidian Crown."

Vaughn became immediately interested. "It's a magical tournament!"

Winnie continued reading, "A series of magical challenges will test your skills, creativity, and courage: Winner to receive the Obsidian Crown title, a larger dorm room for the following year, and one personal wish fulfilled by the Council of Night (with the caveat that it must be within the bounds of magical law). This flyer will act as your entry ticket and only those with a ticket will be admitted into the tournament."

Vaughn's face lit up with excitement, and he chimed in with a dramatic flittering of his fingers. "Oooo... drama!"

Winnie raised an eyebrow, a hint of amusement on her face. "Hmph," she said, shrugging her shoulders as she laid the invitation on her desk.

Vaughn turned to her, his expression serious. "You gonna enter?"

Winnie shook her head emphatically. "Me? No way! I'm nowhere near prepared for a magical tournament. I haven't even successfully summoned a shadow yet, and it's supposed to be the easiest thing to do."

Vaughn chuckled. "You're acting like you've never cast a spell before. Let's see, so far you've taken down two vampires, cloaked a home from a witch, given a rather large angry kitty cat creature a makeover, summoned a swarm of bugs, blasted through the earth with pure beams of magic, stopped time, and protected an eraser from being harmed!"

Winnie tilted her head, her eyes narrowing slightly at the last comment, while Jynx and Vaughn shared a chuckle. Vaughn's expression turned serious again. "But seriously, though, you're not as useless as you think you are and I think you should do it."

Winnie's face softened, and she hugged Vaughn tightly. "Thank you, maybe next year, though. We've got more important things to focus on right now."

"Fine" Vaughn exclaimed; frustration etched on his face. The three of them sat back down, continuing their breakfast discussion about gathering the others. "We'll stop by Aridia first and get Wraps, then head to Brindlemire for Wyatt and Freddy," Winnie said as she laid out her plans. "We'll finish up at Sweet Screams with Boo. Since we're using the shop as our headquarters, it makes sense to end where it'll all begin."

Vaughn nodded, his expression softening, "Got it."

After breakfast, Winnie gathered the items she needed for the spell: six different colored candles and a seventh for the center portal. She examined the room, the spell, and her satchel, feeling a sense of preparation wash over her. With a wave of her hand and a whispered incantation, the traveling door materialized once more. Winnie secured her satchel around her neck; Jynx snuggled inside, and stepped through the doorway with Vaughn following closely behind.

As the door closed behind them, a familiar sound echoed from outside the dorm room window. Midnight,

Ravyn's familiar, took to the skies, her wings beating rapidly as she let out a shrill cry, flying away from the windowsill once more.

As the six companions, plus Jynx, arrived back at Sweet Screams in the Land of Lost Souls, the shop's eclectic atmosphere enveloped them once more. The group's enthusiasm was noticeable, but Wyatt's unease was just as evident. He'd had a chance to discuss the mysterious letter and ring with his parents, as well as the strange woman who'd left him with them but the more he learned, the more perplexed he became.

Meeting Freddy had been a shock, but that was just the beginning. Now, surrounded by a mummy, a ghost, and the others, Wyatt felt like an outsider in a world that seemed to operate on a different plane of reality. He'd always thought of himself as a normal human boy but the truth was slowly unraveling before him and he couldn't shake the feeling that he was in over his head. As he looked around at the supernatural creatures he'd befriended and those he was just meeting for the first time, Wyatt's mind became overloaded with questions: What did any of this mean? Where did he fit in with all of this? Who were his parents? And what lay ahead?

Winnie could sense Wyatt's unease and made her way over to him. "Wyatt," she said softly, her eyes locking onto his. "I know everything you've been through recently has been a lot to process and I just wanted to say thank you."

Wyatt's expression was puzzled. "Thank you for what? I haven't done anything. I don't even know why I'm here or who any of you are."

Winnie's smile was warm and understanding. "I know, and I'm sorry everything's been thrown at you so quickly. To be honest, I don't know much about your involvement either, except that my crystal ball said you were part of this. And if I'm being completely honest, I'm not even sure what this is yet. But I promise you're not alone. We're all in this together and we'll figure it out as we go."

Wyatt's tension eased slightly and he nodded, a small smile forming on his face. Winnie and the others decided to enjoy the shop's unique atmosphere until it closed and as they spent more time together, Wyatt began to relax and have a good time.

Winnie could barely contain her excitement as she rounded everyone up, now that the day was finally winding down and the shop was closing. "I'm so excited, guys!" she burst out, pulling the spell book from her satchel. She flipped through the pages to the section on "The Shadowfel," her eyes scanning the ancient text.

The group held their collective breath, unsure of what was about to transpire. Winnie began to read from the book. "Step one: This spell needs a rather open area in order to summon its power."

Boo spoke up, "Well, the shop is small in most places but the virtual reality gaming room is pretty open. We could use that!" The group agreed and they made their way to the gaming room. The room was spacious, with no obstacles to hinder their workings.

Winnie continued reading, "Step two: Draw the pattern of the sigils on the floor." Boo's brow furrowed in concern. "We're not going to mess up the floor, are we?"

Winnie reassured him, "No, not at all. Maybe we can just lay some paper plates down on the floor in the same order? That's still drawing it out, kind of...right?" The group shrugged as Boo floated off to fetch some plates from the storage room.

"They're not paper, they're Styrofoam. Will that be okay?" Boo asked.

Winnie nodded. "I'd say if a paper plate works so will Styrofoam." Together, Winnie and Boo laid out the plates, forming the sigil pattern on the floor.

As Winnie finished the diagram, she took a deep breath and moved on to the next step. "Step three: The six individuals will stand on a circle, each holding one of the six different colored candles." The group stepped forward, and Winnie handed out the candles. "Wyatt, you're the blue blueberry. Wraps, you're yellow pineapple. Boo, you're white coconut, of course," she said with a wink. "Freddy, green apple for you, and Vaughn, you'll be the red cherry. Jynx and I will be the purple plum one then."

Vaughn raised an eyebrow. "Umm...who's the last candle, and why is it pink, green, and black?"

Winnie explained, "It was the only other candle I could find that wasn't the color of any of the others. It's going to be our center candle, and it's magenta, lime, and black." Vaughn threw his hands up in a mock "sorry" gesture and Winnie added, "And it also smells like strawberry kiwi."

Vaughn leaned over and whispered to Wraps, "I'm gonna go ahead and make a guess here; in the ballroom with the candlestick and one of the fruits did it." Winnie shot him a "shh" motion. Vaughn snapped back into place with a contrite expression on his face.

Winnie continued scanning the steps, confirming none were being missed. "Step four, already did. Step five, already did.... Oh, yeah! I need to write the location on the middle candle." She stepped off her plate, carved the name "Sweet Screams" on one side of the candle and "The Shadowfel " on the other. She also needed to place her object of choice beside the seventh candle; the one she wished to transfer the spell to. After placing her crystal ball next to the seventh candle she took one final look then stepped back onto her plate.

"I think everything is finally ready." Winnie announced as she ran her hand down the page revealing the text, prepared to speak the incantation:

"By candlelight, we gather here,
Six souls bound, with hearts so clear.
Our names inscribed, on wax so bright,
Each color unique, in the mystic light.
Wyatt, blue as night's dark shade,
Wraps, yellow as the sun shall fade.
Boo, white as snowflakes fall,
Freddy, green for forests tall.
Vaughn, is red for passions flame,
Jynx and I, purple, in the mystic's name.
In the center, the seventh stands,
A portal's key, to the nightmare lands.
As we ignite, the flames stand true,
The veil between, shall begin to undo.
The dream world's gates, we now unfold,
A portal opens, to the mystic's hold.
By the power, we call to thee,
Connect these worlds for us to see.
Let the portal, be our gate,
To the realm, where shadows wait.
When the portal begins to glow,
We'll step into, the magic's flow.
This crystal ball shall be my sight,
To watch and guide throughout the night.
As we each repeat our name,
Seal that bond to each realm's plane.
With every breath, we weave this spell;
Now open the portal to The Shadowfel!"

As Winnie finished the spell, the group began to chant their names in unison, each person speaking in a clockwise formation: "Vaughn, Freddy, Wyatt, Wraps, Boo, Winnie" Jynx added a soft meow to the end of the sequence. With each name, the corresponding candle ignited, casting a warm glow over the room. The plates beneath their feet transformed into glowing sigils, leaving the group in awe of the unfolding magic.

The sigils pulsed with energy, gradually connecting to one another as the middle plate morphed into a unique, glowing symbol. Winnie recognized it as the same marking that adorned the front of her diary. The room began to rumble, and the sigils extended glowing lines that reached out to the central sigil.

A vibrant magenta light morphed into an orb within the group's circle as the lines completed their connection. The orb expanded and transformed into an electrified portal, crackling with magical energy. When the portal reached its full form, the rumbling ceased, the candles extinguished, and the sigils dimmed.

The group stood frozen in silence, mesmerized by the portal's power. Vaughn broke the silence, suggesting, "I say we send the cat in first." Jynx shot Vaughn an unhappy glance, accompanied by a warning hiss.

The group gathered before the portal, marveling at its grandeur. Winnie slung her satchel over her shoulder, Jynx peeking out from within, ready to follow. As Winnie stepped forward, she turned to face the group, her voice filled with gratitude. "I couldn't have done this without each of you. Thank you!"

Just as she turned to step into the portal, Vaughn's voice cut through the air, his tone intense. "That's it?" Winnie paused and turned back to him confused. "Huh?"

Winnie's concern spilled out. "I don't know where this leads or what's on the other side. It could be too dangerous?" Vaughn's expression hardened as he replied, "What if it is?"

Vaughn's voice rose. "I know you're going to need help and I want to be there to help you!" The others chimed in, their voices echoing Vaughn's sentiments. Freddy approached Winnie, his teddy bear clutched tightly to his chest. "Winnie, you've already done so much for me. I'm not afraid to go in there since you'll be in there with me."

Winnie's eyes welled up with tears as she felt a deep sense of friendship unlike any she'd ever felt before. She wiped her eyes with her sleeves, a determined smile spreading across her face as she looked at the faces staring back at her. "Alright then, what are we waiting for? Let's find out just what The Shadowfel really is!"

With her friends behind her, Winnie felt even more empowered to take on whatever this new world was about to throw at them. The six of them shared a group hug. Winnie picked up the crystal ball and then, one by one, they stepped through the glowing portal united in their determination to face whatever unknown that was still to come. As they disappeared into the portal's glow, their bond and collective strength seemed to grow, a testament to the unbreakable ties they had already formed and the ones they were about to.

Lor'd to the Dark Side

As the last member of the group stepped through the portal in the shop, it closed behind them, only to reopen in a realm unlike any they'd ever seen. The plane they stood on stretched out endlessly, with magenta skies and lime green mist swirling above. Flashes of black lightning illuminated the darkness. It was clear that the atmosphere had taken on similar characteristics from the candle that had been used. "Couldn't have found a scented candle from the beach or a meadow with cute animals roaming about?" Vaughn quipped as his eyes took in every detail of the nightmare before them.

The team gazed around, taking in the desolate landscape. There was nothing in sight – no terrain, no vegetation, and no creatures – just the sound of lightning crackling above. It wasn't until Wyatt asked, "Uh, guys, where's the portal?" that they realized their way back was no where to be found either.

Boo's anxiety spiked and he began to float back and forth in a pacing motion, his voice rising. "We're all going to die in here!" Vaughn shot back, "Aren't you already dead?" Winnie elbowed him and he muttered, "Ouch."

Winnie stepped in, her voice soothing. "Boo, it's going to be okay. We'll figure this out together." Freddy offered Boo a reassuring smile and took his hand, helping to calm him down.

The group took a few moments to assess the situation and compose themselves before they decided to set off across the endless plane. Time lost all meaning as they trudged forward, the unchanging atmosphere making it impossible to gauge their progress. Eventually, Wraps stumbled and fell to the ground, exhausted. "I need a break," he labored.

The team huddled together, sharing stories and opening up about their pasts. As they spoke, they realized that despite their differences, their experiences were eerily similar. The connection between them grew stronger, forged in the uncertainty of their situation.

As the group continued to share stories, a dark wall of fog emerged in the distance. "Look!" Wraps exclaimed, pointing to the side. "That looks scary," Boo said, his voice trembling. Winnie's gaze fixed on the fog, her expression solemn. "That's where we need to go."

The group stood up, brushed off their clothes, and began walking towards the thickening fog. As they drew closer, the fog grew larger and more ominous, its darkness impenetrable. They reached the edge and hesitated.

"Ok, now what?" Vaughn asked. Winnie's reply was definitive: "We go in." Wyatt spoke up, concern etched in his voice, "We don't know what's in there, though. What if there's a cliff on the other side or something?" Winnie held out her hand to Vaughn as she said "We'll just have to take that chance then." Vaughn looked at it and responded, "Well, that's not very reassuring. This just means you'll step off the cliff first and pull me off behind you!" Winnie's expression remained calm. "Just take my hand."

The group formed a tight line, hands clasped, as they stepped into the fog. The darkness was impenetrable and the air grew thick with the scent of damp earth. The wind picked up, whipping the fog into a frenzy and the group struggled to stay upright. "Don't let go!" Winnie shouted above the chaos.

Jynx was safely nestled in the satchel and the only one spared the worst of it. Despite the turmoil, the group held fast, their determination to stick together driving them forward.

As suddenly as it had begun, the storm began to subside and the fog began to clear. The group found themselves standing in a dimly lit chamber, its purpose unclear. Vaughn's eyes darted around the room before focusing back on the fog-shrouded entrance. "Uh uh...I've seen too many scary movies to know how this plays out," he said, tugging back on Winnie's and Wyatt's hands as if to retreat.

Winnie's grip held firm. "Get back here," she said, pulling him back into the room.

The room was breathtakingly beautiful, a surreal oasis amidst the chaos they'd endured. The ceiling was a vast, star-filled expanse and the fog swirled around the perimeter like a stormy halo. Inside, the air was calm and peaceful, filled with a sense of wonder.

"What is this place?" Wraps breathed. The group wandered, entranced, taking in the details. As they reached the front of the room, a large stone caught their attention. Etched into its surface was a symbol Winnie recognized.

"It's the same symbol," she exclaimed, her eyes grew wide with awe. "The one from my spell book and the spell we cast to get here." Freddy's question was inevitable: "What does it mean?" Winnie's reply was thoughtful. "I don't know but one thing's for sure, they're definitely connected."

The group fell silent, lost in their own thoughts. Vaughn's dry humor broke the tension: "Well, is there a bell to ring or something? How do we get service around here?" The others chuckled and the group dispersed, exploring the room.

The group searched high and low inside the room, but there was no one. Winnie sank to the floor with her spell book, frustration etched across her face. "There's nothing in here," she muttered. "No mention of this place or what we're supposed to do."

The others exchanged uneasy looks. The room offered nothing—just an open sky overhead and the massive stone looming at the front. They'd been led here for a reason, but that reason felt just out of reach, and their patience was wearing thin.

With a sharp huff, Winnie tossed the book aside. It skidded across the floor and came to a stop at the base of the stone. The symbol carved into it flared to life, and the book's symbol lit up in response, drawing a gasp from the group as both began to glow.

"Winnie, look!" Wyatt exclaimed. Winnie's eyes widened as she realized the sigils were connecting. "Guys, the book is the key!" she cried out, rushing to retrieve it.

As she examined the stone, she noticed a slight indentation carved into it– what looked to be a perfect fit for her book. "I wonder," she murmured, placing the book in the indentation.

The symbols flared to life, blindingly bright. As the light began to fade out the group realized it wasn't from it losing power, it was from a black fog that had started to form once again; this time surrounding the stone. Confusion and fear forced the group to slowly step back as the fog grew larger and heavier only this time, it was different. The fog began to speak and its voice was like thunder...

The words echoed throughout the chamber, spoken in a voice that was both ancient and ageless.

"From the veil of mist I emerge, as I have since the first dream was woven," the voice declared with an archaic authority. "I am Lor, the Liminal Warrior of The Shadowfel—keeper of thresholds, custodian of balance.

"Long before your steps touched this realm, I awaited you," Lor continued, their gaze sweeping across the group. "Your ancestors stood where you stand now, and I clothed them in shadow and light. Through me, they became defenders of the dream, guardians against the tide of nightmare.

"But I see the threads of fate that bind you, the sigils that mark your ancestry. The portal you opened to get here was not an easy task. It required very specific components, specifically the harbingers; six precise characters with a duty to justice, loyalty, and compassion. These six sigils are your ancestry."

Lor's gaze locked onto Wraps. "The Pharaoh: a descendent of royalty with skills of ingenuity unlike any other."

His gaze shifted to Freddy. "The Created One: a soul reborn from loss with a pure heart and strength beyond any other."

Next, Lor's eyes fell upon Vaughn. "The Vampire: a creature of the night bound to his legacy not by name but by blood."

His gaze moved to Boo. "The Spirit: a symbol that existence extends beyond the veil of what we know and see."

Then, they looked at Wyatt. "The Lycan: a lineage born from punishment but resounds in strength and agility."

Finally, Lor's eyes settled on Winnie, "and finally, The Spell Weaver: a mystic source of pure arcane energy."

Lor's voice rose filled with a sense of purpose "Now, the cycle turns once more. You are the Shadowborne – heirs to the dream's eternal covenant. With my breath of smoke, I bestow upon you the mantle of Dream Defenders. With my power you shall wield the strength to battle the nightmares that claw at the edges of The Shadowfel.

"Know this: I grant not favor, nor curse, but necessity. You are chosen not for glory but for balance. Stand as your ancestors stood. Defend as they defended. Dream as they dreamed."

Rise, Shadowborne. The dream world endures because of you."

As Lor finished speaking, he exhaled a dense cloud of black smoke that enveloped the group. The sound of coughing and hacking filled the air as the smoke slowly dissipated. Vaughn waved his hands in front of his face, coughing, trying to clear the smog before him. "You know, secondhand smoke is just as deadly, buddy," he muttered.

Once the smoke had cleared, Winnie stepped forward more confused than ever before. "I don't understand," she said. "I thought my parents were like most of the monsters in these realms?"

Lor's expression turned solemn. "Your parents were vigilant members of the Defenders of Dreams but they were not Defenders themselves. They possessed the book and kept it safe, just as many did before them. It wasn't until you were born, Winnie, that these roles were destined to be fulfilled once again. You have yet to realize your full potential or fulfill your greatest destiny but in time, you will."

Winnie nodded, stepping back into the group. Wyatt took her place, hesitating for a moment before speaking. "I have a question, if you don't mind, sir?"

Before he could ask his question, Lor seemed to sense his thoughts. "Wyatt, you have many questions about many things. I may not have all the answers but I can help you with some. The parents who raised you love you dearly but know that your biological parents loved you unconditionally as well. I'm uncertain what became of your father but I do know your mother gave her life for your safety. And I sense that you possess a powerful artifact known as the moonstone."

Wyatt's eyes widened. "A creature nearly killed my family for the moonstone but I don't know what it is or what it does."

Lor's eyes took on a faraway look, as if recalling a story from a time long forgotten. "Centuries ago, a lone Lycan warrior was gravely injured in battle. A Nyxen, an enemy of the Lycans, stumbled upon him but chose to spare his life and even nurtured him back to health. The two eventually fell in love and their union gave birth to a new species: the Baraffinx. However, the Baraffinx inherited the feud between their parents' kind and have been searching for the moonstones ever since."

Lor paused, his gaze refocusing on Wyatt. "The moonstone you possess allows you, dear Wyatt, to transform between human and Lycan form. But for a Baraffinx, it grants them the ability to venture beyond the forest's edge during the day in their mystical form. The Baraffinx are a mystical feline version of the Lycan species, with the ability to camouflage themselves in their

182

forest surroundings. They have become a formidable species driven by a quest for power."

Wyatt pulled out the moonstone ring and held it up, curiosity etched on his face. "How does it work?" he asked Lor. Lor's response was calm and measured. "The moonstone enhances the natural abilities of your species. When you wear the ring, simply envision the change and it will take form."

Wyatt nodded, tucking the ring away and thanked Lor before stepping back into the group. Lor's gaze shifted to Freddy, who suddenly looked terrified. "Freddy, please step forward," Lor said gently.

Freddy hesitated, hiding behind Wraps and clinging to his teddy bear. Lor's soothing voice reassured him, "its okay little one." Freddy slowly emerged from behind Wraps, his eyes wide with wonder. Lor continued, "You have been given a second chance at life, young one but that was always your path to walk. Just like Wyatt's mother, the love from your father showed no bounds, willing to give up everything for his everything. Your new body was born from a place of strength and your soul was revived from a source of undying love. This is what powers you. You possess the touch of a mother's love from the heart that was placed within you and an empowered strength from your father's unwillingness to let go. While a creation stitched from cloth, you are still complete because of your mother and father."

Freddy's face lit up with a smile as he hugged his teddy bear tightly. He stepped back into the group and Lor turned to Wraps. "Wraps, you were born into a world asking so much of you already, a world you can't deny nor a world you wish to accept. You believe your role in this world is to conform to those around you that your life has already been laid out for you. The truth is, little inventor, you haven't even begun your true destiny yet. Challenges will await you and nothing comes without cost but consider both a blueprint. Your job is not to conform but to re-invent."

Wraps smiled, nodding slowly and began to step back into the group but his moment was interrupted when he tripped on his bandages and tumbled to the ground. He quickly got up, dusting himself off with a sheepish grin.

Lor's gaze moved on to Vaughn. "Vaughn, you have been blessed with a new family – this family. A family is not defined solely by blood ties but by the unbreakable bonds you form with those you truly love and trust. You've been given a rare gift – the chance to experience something that few other vampires will ever know..." Vaughn, being Vaughn, couldn't help himself and he interjected, "Pet allergies?" Lor's expression remained serene as he continued, "Loyalty. A vampire's home is unlike any other. While you may have a mother and father, you live as part of a larger colony, bound by the rules of legacy rather than individual allegiance. But here, you've learned the true meaning of loyalty. This understanding will shape you into the leader you're meant to become." Vaughn's face softened and he smiled, his cheeks flushing slightly as he stepped back into the group.

Lor's gaze moved to Boo, who looked both frightened and awestruck. "Boo, you may feel small and defeated but your bravery has yet to shine through. You possess an almost premonition-like ability that will play a crucial role in guiding your teammates through The Shadowfel."

Boo's expression remained frozen, unsure how to respond. Lor chuckled softly, his attention finally turning to Jynx, who was still hiding in Winnie's satchel, trying to stay off the radar. "I have one more to address—Jynx." Jynx, surprised that Lor knew she was even there, popped her head out of the bag with a quick "meow." Lor continued, "You may not be one of the six needed to get here but you're definitely one of the seven needed to protect this realm and all it stands for. You will play a larger role in this journey than you may have even realized and so with that in mind, I bestow my powers to you as well."

With that, Lor blew a puff of smoke toward the satchel containing Jynx. The sound of Jynx's sneezing fit filled the air and when the smoke cleared, she looked up with a curious expression.

Winnie stepped forward, a puzzled expression on her face. "Lor, what exactly is a Dream Defender? What's our role?" Lor's gaze shifted back to her. "Dreams are the subconscious of one's reality but in a different form. When mortals dream, they often project their personal experiences into this realm. However, the nightmares here feed on their weaknesses and insecurities, taking control of the dreams and causing harm to those in the real world. Your role as a Dream Defender, Winnie, is to free these individuals from their nightmares."

Winnie's eyes shimmered with tears and determination as she nodded. "There's one more thing, Winnie," Lor added. "Your crystal ball is now a beacon; a portal to the dream world. Use it to locate troubled dreamers and access their dreams. But be warned, the portal to return will only reopen once the dream is over or the subject awakens."

The group stood before Lor, looking both overwhelmed and inspired. "With my breath, I bestowed upon each of you a tiny button on your clothing," Lor continued. "Once pressed, it will act as an intercom system between you in either realm. Don't worry about others around you; only the seven of you can hear what's coming through it."

As the group began to search for the buttons on their clothing, Boo looked concerned. "Uh...I don't have one?" he said. Lor's response was reassuring. "You don't need one Boo. In times of distress, your special ability will allow you to pick up what's needed."

Lor's expression turned serious. "I know the seven of you will do remarkable things for the mortal realm, just as those before you did. You now have everything you need to begin your new roles. Save the dreamers in the nightmare world and you'll save them in the real one. I bid you farewell, little defenders."

As Lor finished speaking, the black mist began to dissipate, dissolving back into the stone altar.

The group stood frozen in shock, their eyes fixed on the altar as the weight of Lor's words sank in. Minutes seemed to pass in silence until Vaughn finally broke the tension with a dry, offhand remark: "He's gonna be a hard one to buy for come Christmas time." His tone was light, almost teasing and it was enough to make the others snort with reluctant laughter. Their gazes shifted toward one another, the heaviness in the room easing just a little.

Winnie nodded; her expression practical. "We should probably head back, guys. We can talk more there." She hesitated, glancing at her spell book and the crystal ball. "I wonder if this thing works for that too now?" she questioned. She pulled out the crystal ball and as she did, she asked the others, "Sweet Screams?" The crystal ball glowed and a magenta and black portal opened before them.

"Wow!" Winnie exclaimed, surprised. "I didn't even need to recite a spell to summon it!" She beamed with pride, tucking the crystal ball back into her satchel. With a glance at the others, she stepped forward and the group followed her through the portal. One by one, they disappeared into the shimmering light, their forms dissolving into the darkness. Finally, the last of them stepped through and the portal closed behind them with a soft whoosh. As the light faded, the group found themselves back in the virtual reality room of Sweet Screams, the familiar sights and aroma of the candy a stark contrast to the mystical world they had just left.

Sweet Screams Are Made Of These

The group stood in stunned silence, the Virtual Reality Room of Sweet Screams fading into the background as they reflected on the revelations they had just received. Winnie felt a deep connection to her parents and the legacy they had kept alive, a sense of purpose and belonging that she had never known before. Vaughn, too, felt a sense of belonging, realizing that he had found a new family among his friends, one that valued the same virtues he did.

Freddy's thoughts turned to his mother and the heart he had carved out of wood, a symbol of his love for her. But now, he felt like that love had given him a second chance at life, thanks to his father's sacrifice. He felt truly blessed to be surrounded by such incredible people.

Wraps was thinking about his future and how his passion for engineering didn't have to be limited by his destiny. He could still make his parents proud while forging his own path.

Boo was feeling a sense of pride and purpose, realizing that his empathy was not a weakness but a strength. He had always struggled with self-doubt but now he saw his ability to understand and connect with others as a valuable asset.

Wyatt, meanwhile, was processing the answers he had received but still had questions lingering in his mind. However, looking around at his friends, he knew that he wasn't alone on this journey. They all truly were in this together and that gave him a sense of comfort and gratitude.

"It's been a really long day, guys," Winnie said, breaking the silence. "How about we take the night to process all of this and meet back up here tomorrow, same time?" The group agreed and Winnie pulled out the crystal ball, tempted to test its limits. She held it tightly, said the word "Aridia" opening a magenta and black portal before them once again.

"I could definitely get used to this," she declared, as Wraps hugged the group and stepped into the portal. One by one, Winnie summoned portals for the others, sending them back to their respective destinations. Finally, it was just Boo, Vaughn, and Winnie left. Boo hugged Winnie and Vaughn before they called for their portal to head back to the dorm room in Darkspire Academy.

The portal opened up inside Winnie's dorm room at Darkspire Academy where she and Vaughn stepped out, only to be met with an unexpected surprise. The Council of Night was waiting for them, their faces stern and unyielding. Winnie and Vaughn exchanged a shocked glance before Vaughn ducked behind Winnie, trying to avoid detection.

But it was too late. Professor Wychwood, Ravyn's father and head of the Council of Night, stood up, his eyes fixed on Winnie. "We've been waiting for you, Winnie. It's come to our attention that you've been harboring an out-of-realm guest within the school. Not to mention in the realm itself, for that matter." Winnie stammered, trying to come up with an excuse but nothing came out.

Professor Wychwood's expression was unforgiving. "We have no choice but to expel you from Darkspire Academy, effective immediately. Pack up your belongings; you'll be escorted off the premises within the hour." Winnie's eyes welled up with tears as she grabbed Professor Wychwood's arm, pleading with him. "No, please! You can't!"

"You brought this upon yourself," he said in a cold voice as he ripped his arm out of hers. He turned to leave, instructing another council member to escort Winnie off the premises.

As Winnie gathered her things, Vaughn whispered words of reassurance. "This isn't over, Winnie. Your parents don't have to know anything just yet. We can just stay with Freddy and Wyatt for a while until we figure something out." Winnie nodded, wiping away tears.

Once they were outside the academy gates, Winnie turned to Vaughn, her eyes welling up with tears again. "I just don't understand. We've been so careful. How did they know?" Her voice cracked with sadness and confusion. Vaughn's expression was sympathetic but before he could respond a voice spoke up from behind them with a sense of sarcasm and sorrow.

"I'm just heartbroken that this happened to you" Winnie and Vaughn turned around and Winnie's expression changed from sadness to shock and then one of fury. "Ravyn!" she exclaimed, her voice rising in anger. Ravyn stood behind them, a malicious grin spreading across her face. "You never should have started something you weren't able to finish, Winnie." Midnight flew overhead, perching on the spindle of the iron gate between them as Ravyn taunted them. Winnie's face turned red with rage and she stomped her feet in frustration. "This isn't over Ravyn!" Winnie shouted but Ravyn had already turned and walked off, laughing at her victory, as Midnight followed her.

Winnie's anger boiled over and she stomped her feet in frustration. Vaughn placed a calming hand on her shoulder. "Come on; let's just get to Freddy's. We'll figure this out. This isn't over yet." Winnie took a deep breath, her anger slowly subsiding.

As she furiously opened her satchel to grab her things, Jynx's scared face peeked out and Winnie's expression softened. "Oh, Jynx – I'm so sorry. I almost forgot you were in there." Jynx meowed reassuringly and Winnie began to pet her.

With a brand new outlook on the situation, Winnie pulled out her crystal ball, wiped away her final tear, and spoke the word, "Brindlemire!" The magenta and black portal opened before them and Vaughn helped Winnie gather her belongings. "Don't worry, we'll be back." he said with a reassuring smile.

Winnie nodded and together they stepped through the portal, leaving Darkspire Academy and the wrath of Ravyn behind. As the portal began to close Winnie cast a defiant glance back at the iron gate. Her spirit was unbroken and a fierce fire now burned within her.

Winnie, Vaughn, and Jynx arrived at Freddy's house, where they filled him and his father in on the events that led to Winnie's expulsion from Darkspire Academy. Mr. Sutorre welcomed them warmly. He was actually thrilled that his home was filled with the sound of voices and laughter once again. As evening fell, the group gathered around the fireplace, discussing their individual concerns and the challenges they still faced.

Winnie expressed her frustration, feeling more overwhelmed than before. "I was so excited to finally have some answers but now I'm more lost than ever," she admitted. The others nodded in agreement and Winnie pulled out the crystal ball, setting it on the floor in front of them. "This thing has added so much responsibility to us all and I don't know how to handle it. How am I supposed to help save the dream world when I can barely take care of myself?"

Vaughn placed a reassuring hand on her shoulder. "Winnie, what happened at school wasn't your fault. You were set up." He paused for a moment before continuing, "Not only are we going to find a way to get you back in that school but we're going to become the best defenders the dream realm has ever seen!" He looked around the circle, his eyes locking onto each of them. "Who's with me?" Vaughn threw his hand out over the crystal ball and one by one they placed their hands on top of his with Jynx adding both her paws to the top of the pile.

As they broke the circle, the crystal ball began to pulse with a soft, golden light. "Look!" Winnie gasped. The pulsing grew more insistent and Winnie felt an inexplicable pull towards the crystal ball. Without thinking, she reached out and placed her finger on the top of the ball. The pulsing stopped and the light immediately transformed into a clear image.

A little girl lay in her bed, clutching the covers to her chest as she gazed up at the dark ceiling with wide, fearful eyes. The room was dimly lit with only a faint glow from a nightlight casting shadows on the walls. The little girl's voice trembled as she finally yelled "Daddy?" while her eyes darted towards the closet then under the bed. Her father raced into the room to reassure her, checking under the bed and in the closet but the little girl's fear didn't dissipate. "Can you leave the closet light on?" she asked, her voice cowardice and gentle. Her father nodded and turned on the closet light, casting a warm glow into the room. The little girl's eyes still looked scared but she seemed to relax a little, her breathing slowing as her father sat beside her, stroking her hair. "They must be having a tough night," Winnie whispered, her eyes fixed on the scene unfolding before them. The group watched in silence, feeling a sense of empathy for the little girl's fear.

The group continued watching and the little girl's eyelids finally drooped, drifting off to sleep. "I guess there's nothing to do here," Wyatt said but before he could finish, the closet light flickered and died. "What's going on?" Wyatt asked.

As they watched in horror, glowing red eyes materialized in the darkness of the closet. Black, twisted hands and arms began to writhe out from under the bed slowly emerging into view. The scene was almost too terrifying to behold. The little girl's nightmares weren't just fears – they were real and they were escaping into the mortal realm.

The group panicked. "What do we do?" Freddy asked, his voice shaking. The hands and arms under the bed began to morph into a single, twisted creature – a dark, formless mass that loomed beside the little girl's bed. It reached out and placed a twisted hand on her face, causing her to twitch and writhe in her sleep.

"We have to save her!" Winnie exclaimed. Vaughn sprinted into the kitchen and returned moments later, wearing a pot on his head like a helmet and holding a lid as a shield. "What are you doing? You look ridiculous!" Winnie asked, torn between fear and amusement.

Vaughn's eyes were wild. "You have your magic but what's the rest of us supposed to do? We need to go in prepared!" Winnie's expression turned thoughtful then committed. "Okay everyone, gather some supplies then. We're going into The Shadowfel."

The group scattered, snatching up anything that might serve as armor or a weapon, with no idea how they were meant to face the nightmares ahead. "I grabbed some stuff for Wraps, too," Vaughn said and Winnie nodded curtly. "Alright, let's get him and head to Sweet Screams for Boo," she commanded.

With the crystal ball in hand, Winnie summoned the portal for Aridia and the group stepped through it. Eventually, they emerged into Sweet Screams, standing before Boo. The group was a comical sight, dressed in makeshift armor and wielding kitchen utensils like spatulas and wooden spoons. Boo's expression turned from surprise to alarm as he took in the scene.

His concern was twofold: he knew they were about to face something in the dream world and the group's makeshift defenses did little to reassure him. The sight of them, armed with kitchenware and looking like children playing dress-up, was almost more alarming than the prospect of whatever danger was still to come.

Boo spoke out, "You know guys, my special ability is pretty much feelings and I have to say that right now I'm not feeling very confident with where this is going." The group exchanged glances with one another when Vaughn said, "We didn't have time to prepare and it's an emergency. We have to go, now!"

Winnie held up the crystal ball, displaying the image of the little girl and the twisted creature looming over her. Boo's eyes widened in distress. "She's in so much pain... I can feel it." As he gazed into the crystal ball, the creature's head jerked up, as if it sensed their presence.

Boo's eyes went dark and his voice dropped to a horrific, menacing growl. "Once I've infected her dreams with nightmares, her life force will be mine. I'll keep growing stronger, one child after another and there's nothing you can do to stop me!" The group stared at Boo in horror, shocked by the sudden transformation.

Wraps shook his head. "No way, that just happened." Vaughn, however, remained unfazed, his eyes fixated on Boo as he slowly starts to hand him a king size candy bar. "He doesn't seem quite like himself today, does he?" he said to the others, his voice deadpan.

As Boo's eyes returned to normal he shook his head, looking disoriented. "What just happened?" he asked, dazed and confused. Vaughn chimed in, "The candy bar thing must have worked." Winnie shot Vaughn an incredulous look but he just shrugged.

Turning back to Boo, Winnie explained, "You somehow connected with the monster and it spoke to us through you." Boo's eyes went wide with fear and he exclaimed, "I don't want to be a monster!" Winnie quickly reassured him, "You're not a monster, Boo. Your special ability just allowed you to tap into its thoughts somehow."

Vaughn, however, couldn't resist adding, "Yeah, you were like a scary intercom we didn't know how to turn off." Winnie elbowed him, muttering, "Not – helping."

"We don't have much time," Winnie urged. "If we're going to save that little girl, we need to act now. She's counting on us and we're the only ones who can help her." Boo hesitated, still shaken by his recent experience but after a moment's pause, he nodded in agreement. "I'm in," he said. "Let's save her."

Winnie held out her crystal ball, its glow illuminating the darkening space. Without needing to say a word, she focused her thoughts on opening a portal to the little girl's dream world. The crystal ball responded, displaying the monster feeding off the girl's dreams. The magenta and black electrified portal burst to life before them and the group prepared themselves for their first encounter of The Shadowfel. With a deep breath, they stepped through the portal and straight into the girl's dream...or so they thought.

Playing in the World Spiri's

As the group emerged from the portal, they expected to find themselves in the little girl's dream. Instead, they found themselves back in the sanctuary where they had met Lor. "This can't be right," Wraps said, confusion etched on his face. "Why are we here again?"

The group approached the altar and Winnie prepared to place the book on the stone pedestal. However, this time it wasn't necessary. The black mist began to swirl above the altar, taking the shape of Lor. "I'm sorry to have brought you here, little defenders," he said mysteriously. "But I felt an urgency that wouldn't allow you to enter the child's dream unprepared."

As Lor spoke, the group continued to approach him, their makeshift armor clanking and clattering. Lor blew a breath of smoke towards them once again and the dark mist enveloped the group. When it cleared this time though, their outfits had transformed into darkened, black and gold versions similar to their original apparel.

"These garments will serve you well in the dream world," Lor explained. "They hold no special powers but they're tied to you and the dream world, adapting to your needs as you enter it. You'll also notice your weapons are gone – I've removed them, as they may prove to be of little use in your current and future endeavors. You will soon face creatures known as Spiri's; shadowy beings that can morph into whatever they desire. They will stop at nothing to claim the dreams of the innocent and you must be prepared to face their ever-changing forms. Your true strength, against the Spiri's, lies within your special traits and skills, which will all be revealed to you in due time."

The group stood before Lor, taking in their new appearances. Each member was now dressed in a sleek black and gold leather version of their original outfit, except for Boo of course. Lor's final words hung in the air: "Your powers and abilities will be stronger in the dream world. Use this to your advantage any chance you can. Now, a little girl's life hangs in the balance. I bid you farewell, little defenders."

With that, the black mist dissipated and the group was left standing in their new attire, feeling like true superheroes. "So cool!" Vaughn exclaimed. The magenta and black electrified portal burst to life once more and Wyatt motioned for the group to follow, "Quickly, guys!" The group charged into the portal, now feeling ready to face the nightmares beyond the gate.

As the group emerged from the portal, they found themselves in a replica of the little girl's bedroom. "Wow, It looks like her room," Freddy observed. Winnie nodded, "Yeah, but I was expecting it to be more..." Wraps chimed in, "...scarier?" Wyatt scanned the empty space, asking, "And where is everyone?"

Vaughn's gaze swept the room, confirming, "It's empty." Meanwhile, Boo stood frozen, his eyes darting wildly between the walls as he struggled to contain his fear. Winnie noticed his distress and asked, "What's wrong Boo?"

Boo's voice trembled as he replied, "Something's not right. I don't know how to explain it but... but I'm getting a weird feeling about that closet." Vaughn's eyes snapped to the closet and he cautioned, "Everyone stay focused. We're in unfamiliar territory and we don't know what we're up against; stick together, move slow."

The group's eyes locked onto the closet, their senses on high alert as Boo's unease became contagious.

As the group crept closer to the closet, the room seemed to stretch and distort like a funhouse mirror reflecting their growing unease. "It's not looking so normal now," Wraps muttered but could barely be heard over the noises of the floorboards.

The closet door inched open with a slow, bone-deep creak as a pair of red eyes appeared in the crack between the door and the frame. The eyes were level with the group and they seemed to be staring directly into their souls. "I think this just got a whole lot worse," Wraps said with concern.

As if on cue, three more pairs of eyes materialized in the darkness behind the first pair, their gazes fixed on the group with an unblinking intensity. Freddy's grip on his teddy bear tightened, his eyes widened with fear. "I'd have to agree," he stammered.

The eyes drew closer and the group saw that they were attached to a massive, shadowy form that resembled a giant spider. The creature's body, however, flickered and danced like a flame, its legs twitching with an unnatural energy. As it emerged from the closet, it let out a deafening screech, its high-pitched wail sending shivers down the group's spines.

Vaughn gave Wyatt a slight push forward but Wyatt resisted, digging his heels into the ground as Vaughn grunted out as he pushed, "Just go smack it with a newspaper. We'll be right behind you." Wyatt's eyes locked onto the charging creature and without hesitation, he yelled "Everyone run!" The group turned to flee but the room seemed to stretch on forever, offering no escape from the monstrous creature bearing down on them.

The giant shadowy spider hurtled towards the group with increasing speed. "Everyone split up!" Wyatt yelled and the group scattered in all directions, like mice fleeing across the vast, cluttered bedroom floor. The furniture loomed like skyscrapers with toys and shoes strewn about providing uncertain hiding spots.

Winnie and Jynx ducked behind the massive wooden leg of the bed, gasping for breath. Winnie slid down the post, her back against the bed frame, and rummaged through her bag for her spell book. "There has to be something in here, Jynx," she muttered, but her heart sank as she flipped through the pages – they were all blank. Panic set in as she frantically flipped through the book, her voice rising in desperation. "I don't understand. It's gone! It's all gone!"

The spider's thunderous footsteps shook the floor, its roars and hisses growing louder. Winnie's eyes welled up with tears as she remembered the crystal ball. She yanked it out of her satchel but it was just a hollow orb. "Jynx, what are we going to do now?" she whispered, her voice trembling.

Jynx turned to Winnie offering a confused meow before refocusing on the scene unfolding across the room. The spider stood atop a sneaker, its shadowy legs probing for Freddy, who cowered at the back of the shoe, his terrified cries echoing through the room.

With everyone watching and listening to the horror unfold before them; Wyatt finally emerged from behind a water bottle, his face twisted in rage. He patted his pockets, produced the ring, and slid it onto his finger. "I'm coming, Freddy!" he bellowed, his eyes blazing with fierce intent. As soon as the ring settled onto his finger, Wyatt felt a searing pain coursing through his veins. His body began to contort and shift, his muscles stretching and growing in ways that seemed impossible. His bones cracked and realigned, his senses heightening as his body hair began to grow and thicken. His hands transformed into razor-sharp claws, and his face elongated into a wolf-like snout. Wyatt's vision blurred as his senses were overwhelmed by the transformation. He felt his body surge with newfound power and strength. As the transformation reached its peak, Wyatt let out a mighty howl, unleashing his inner beast. He stood tall, his eyes glowing with an overpowering inner light, and his fur bristling with power.

The spider, still focused on Freddy, didn't notice the new threat. The others watched in awe as Wyatt transformed, their fear momentarily forgotten in the face of this unexpected turn of events.

As the transformation took hold, Wyatt felt a surge of power coursing through his veins. His senses heightened and his vision shifted to a more nocturnal spectrum, allowing him to see the room with a newly discovered clarity. He knew his sense of smell had improved as he could now pinpoint Jynx's location across the room. Freddy's pounding heart was like a drumbeat in his ears and he could feel his friend's fear pressing in on him.

Wyatt's new form felt both foreign and familiar, like a second skin waiting to be worn. He launched himself into a sprint, his quickened reflexes allowing him to cover the distance in a flash. With his claws extended, he leapt into the air, striking the spider's side with a resounding thud. The creature let out a deafening wail as Wyatt landed on the floor.

The spider spun around, its body a blur as it lunged at Wyatt. He dodged to the side, avoiding the snapping fangs by mere inches. The spider adjusted its aim and Wyatt darted in the opposite direction but the creature was relentless. It feigned a strike then swung its leg in a vicious arc, catching Wyatt off guard and slamming him into the toe of the shoe. The spider pinned his leather jacket to the ground with another leg and Wyatt found himself now trapped as well.

As the spider raised its front leg to deliver the final blow, Wyatt raised his arm to defend himself. But the strike never came. Instead, he heard a loud roar. He lowered his arm and saw the spider's leg was being pulled back. Wraps had unwound his bandages and created a makeshift lasso again, ensnaring the spider's leg.

Vaughn, meanwhile, had found a pair of dolls near the nightstand and climbed up onto them. Donning a tiny cowboy hat from one of them, he yelled "Yee-haw!" and leapt onto the spider's back. The creature bucked and twisted beneath him but Vaughn held tight, riding it like a bucking bronco. "Git along, little doggie!" he hollered with his cowboy hat clutched in one hand.

The spider's frustration boiled over into a violent frenzy, tossing Vaughn off its back, slamming Wraps across the room, and kicking Wyatt out from under its leg. The three of them landed hard, sliding across the floor towards the foot of the bed. The spider reared up on its hind legs, unleashing a piercing screech as it displayed its dripping fangs. It stood motionless next to the shoe, as if sizing up its opponents.

Vaughn, Wraps, and Wyatt struggled to their feet, wincing in pain. Winnie peeked out from behind the bed, "Guys, the book is empty!"

Vaughn's said confused, "What do you mean?"

Winnie's eyes locked onto his. "I mean, the spell book is blank!"

The three of them stood there, their faces falling in unison. They murmured a long, drawn out "Oh…" until the realization dawned on them. Another collective "Oh…" followed, this time showcasing a sense of hopelessness. The spider, still towering over them, seemed to sense their despair, its gaze redirected back to the shoe that held Freddy captive.

Vaughn turned to Winnie with a hopeful expression. "You know, your book was basically just words. Can't you just make some up yourself to cast a spell?" Winnie's face scrunched up in thought, her shoulders shrugging with intrigue. "I don't know, I've never tried before."

Freddy's terrified screams grew louder as the spider began to tear at the shoe. Vaughn's urgency was quite noticeable. "Well, there's no better time than now to try it." He gestured for Winnie to take the lead.

Winnie hesitated then turned to face the spider. She clasped her hands, popped her knuckles, and began to chant:

> *"Sizzle, fizzle, pop and blaze,*
> *Toast my marshmallows in a daze!*
> *Tiny fire, don't be shy,*
> *Dance around and kiss the sky!"*

Vaughn raised an eyebrow as Winnie finished. "Those were the first words that popped into your head? Sizzle, fizzle, marshmallows?" Winnie shrugged. "Well, I was thinking fire and I'm also hungry, which made me think of s'mores, so… yeah, Vaughn – marshmallows."

Before Vaughn could respond, Wyatt interrupted. "Hey! I think it's working!" Tiny flames erupted on the floor around the spider, shooting sparks into the air like a miniature fireworks display. "Well, it sort of worked," Wyatt said with a slight disappointment in his voice. Vaughn leaned in with his trademark jab, "All we're missing now are the back up dancers and then we can take this act on tour." Winnie's glare could have melted steel. While it had not performed the way Winnie had hoped, the truth was that it had indeed worked. The spider let out a shriek, momentarily startled, and backed away from the shoe. The group took advantage of the distraction to rush over in order to free Freddy.

Winnie knew her magic was limited and the sparks from the flames had barely lasted a moment before fizzling out. "First the sizzle and now the fizzle," Vaughn quipped as they pulled Freddy from the shoe. The spider, enraged, turned back when it saw the group escaping. It reared up on its hind legs, its eyes blazing with fury as it let out a shrill cry.

Freddy yelled, "My foot's caught!" with panic in his voice. Vaughn and Wyatt sprang into action, trying to pull him out of the shoe as the spider charged towards them. "Hurry, it's coming back!" Winnie shouted.

Just as the spider was mere feet away, a large piece of cloth dropped onto it, momentarily trapping it. The group looked up to see Boo floating above, a sheepish grin on his face. "I found a napkin," he said, as if it was the most normal thing in the world.

The napkin acted like a net, pinning the spider beneath it. Vaughn and Wyatt took advantage of the short intermission to free Freddy's foot and help him down from the shoe. "You're okay now, Freddy," Winnie said, hugging him tightly.

But they knew the spider wouldn't stay trapped for long. "This is our best chance to take this thing out," Wraps said, his eyes locked on the struggling creature. "Right now, he's trapped and can't see where anything's coming from. I have an idea if you can buy me a little more time, though." he said with a hint of excitement in his voice.

The group looked at Wraps and nodded in agreement. Wraps, now on a mission, just needed a few moments for his plan to play out. "Quick, everyone grab a corner of the napkin and hold it down!" Vaughn shouted. One after the other each of them ran towards the spider and grabbed a separate corner of the napkin, struggling to hold it in place. "It's too strong!" Winnie yelled, "I don't know if I can hold it down by myself!" Jynx took hold of the same corner Winnie was holding with her mouth and Boo floated down to help her adding his weight to the effort.

Meanwhile, Wraps made his way back to the nightstand area. He placed his hands on the side of the water bottle and started to push on it but it was too heavy to budge alone. "Wraps, hurry!" Wyatt shouted as the spider continued to kick and scream from beneath the cloth. Wraps knew he didn't have much time. He unwrapped his bandages once more and fashioned another lasso; he was really starting to get the hang of it at this point. He slung it across the top of the water bottle and latched it around the mouth of the bottle then began to pull on it. He stepped back, loosening his bandages more and more to get more traction, stumbling backward as he pulled. The spider was making headway with the napkin, tearing a tiny hole in the fabric above it. "We're running out of time!" Wyatt shouted again.

Wraps continued to pull and tug with all his might and finally, the water bottle toppled over, spilling its contents onto the floor in the direction of the spider. He quickly unhooked his lasso and started wrapping himself up as he ran for the next components. "I'm hurrying – I just need a few more minutes!" he shouted. "I don't think we have a few more minutes!" Vaughn shouted back.

Wraps dove under the nightstand, grabbing the battery and paperclip he had spotted earlier. He dragged the paperclip behind him as he rolled the battery out into the open. The water continued to spread across the floor, eventually reaching the group and soaking the napkin, which actually helped to weigh it down. Wraps quickly got to work. He began uncoiling the paperclip into an arc shape and wrapping one end around the positive terminal of the battery with the middle of the arc lying inside the water.

The group scrambled to safety, jumping off the soaked napkin's edges onto the dry flooring. The spider thrashed about, throwing the napkin off its back as it roared in anger, its mouth frothing with venom. Wraps wrapped his bandage around the other end of the paperclip and pulled back on it. As the open end touched the negative terminal of the battery, it created an electrified surge that ran through the water and straight into the spider. The creature's body convulsed, twitching and screaming in agony.

As the electrical current coursed through its body, the spider's movements slowed, its screams fading into a pitiful whimper. Finally, it slumped forward, its body motionless. Wraps let out a deep breath, releasing the paperclip from the battery. Vaughn strolled over patted the spider on its side and said, "You sir, are no longer current." The others chuckled and rolled their eyes at the terrible pun. The tension in the room dissipated but was quickly replaced with bouts of laughter and ragged breathing. They had done it. They had survived their very first battle against a spiri but they also knew it wasn't going to be their last one either.

A Little "Light" Reading

The group collapsed onto the floor, exhausted but exhilarated by their recent triumph. As they gazed up at the vaulted ceiling of the little girl's bedroom, their awe was tempered by the realization that their accomplishment had been more a product of luck than skill. Wraps strode over; a triumphant smile plastered on his face, unwinding his bandages as he walked due to the paperclip still taped to his wrappings trailing behind him. The others couldn't help but laugh at the sight but they applauded his quick thinking nonetheless.

As Wraps approached, still smiling, he suddenly realized what was happening and his eyes widened in embarrassment. He turned around, starting to rewind the bandages back up, muttering under his breath as the paperclip clinked and tangled its way back into place. "Piece of cake," he said, trying to play it cool despite his momentary fluster.

The group exchanged blank stares, with Winnie looking particularly lost. She was still reeling from the discovery that her spell book's pages were blank. Self-doubt crept in as she wondered if she was cut out for this magic thing. Why did others seem to grasp it so easily, while she stumbled from one mistake to the next?

"Boo, what do ya think buddy? Where should we go?" Wyatt asked, grinning. Boo looked back and forth between everyone's face, all staring back at him expectantly. "Me? You want me to decide where we go next?" he said in a doubtful panic state. "Of course, you were the one that figured out the closet situation earlier," Wyatt said, nudging him encouragingly. Vaughn added a quick insight, "Yeah, you're like a little ghost detector."

Vaughn giggled at his own pun and the others followed suit. Boo, however, didn't find it funny, especially being put on the spot as the de facto leader. "Uh...well, let me see here," he said, frantically scanning

the room as he tried to come up with a plan. His eyes
darted wildly and he looked like he might even
hyperventilate at any moment. Vaughn leaned over to
Freddy and whispered, "I've never seen a ghost with stage
fright before." The others were watching Boo attentively
but Winnie was oblivious, lost in thought as she stared at
her spell book.

Boo's frustration finally boiled over and he shouted,
"I DON'T KNOW!" The sudden outburst snapped Winnie
out of her trance-like state. She looked at Boo with a
mixture of concern and understanding. "Boo, it's okay.
You've already helped us so much. We need to approach
this like a puzzle, one piece at a time." The others agreed
but it didn't help them figure out what their next move
was.

Boo suddenly picked up on a feeling of concern and
directed his attention towards Winnie. "You seem sad,
Winnie. What's wrong?" he asked, his voice softening.
Winnie hesitated and then lowered her head. "I'm just
not very good at any of this," she admitted. "Everything's
changing in my life. I have no school, no home...my spells
never seem to work right and now my spell book has
erased itself. I feel like I just keep messing things up even
more."

The group tried to offer words of encouragement,
with Vaughn apologizing for his earlier joke. Winnie
shook her head. "It's not that. I just feel lost and unsure
of myself." She sat down on the floor, her legs pulled up
to her chest, and her head resting on her arms. Freddy
stepped up beside her, offering his teddy bear in a gentle
gesture of comfort. "Thank you, Freddy," Winnie said,
her voice slightly strained from holding back tears. "I'll be
okay though." Her words were unconvincing, and she
forced a weak smile onto her face.

Vaughn pulled out Winnie's spell book and began
flipping through its blank pages, trying to find a solution.
He even held it upside down, shaking it gently, but
nothing worked. "I'm sorry, Winnie. I tried," he said,
handing the book back to her. As he did, Jynx's collar

suddenly began to glow again, catching everyone's attention. "What the..." Vaughn quickly stated being caught off guard. "Winnie, Jynx's collar – it's glowing again; just like before."

Winnie raised her head off her arms, her eyes locking onto Jynx as the cat's collar pulsed with that strange ethereal glow. "What do you suppose it means?" Wraps asked. Winnie's gaze was fixed on the emerald, watching as it blinked faster and faster before stopping abruptly. The silence that followed was heavy with anticipation.

"Well, that was weird," Wyatt said, voicing the group's collective confusion. They sat in stunned silence, waiting for some sign or hint as to what the glowing collar might mean. Then, without warning, the symbol on Winnie's spell book began to pulse in the same rhythm as the emerald had.

Winnie's eyes snapped back to her book. "It's glowing now too," she said softly. Like the collar, the symbol eventually stopped pulsing, leaving them with more questions. Winnie flipped open the book but the pages were still blank. Incredibly annoyed, she shouted, "Why does everything have to be a mystery!?" Slamming the book shut. However, she was surprised when it bounced back open.

"Now what?" she wondered aloud. Closing the book again, she watched as it swung open once more, revealing the same blank pages. Winnie's eyes examined the pages, searching for any sign of meaning. That's when she saw it – tiny paw prints walking across the left page onto the right before disappearing.

"What is it, Winnie?" Freddy asked, noticing her intense focus. "Paw prints," she replied. She flipped through the pages again but they remained blank. She closed the book for a final time and this time it stayed shut. "I'm so confused," she admitted, her voice laced with defeat.

Vaughn stepped in, reminding her of her own words: "We treat it like a puzzle, remember?" Winnie's mind was already working in overdrive as she tried to piece the connection between Jynx's collar and the paw prints on the book. There had to be a meaning behind what it was trying to tell her.

Suddenly, the room around them began to dissolve into darkness, like paint swirling down a drain. Vaughn asked as his head looked around the room "Everyone else is seeing nothing too right?" The group stood frozen, surrounded by an endless, pitch-black void. It was as if they'd been swallowed whole by nothingness.

A low, menacing laugh echoed through the emptiness, seeming to come from all directions at once. "It seems I may have underestimated your willingness but I won't make that mistake a second time. I'm getting closer to completely infecting the girl's dream. You may have taken care of my little shadow pet but you'll never find your way out of my darkness."

"That voice! It's that monstrous hand creature again!" Wyatt exclaimed.

"Where do we go?" Freddy asked as he clung to his teddy bear tighter. "There's nothing around here." The group stood together, looking around at the emptiness. Oddly, they could see each other but nothing else.

"There must be some kind of block that prevents the monster from shading us out, like he's done with everything else around us," Wraps suggested.

"I suppose but where do we go from here? How do you fight something when that something is nothing?" Winnie wondered aloud.

The group decided to start moving, hoping to stumble upon a clue or a way out. As they began to move, Boo noticed something—every step Jynx took left behind a glowing paw print.

"Winnie – Paw prints!" Boo shouted. Winnie turned and looked down at Jynx and sure enough, the glowing paw prints were there, just like the ones on her spell pages.

She pulled out her book and started to open it only the pages fluttered open on their own. The paw prints started walking across the left page again, this time in a specific sequence. "Wait guys – I think it's a map!" Winnie exclaimed. "Three steps forward, two steps to the left," she started calling out the patterns with even more certainty.

The group quickly fell into formation behind Winnie and Jynx, following the glowing paw prints through the void. With Jynx leading the way, they moved forward, one step at a time, into the unknown.

Jynx padded carefully through the darkness, following the path Winnie's directions had laid out. The faint glow of her paw prints illuminated the way for the others, who followed closely behind. Winnie's eyes were fixed on the book, watching as the paw prints moved from one of the pages, to the next, and then the next. Suddenly, Jynx vanished from sight. A faint, distressed meow echoed through the darkness, growing fainter. "JYNX!" Winnie shouted into the darkness. "WHERE ARE YOU?" She spun around, her eyes scanning the emptiness for any sign of Jynx. Winnie's concern for her friend drove her to action. "We have to go after her," she said urgently.

Without hesitation, Winnie stepped forward, and found herself falling. The wind rushed past her, her stomach dropping as she plummeted downwards. As quickly as she found herself falling, however, her fall now slowed, and she landed softly on a glass floor below. Jynx was standing a short distance away, her eyes fixed on something in front of her. Winnie's relief was short-lived, her gaze taking in the vast, crystal-filled library. The walls and floor were made of a glittering white marble infused with threads of glass that refracted and reflected the glass in dazzling patterns. The light from the fixtures above bounced off the glass, casting a kaleidoscope of colors across the walls and floor. Rainbows danced and swirled around them, adding to the ethereal beauty of the space.

The others began to arrive, falling from the void and landing softly on the glass floor. "Where are we now?" Wyatt wondered, his voice full of awe. "This place is absolutely breathtaking," Wraps breathed. "Just look at the architecture. The history that these structures must hold within them," he added. Boo's eyes were wide with wonder. "It's so bright in here."

Winnie's gaze followed the others', taking in the beauty of the library. The walls were lined with towering shelves, filled with books that seemed to glow from within. The group walked down the glass floor corridor, their footsteps echoing off the walls. The sound was like music, a gentle harmony of crystal and glass. Eventually, they came to a common area, filled with a single pedestal in the center of the room. On top of the pedestal was a plaque, carved with the most delicate of styling and it held only a couple of words; Vocare lucem.

Winnie approached the pedestal, her footsteps echoing off the glass flooring. Jynx walked beside her, while the others watched from the entrance of the room. As she drew closer, Winnie felt an inexplicable pull towards the pedestal. She reached out and placed her hands on either side of the pedestals top, her curiosity getting the better of her. She whispered the two words inscribed on the plaque, "Vocare lucem," as if she was just simply examining the piece before her.

The moment the words left her lips though, the room began to shake violently. The lights flickered and burst, casting random patterns across the walls. The group panicked as the walls started to split and crack. "Winnie, we need to go!" Wyatt shouted, rushing towards her. The glass floor was cracking and pillars were tumbling down. Winnie turned to see the pedestal crushed beneath the rubble. Her eyes widened in fear and realization.

The group started to run but Wraps fell behind. A chunk of pillar had fallen and rolled, catching his bandages and pinning him down. Winnie was the last to make it to the door and turned, realizing Wraps was stuck. Without hesitation, she sprinted back towards him, Jynx following closely behind. The room continued to crumble around them, the floor breaking apart in sections. Jynx grabbed hold of the bandages and started pulling but the chunk of pillar was too large for her to maneuver it out of the way. Winnie ran around and started pulling on the bandages too, her face refusing to give in to defeat.

The others started to make their way off the stoop to head back to help them but the ceiling fell, blocking their path. Wraps looked up at Winnie, his eyes locked on hers. "You have to get out of here," he said. "If you stay here, we're all three going to die." His voice was hollow with understanding — he knew exactly what staying meant, and he was choosing her over himself. "You need to go, NOW!" The floor cracked open next to them but Winnie refused to leave Wraps behind. "I'm not going to leave you!" she yelled back at him.

She looked at Jynx and said, "Jynx, head for the door. No matter what happens, I need to know you're safe." Jynx looked back at Winnie with a defiant glare, but the pleading in Winnie's eyes softened her stubbornness. "Jynx, please!" Winnie begged, but before Jynx could react, the ceiling above them gave way and started falling down towards them.

The three of them looked up and the others at the door watched in horror, knowing that in a matter of seconds they were about to lose three of their friends in a horrifying way. Wraps stopped pushing on the pillar and threw his arms over his head in a defensive stance. Since Jynx was as nimble as she was, she was able to leap out of the way. Winnie threw her hand in the air as a reaction to watching the ceiling fall on them when suddenly a massive blast of light emerged from her palm up towards the falling ceiling, blasting it to pieces.

Winnie stood there in shock, as did the others. Wraps removed his hands from his eyes, wondering why he was still alive, not witnessing what had just happened. The room continued to crumble around them, and the floor opened up even more. Freddy remembered how easy it was to rip open the cage he had been trapped in and wondered if that had been a one-time fluke or not. He grabbed a hold of the piece of rubble that had fallen in front of them with one hand, keeping his teddy bear close to him in the other. "What are you doing? Are you crazy?" Vaughn asked, but with barely any effort, Freddy lifted the chunk of rubble and hurled it aside. The others froze, stunned all over again.

"What is going on right now?" Vaughn shouted, his voice barely cutting through the chaos. Freddy quickly sprang into action, making his way through the collapsing structure with an unnatural strength. He tossed aside massive chunks of rubble and debris with ease, his movements swift and precise. As he navigated through the wreckage, he busted through walls and pillars, creating a path for the others to follow. Finally, he reached the pillar that pinned Wraps down, and with a single, powerful motion, he lifted it off and threw it aside. Wraps stumbled out from under the rubble, his eyes wide with gratitude. Freddy smiled at him and nodded his head, as if to say "no problem."

With Freddy leading the way, Winnie, Wraps, and Jynx followed closely behind, as Freddy continued clearing the path back. They made their way back to the steps at the door, dodging falling debris and leaping over chasms in the floor.

Without hesitation, they stepped through the mirrored door as the room behind them reached its breaking point. The walls gave a final, deafening groan, and the sound of crashing rubble filled the air. The door swung shut behind them, sealing itself with a soft click. The sudden silence was suffocating, and as their eyes adjusted to the darkness, they realized they were back in the twisted realm of the nightmare. The darkness seemed to swallow them whole, leaving only the echoes of the fallen room behind a wall that now seemed to no longer exist either.

"Hey, where'd the door go?" Wyatt asked. The group stood in the darkness, staring at the spot. "It's gone now too," Boo said, his voice confused but truthful. "Everything's gone." Vaughn turned to Winnie, his eyes searching for answers. "Hey, what happened in there just now?" Winnie stared at her hands, her expression unreadable. "I'm not really sure. I've never done anything like that before."

Freddy spoke up, his voice shy and quiet. "How do we get back out of here though?" Wraps nodded in agreement. "Good question." The group began to look around, trying to get their bearings. Jynx darted around, but her paw prints didn't glow this time, leaving them in an unsettling darkness.

The group stood around, unsure of what to do, until Winnie's satchel suddenly lit up from within. The soft glow emanating from the bag was mesmerizing, and the group couldn't help but peer into it. "What's going on?" Vaughn asked. While still staring into the bag, he started swaying back and forth and began to sing "This little light of the mine..." in a goofy, off-key tone. Wyatt let out a quick chuckle and shook his head, before slapping Vaughn across the stomach with the back of his arm, taking his breath away momentarily. "What?" Vaughn asked, still grinning, "It seemed fitting."

Winnie pulled out the spell book, and the symbol on the cover pulsed with a soft, golden light. The pages seemed to shimmer and glow, as if infused with an inner radiance. As she opened the book, the light spilled out, illuminating the entire space they were standing in. The group watched in awe as the light cascaded from the book to the walls, painting every surface with an ethereal glow as warm as honey. However, one corner of the room remained dark and the surface of that darkness rippled like gentle waves on a breezy day.

"I think it's safe to say, we know where we need to go now," Wyatt said. Winnie held the book before her, using the light as a guide leading their way. The closer they got to the blackened portal, the larger it seemed to become. The group stood before it, looking up at its expansive form in awe.

"It's large enough for us to go through it in pairs," Vaughn said. "So, I say we do that. Winnie and I will go last." he suggested. Wyatt raised an eyebrow. "Why do you get to go last?" but before Vaughn could respond,

Winnie chimed in and said, "Boo and I will go in last.
Vaughn, you and Wyatt go in first, and Freddy and Wraps
will be right behind you."

Vaughn pouted loudly, "Fine!" he said as he paused
for a moment. "But I'm taking the cat for leverage," and
scooped up Jynx from the ground, causing her to grunt
out a meow of protest. Jynx squirmed in his arms, but
Vaughn held tight. As Vaughn and Wyatt stepped through
the blackened portal, Freddy and Wraps followed closely
behind. Winnie looked at Boo and said, "Alright Boo, let's
do this." She continued holding the book out for a source
of light, and both she and Boo walked through the portal,
taking the light with them and sending the room back
into complete darkness behind them.

All "Hands" On Deck

s the team emerged on the other side of the blackened portal, they found themselves in a twisted celestial throne room. The void above and around them was a deep, starry expanse that seemed to spin like a carnival attraction. The only structure in sight was a hovering path of black reflective tiles, lined with six purple-flamed candelabras that led to an elevated throne. The disfigured monster sat motionless on the throne, a cage made of shadowy tendrils dangling beside him, holding the terrified little girl captive. His voice boomed through the void, "Your group has proven to be more of a nuisance than expected. You'll not be so lucky escaping me though."

The monster rose from his throne, revealing seven hands scattered across his torso, each one opening an eye that gazed at the group. Wraps whispered, "It's almost like the spider." The monster's arms swayed in a sinuous, snake-like motion, the eyes on the palms watching the group. "I know what scares each of you," the monster taunted, "and your fears will feed my power."

Six of the seven hands opened their eyes wide, glowing crimson red as the candelabras erupted in purple flames that danced down to the black tiles. The flames morphed into shadowy duplicates of the team members, each one twisted and menacing. The monster's voice echoed through the void, "You are your own fear."

The team stood frozen, their eyes fixed on the dark reflections of themselves. Vaughn, trying to break the tension, whipped his cape behind him and sneered, "We're not afraid of a bunch of killer clones from outer space, handyman." He assumed a fighting stance, ready to face the twisted duplicates of himself and his friends.

The room erupted into chaos as the evil laughter faded away, replaced by the monster's voice, "...then let's get to it." Vaughn shouted to the group, "Everyone spread out! It's go time!" The clones immediately gave chase, each one fixated on its original. The dark versions of themselves proved to be formidable opponents, stronger and more powerful than they had anticipated.

Shadow Wraps and Wraps faced off, their eyes locked in a fierce stare-down. Wraps lunged forward, trying to take control, but Shadow Wraps was one step ahead. With a swift motion, he loosened his bandages and used them as a whip, striking Wraps' foot and sending him tumbling to the ground. Before Wraps could recover, Shadow Wraps wrapped his bandages around his neck, pulling him up into a chokehold.

Meanwhile, Shadow Freddy was a force to be reckoned with, his teddy bear even twisted into a grotesque parody of its former self. He pummeled Freddy with punch after punch, sending him crashing to the floor. Shadow Freddy had even found a way to turn his lovable teddy bear into a makeshift flail that repeatedly struck Freddy's chest sending him backwards. Freddy tried to defend himself, but Shadow Freddy's relentless assault continued, the teddy bear flying through the air to strike him again and again, until Freddy slid across the room, already tired and lying in pain. Freddy's eyes were already swelling, and he struggled to get back to his feet.

Boo's terrified squeaks filled the air as Shadow Boo stalked him, an unworldly aura surrounding him. Boo darted and weaved, trying to evade Shadow Boo's grasp, but his dark counterpart was relentless. Shadow Boo chased him through the room, over and through objects, with an unnerving determination.

Wyatt and Shadow Wyatt faced off, their eyes locked in a fierce stare. Shadow Wyatt lifted his hand, displaying the ring on his finger, and gave Wyatt a smug smirk. With a fluid motion, he transformed into a twisted version of Wyatt's Lycan form. Wyatt followed suit, his body shifting into its familiar shape. Shadow Wyatt was a blur of motion, leaping through the air and landing on Wyatt's shoulders, kicking him forward and sending him stumbling to the ground. Wyatt quickly rolled out of the way just in time, avoiding Shadow Wyatt's claws as they struck the floor where he once lay. Wyatt had narrowly avoided the attack, but he was unsure how much longer he could keep this up.

In a distant corner, Vaughn faced off against his own shadow, the two of them engaged in a fierce stare-down. Vaughn sneered, "You know, you should really talk to someone about these issues you have." Shadow Vaughn laughed, charging forward with a flurry of punches and kicks. "Great, then let's talk," Shadow Vaughn taunted. Vaughn seemed to hold his own though; thanks to the countless hours he'd spent watching karate movies during his dorm room confinement. It wasn't that he was a master fighter, but he'd picked up enough basic moves to block some of Shadow Vaughn's lightning-fast attacks. Then he noticed it: Shadow Vaughn wasn't just fighting him — he was copying him. "Great," he thought. As if battling himself emotionally wasn't enough, now he had to deal with the literal version too. Still, it was clear Vaughn was starting to tire under the relentless assault.

Winnie was in a desperate battle, dodging and weaving to avoid the dark magic hurled by Shadow Winnie. Shadow Winnie stood frozen in place, her eyes blazing with malevolent intent as she summoned the darkness to do her bidding. With a mere flick of her wrist, tendrils of shadowy energy shot forth, striking with precision and force; the flames of darkness seemed to have a life of their own, twisting and turning in mid-air as they barreled towards Winnie. Winnie's eyes darted back and forth searching for an opening to counterattack, but Shadow Winnie's magic seemed almost effortless. She didn't need to move from her spot, her confidence and precision allowing her to wield the darkness with deadly accuracy. Winnie, on the other hand, was a frantic blur of motion, dodging and weaving behind pillars and leaping over obstacles in a desperate bid to avoid the surges of darkness flung her way. She cowered behind a pillar, her chest heaving with exertion, as the darkness continued to probe and pierce the air around her. It was everything she could do to avoid being hit, trapped in a desperate game of cat and mouse with her own shadow.

The room was a maelstrom of chaos, the team fighting for their lives against their own twisted reflections. The disfigured monster watched with a twisted grin, his eyes gleaming with malevolent pleasure.

Winnie's voice was laced with desperation as she cried out to her friends, "I'm really sorry, guys! I thought we could do this, but they're just too strong!" Shadow Winnie stalked towards her, a menacing smile spreading across her face as she conjured a dark orb in the palm of her hand. She seemed to be savoring the moment, teasing Winnie with the promise of impending doom. Winnie's eyes welled up with tears as she stared up at her shadow clone, resigned to her fate.

Just as Shadow Winnie was about to deliver the final blow though, Jynx launched herself at the shadowy duplicate, sinking her teeth into the back of her neck and clawing at her back. Shadow Winnie shrieked in pain, the dark orb dissipating in her hand. Enraged, she grabbed Jynx by the neck and hurled her across the room, blasting her with a dark orb before she could land. Jynx slid across the floor, crashing into the steps of the throne, and fell limp to the ground.

Winnie's eyes blazed with fury as she watched her friend fall. A surge of emotion coursed through her, and she stood up, her body trembling with rage. As Shadow Winnie turned back to face her, Winnie grabbed her shadow clone by the neck, her hands glowing with an intense light. The disfigured monster sat up in his throne, his eyes fixed intently on the battle unfolding before him. "That's impossible," he breathed.

The light coursed through Winnie's hands, illuminating the dark form of her shadow clone. For the first time, Shadow Winnie's face twisted in fear as she realized that it was in fact her fate that was sealed. She clawed at Winnie's hands, trying to pry them off her neck, but Winnie's grip only tightened. The love and friendship Winnie had for Jynx had unleashed a power within her, a power that was now consuming her shadow clone. Shadow Winnie's screams of "Nooo..." echoed through the chamber as she dissolved into nothingness, banished by Winnie's fierce determination and the power of her own emotions.

A surge of power erupted within Winnie, taking complete control of her. The light emanating from her body intensified, overflowing from her eyes like a tidal wave. Still standing, she glanced over at Shadow Wraps, who was strangling Wraps with his bandages. Without hesitation, Winnie raised her hand, firing a blast of light that disintegrated Shadow Wraps instantly. She didn't even flinch, raising her other hand to summon a beam of light that struck down Shadow Boo from the air. The power coursing through her proved too much, and she collapsed to the floor, unconscious.

Wraps slowly got to his feet, gasping for breath, and stumbled over to Winnie's side. He checked her pulse, relieved to find that she was still breathing. Knowing he couldn't stay with her, he quickly assessed the situation and saw that Freddy was in dire need of help. Shadow Freddy had already done a number on him, and Freddy was barely clinging to consciousness. Wraps knew he had to act fast. He rummaged through Winnie's satchel, searching for anything useful. His fingers closed around a few random items: a coin, a bottle of perfume, and a small eraser. He had an idea, though he wasn't sure if it would work. He laid the coin and eraser down on Winnie's chest and grabbed the perfume bottle, stood up, and rushed towards Freddy. "I'm coming, Freddy, hold on!" he shouted, but his feet got tangled in the iron footing of a candelabra. "Oops," he said as he crashed to the floor.

The perfume bottle shattered, releasing its contents, and the candelabra fell next to him, its purple flame igniting the liquid. Shadow Freddy was engulfed in flames, screaming in agony as he ran and rolled around the room, trying to extinguish the fire. Wraps lay there, stunned, as Shadow Freddy's darkness dissipated, leaving him lifeless. The silence that followed was a stark contrast to the chaos that had erupted just moments before.

Meanwhile, Boo — still drifting high above after narrowly escaping his own shadow clone — caught sight of Jynx slumped against the stairs of the throne room. The disfigured monster loomed just above her. Normally, Boo would never willingly drift anywhere near a creature like that, but the moment he saw her still form, hesitation vanished. He dove toward her without a second thought.

Boo hovered above Jynx's lifeless body, his eyes fixed on her pale face. The disfigured monster stood up, its eyes fixed on Boo and Jynx, and began to make its way towards them. Boo's face twisted in anger as it raised its arms to deliver a crushing blow. But Boo summoned an unexpected strength, creating a force field around himself and Jynx that blocked the monster's attack. The creature slammed its fists against the dome, but Boo's determination held strong, fueled by his love for his friend.

Wraps helped Freddy to his feet, supporting him as he swayed unsteadily. "Can you stand?" Wraps asked. Freddy nodded, wincing as he tested his weight on his battered body. One eye was already swelling shut, and his lip was bleeding, but he was determined to keep going. Wraps helped him to a safer spot to sit then turned to assess the situation with Wyatt and Vaughn.

Wyatt was still dodging and weaving, trying to avoid Shadow Wyatt's relentless attacks. However, his stamina was starting to wane, and Shadow Wyatt's blows were landing with increasing frequency. Just as a result, Wyatt stumbled backward, his agility and reflexes compromised by his exhaustion.

Shadow Wyatt seized the opportunity, landing a solid blow that sent Wyatt crashing to the floor. Wraps sprang into action, racing towards Shadow Wyatt. But Wyatt's exceptional hearing picked up the sound of Wraps' approach, allowing Shadow Wyatt to back flip over Wraps and extend his claws to strike as Wraps turned around. In his haste however, Shadow Wyatt failed to notice just how closely he had positioned himself to Freddy, who was supposedly defeated and no threat.

Freddy, however, had other plans. He stood up behind Shadow Wyatt and grabbed his paw, before the strike could land on Wraps, sliding the ring off his finger. Shadow Wyatt spun around, his face exuding a mixture of rage and confusion, only to find Freddy standing behind him, the ring held triumphantly in his hand. For a moment, Shadow Wyatt's eyes locked onto the ring, and then he watched in horror as Freddy crushed it in a single, swift motion. The ring's destruction transformed Shadow Wyatt back into his human-like form.

Wyatt watched the scene unfold before him as he struggled to his feet, the loyalty of his friends giving him the strength to keep going. Snarling at his human shadow form, Wyatt launched himself at Shadow Wyatt with a fierce cry, claws extended. The two clashed in a flurry of strikes, Wyatt's claws tearing through Shadow Wyatt's form with relentless ferocity; with one final blow, Shadow Wyatt combusted into a cloud of black smoke, dissolving into nothingness before their eyes.

Only Vaughn's shadow remained, and it was clear he was starting to tire. The two mirrored each other's movements, exchanging blows with eerie synchronicity. It was like watching a reflection come to life. Wyatt dashed across the room, using his super speed to catch Shadow Vaughn off guard. He knocked him to the ground, sliding him across the room but to Wyatt's confusion, the original Vaughn was also sent flying, as if the two were somehow linked. "They're connected," Wyatt muttered, just as Shadow Vaughn sprang back to his feet.

Shadow Vaughn spun around, his cape fluttering behind him, and landed a palm punch that sent Wyatt crashing across the room. Freddy tried to intervene, but Wraps held him back. "I don't think we can help with this one," he said. "Vaughn's fear is different somehow."

Vaughn struggled to his feet, his mind compiling all sorts of questions. How were he and his shadow linked?

Wyatt's shout cut through the chaos: "Vaughn, you have to face your fear! He is your fear!" The words sparked a realization in Vaughn. If his shadow was a part of him, then he was the one holding himself back.

Vaughn's eyes locked onto his shadow form, and he felt a sense of peace wash over him. "It's time to let you go," he said, his voice firm. Shadow Vaughn sneered, but Vaughn continued, "I have to accept that you're a part of me, whether I like it or not but I don't have to fear you taking control. Today, I decide which part of me moves forward and that part isn't going to be you."

The words struck a chord, and Shadow Vaughn's demeanor shifted. He stumbled back, his confidence faltering, as Vaughn's acceptance washed over him. The air seemed to ripple, and Shadow Vaughn began to dissolve into the black tiled floor, disappearing from view. In that moment, Vaughn realized that sometimes words were more powerful than physical strength, and that his greatest battle was in fact the one he'd been holding within.

As each shadow faded away, the disfigured creature grew weaker, its power waning with each lost form. The eyes on its palms began to vanish, one by one, until only the central eye remained, glowing with an eerie light that would have been at the center of its face if it had one. Despite its weakening state, the creature's rage intensified, its twisted body contorted in a snarl. Boo continued to shield Jynx from the monster's attacks, his eyes fixed intently on the creature as he absorbed the blows. Meanwhile, the others tended to Winnie, trying to revive her from her unconscious state. The mortal child, still trapped in the shadow cage, sobbed uncontrollably, her small body shaking with fear.

The creature, realizing it couldn't breach Boo's defenses, turned its attention to Winnie; the witch that started unraveling everything from the start. She lay helpless, unaware of the danger looming over her, her chest rising and falling with each shallow breath. The creature's body began to glow with dark energy, and it let out a deafening roar as a shadow tendril shot towards Winnie.

The group stumbled back, caught off guard by the force of the creature's spell, but Winnie remained untouched, the tendril stopping mere inches from her face.

Vaughn's eyes widened as he realized the eraser was the same one she cast the spell on earlier and it was protecting her. With newly gained courage, he stood up, resisting the force of the creature's spell. As he planted his feet, his body began to feel heavy and rigid, and his eyes turned a deep, inky black. The others watched in confusion and concern as Shadow Vaughn emerged from Vaughn's form, his shadowy body rippling with power.

But to their surprise, Shadow Vaughn didn't attack. Instead, he winked at the group, a mischievous glint in his eye, saying "Don't worry, I've got this" and dashed into the monster's spell, disappearing from view. The creature stumbled back, its spell broken, and Shadow Vaughn vanished into nothingness. Vaughn's eyes returned to normal, and he fell to his knees, clutching his head. "Ugh…" he groaned "my head is splitting." Wyatt helped him up, "You have no idea how true that is" laughing and nodding in understanding, as the others watched and nodded in amazement too. As they watched, Winnie began to stir, making painful noises as she slowly came back to life, her eyes fluttering open.

The monster's voice was softer this time, its words heavy with a sense of desperation. "It…It can not be. I hold the power here, not you." Winnie finally came to, sitting up and shaking her head. "What…what happened?" she asked, still partly dazed. Boo released the force field around Jynx and himself, seeing that the monster was now stumbling backwards, attempting to reach its throne. Boo quickly flew over to the group, Jynx limp in his arms.

As Winnie saw Jynx, she remembered what had started the battle. Tears welled up in Boo's eyes as he handed Jynx over to Winnie, who began to sob as she held her friend's lifeless body. The others gathered around, running their hands over Jynx's silky black fur as they wept.

But their grief was short-lived, as a massive explosion rocked the throne area. The wall next to the throne imploded, revealing a beautiful and regal woman dressed in all black. The monster cowered, pleading with her. "Hexus, please—wait. You don't understand. It's not my fault..."

The woman, Hexus, interrupted the monster with a soft, motherly tone. "Shh, shh, shh, there, there, my sweet child, everything's going to be okay." She began walking down the stairs, her long black dress flowing behind her like a dark mist. As she reached the monster's side, she knelt beside it, her expression compassionate. She gently reached out and cradled the monster's disfigured hand, the one with the central eye still glowing with an eerie light, in her own. Her fingers tenderly stroked the creature's palm, as if soothing a wounded child. "I tried to do what you asked of me," the monster whispered. Hexus's voice remained gentle, "I know..." Her eyes, still filled with a deep sadness, seemed to hold a hint of disappointment. But in an instant, her tone and expression shifted. Her voice turned cold and detached, "but you failed." As she spoke, her hand closed around the monsters, and a dark, fiery energy coursed through her fingers. The monsters body ignited, its screams echoing through the chamber as flames engulfed its form, fueled by Hexus's touch.

Hexus stood, her expression returning to its calm, collected state. She walked down the stairs towards the group, who backed away in fear. "Well, it seems we ended up meeting much sooner than I had anticipated," she said, her voice smooth. Winnie, still holding Jynx, asked, "Who are you and what do you want with us?"

Hexus began pacing, her movements fluid and almost bored. "My official title is Lady Hexus, the Shaper of Shadows. But you may call me Hexus. Since you're standing here, it means you've met Lor, and you're the new chosen defenders of the realm." Vaughn spoke up, "We asked who you were, not what we are." Hexus shot him a cold glance, but her expression softened into a smirk. "Let's just say it's my job to keep things interesting in this realm. And it has been since the beginning of time."

Wyatt asked, "So, you're like Lor, then?" Hexus shrugged. "Something like that." She stopped pacing and looked at the group. "I feel we've gotten off to a bad start here. How about we have a do-over?" Wraps repeated, "A do-over?" Hexus's eyes lit up. "Yes, you know a fresh start. I know this was your first time entering the Shadowfel, and let's be honest you weren't very good at it. This way you'll have more time to practice and I'll definitely have more time to prepare for the next round. I'd hate to have to wait another century for the next group to come along..."

Vaughn asked, "What's the catch?" Hexus's expression turned serious. "Catch?" "Yeah, the fine print," Vaughn replied. Hexus continued, "Oh, I did forget to mention that part didn't I? It's not really a catch I'd say but more like a sacrifice for a sacrifice. If we pretend this night never happened, you'll forget everything that occurred in this room. You won't remember me, or even making this deal." Winnie's voice was laced with anger. "And why would we ever agree to that?" Hexus's tone turned menacing as she leaned over to Winnie, placing a hand under her chin. "You're holding it," before standing upright again. Winnie looked down at Jynx in her arms. Her loving friend had already sacrificed the biggest sacrifice she could for her, giving her life for hers and she'd do anything to give it back to her.

"What about the girl?" Wyatt asked, his eyes fixed on the cage where the little girl lay exhausted, her small body shaking with sobs. Hexus followed his gaze, her expression unreadable for a moment before she nodded. "Who – her?" Hexus asked with bored amusement. "Tell ya what. You make this deal, and I'll not only send her back to her home safely, I'll even take her off my list.

You'll never have to worry about her being bothered by the nightmares again." The group exchanged anxious glances, their faces reflecting their desperation. Winnie's voice was firm as she spoke up, "It's a deal." Hexus's face lit up with an unnatural giddiness, and she clapped her hands together, her eyes sparkling with excitement. "Oh, goody!" she exclaimed, slightly hopping up and down in place. "Now, don't forget...you have to forget!" she said somewhat jokingly, her violet colored eyes intensified as she waved her hand over the group, starting the day over once more.

The morning sun streamed through Freddy's window, gently rousing him from his peaceful slumber. He sat up in bed, rubbing the sleep from his eyes, his teddy bear lying beside him. Stretching his arms, he arched his back, feeling the day ahead. His face was back to normal, the bruises and cuts from the forgotten adventure had become nothing more than a faded memory. The others stirred, one by one, awakening to a new day. Wraps, Wyatt, and Vaughn, slowly sat up in their beds stretching and yawning. None of them remembered anything about the events that had transpired in the Shadowfel but Winnie was different. She shot up in bed, her eyes wide with a sudden realization. One word escaped her lips in a panicked whisper, "Hexus!" as a black, furry; little face sprang up beside her.

Déjà Boo

innie sat up in bed, running her hands through her hair and pulling it back out of her face. "Oh my gosh…" she gasped, "Was that real?" she whispered, her eyes locked on Jynx, who was watching her with an adoring gaze. Winnie's face softened, and she pulled Jynx into a tight hug, maybe even a little too tight. Jynx squirmed and threw her arms out, trying to escape Winnie's grip, as Winnie exclaimed, "Oh Jynx, I thought you were dead – but you're here." Winnie finally released Jynx, allowing her to fall back into Winnie's lap. "Was that real, Jynx? Do you remember going into the Shadowfel at all?" Jynx tilted her head to the side and shook her head no.

Winnie got out of bed and began getting dressed. She made her way downstairs to the kitchen, where the others were already gathered around the table, enjoying breakfast. Winnie paused at the bottom of the stairs, taking in the scene. "Well, everyone looks okay," she thought to herself. She joined the others at the table, grateful that everything seemed normal, but she couldn't shake the feeling that something was off.

"How'd everyone sleep?" Winnie asked, hoping for some reassurance. Freddy replied, "I must have really dozed off. I don't remember waking up once last night." Wyatt agreed, "...me either!" Vaughn, with his face halfway in a bowl of cereal, muttered "...same" between mouthfuls. Winnie decided to drop the subject, but her unease still lingered.

The others started discussing their plans for the day, and Wyatt asked Winnie if she wanted to join them at Sweet Screams. Winnie was lost in thought and didn't catch the question. "Winnie?" Wyatt said, waving his hand in front of her face. "I'm sorry, what did you say?" Winnie asked, snapping back to the present. Wyatt repeated the question, and Winnie replied, "Uh...no. I feel like I need to do something first, but I'll meet you there right after."

Vaughn suddenly shot up from the table, milk dripping down his chin. "Okay, I'm ready! Time for games and candy!" he declared, followed by a proud belch. Wyatt and Freddy laughed, while Winnie's mind wandered off again.

"Can you call the portal for us, Winnie?" Freddy asked politely. "Yeah, sure," Winnie replied in a distant tone. She got up to retrieve her crystal ball and returned to the living room. With a flick of her wrist, the magenta-colored portal to Sweet Screams appeared. The others bid her farewell, telling her to hurry up, and stepped into the portal. Winnie watched as the portal closed behind them, then sat down at the table, lost in thought. She finished her breakfast with Jynx, and the two of them went back up to Winnie's room.

Winnie closed the door to the room and gently placed the crystal ball back in her satchel. As she reached for her spell book, her fingers brushed against the coin and eraser, and she felt a sudden wave of dizziness wash over her. She had to sit down, and Jynx immediately ran to her side, pawing at her anxiously. "I don't know what's wrong with me today, Jynx," Winnie said, closing her eyes and pressing her hand to her forehead. "I must be coming down with something." She laid back on the bed, spell book clutched to her chest, and soon found herself drifting off to sleep.

As she slept, Winnie's mind plunged into a dream. Everything was black, and the focus was solely on Jynx, who sat calmly in the center of the void. The camera-like perspective began to pan around Jynx, rotating slowly in a wide arc, her serene face passing in and out of view. The movement was smooth and deliberate, as if the camera was circling around her, taking in every detail. As the camera continued to rotate, it slowly zoomed in on Jynx, her features growing larger and more defined. The movement stopped abruptly as the camera found its way back around to facing Jynx, and Winnie was looking directly at her. Jynx sat still for a brief moment, and then she stood up. Jynx began to turn around, the emerald in her collar catching a glint of light, sending a tiny spark of green flashing through the darkness. With her back to Winnie, Jynx began walking away, leaving a trail of glowing paw prints behind her. Winnie followed Jynx in her dream, her footsteps echoing through the blackness. Jynx led her to an arched, mirrored door. Winnie made her way to the reflective door and saw a reflection staring back at her. The reflection was of her but somehow she looked different; she looked wiser and more confident than she actually felt in real life.

Suddenly, her reflection broke pattern and motioned for her to open the door. Winnie reached out and grasped the handle, pushing the door open without hesitation. A surge of blinding light spilled out. Winnie raised her arm over her eyes to shield them as she walked forward into the unknown. The light was so intense that she couldn't see anything, and she kept her eyes covered, trying to block out the glare.

As she continued through the room, the light began to fade. Winnie slowly lowered her arm, her eyes adjusting to the sudden darkness once again. The intense brightness gave way to an endless, featureless void like the one she had just left. Winnie found herself standing in a space without walls, ceiling, or floor. The blackness was absolute, with no discernible texture or depth and in the center of this void sat Jynx, her eyes fixed intently on Winnie's. The silence was deafening, and Winnie felt a shiver run down her spine as she gazed back at Jynx. "Jynx, I don't understand," Winnie called out in her dream, "What does any of this mean?" She took a step forward, her eyes locked on Jynx's, hoping for some kind of answer or clue.

Jynx remained still, her expression serene, as she tilted her head to the side. The emerald in her collar caught the dim, non-existent light, sending a tiny spark of green gleaming into the darkness. For a moment, Winnie thought she saw something flicker in Jynx's eyes, a glimmer of understanding or perhaps even a message. But it was gone in an instant, leaving Winnie with more questions than answers. Winnie could feel herself being pulled back into her waking world. As she opened her eyes, the memory of the dream lingered and so did the elusiveness of its message.

Winnie slowly opened her eyes, her gaze falling on Jynx, who was lying next to her on top of the spell book. As Winnie stirred, Jynx's eyes flickered open, and she looked at Winnie with a sleepy expression. "I had the strangest dream again, Jynx," Winnie whispered, as if sharing a secret. "It seemed so real, and there were things about it that just felt...I don't know—familiar." She furrowed her brow, puzzled. Jynx hopped off the spell book and padded over to Winnie, who stretched and propped herself up, reaching for the spell book.

Winnie, still focusing on Jynx, started opening her spell book. "Everything today just seems completely off" she said to Jynx in confession. As Winnie redirected her attention back to her spell book that she had just opened, her eyes widened in surprise. "It's blank, Jynx!" she exclaimed. Jynx let out a curious meow and padded over to investigate. Winnie's thoughts were all over the place. "I knew something wasn't right, but what is it? What am I missing? Why can't I remember?" she asked aloud, her eyes scanning the empty pages.

As she pondered, Jynx sat down beside her, and the emerald on her collar caught a glint of light, catching Winnie's attention. "Your collar...there was something about your collar in my dream," Winnie said, her voice filled with curiosity. She reached out to pet Jynx's head and grasped the emerald, examining it closely. "It looks the same as it always has," she said, but her words trailed off as she flipped it over. "There's something engraved on the back of it, Jynx. This wasn't there before." She paused, her eyes following each letter of the inscription. "Vocare lucem." The moment the words left her lips, Jynx's eyes instantly morphed into pillars of light.

Winnie's eyes widened in shock as Jynx's collar began to glow with the same golden light. The room started to shake, and Winnie found herself backed up against the wall, calling out "Jynx, stop!" The room fell silent, the emerald's glow extinguished, and Jynx returned to normal. Winnie looked around, disoriented, and then her gaze fell back onto Jynx as she made her way back towards her.

Before she could speak, a portal of light burst open in the room. Winnie instinctively grabbed Jynx and backed away, unsure what to expect. But as the portal pulsed with an unusually bright energy, she realized it might be their only lead. "I think the portal might be for us, Jynx," she said with a mix of emotions. Gathering her belongings, Winnie slung her satchel over her shoulder and stepped into the portal with Jynx by her side in hopes to finding the answers she was searching for.

As Winnie and Jynx stepped through the portal, they found themselves back in the sanctuary where they had first met Lor. Winnie's confusion gave way to relief as she recognized the familiar surroundings. She and Jynx walked up the aisle towards the stone, where Lor was waiting for them. "I've been expecting you, Winnie," Lor said, his voice calm and authoritative.

Winnie's eyes narrowed. "Something's happening to me, and I don't understand what it is. I sense I'm forgetting something. My spell book is blank and something weird just happened after reading the engraving on Jynx's collar. And then this portal appeared, leading us to you. Please can you help me understand?"

Lor's expression was sympathetic. "What you're experiencing is a normal transition for the role you're destined to obtain. Let me explain. My role in balance prevents me from intervening, but that doesn't mean I don't watch over you. Everything you believe you're forgetting, you are, but only because of a deal you made with Hexus."

Winnie's eyes widened. "So she was real then?"

Lor nodded. "Hexus is a balancing agent for this world, like myself. Her focus lies on The Shadowfel, but she's yearning for more. She's actively searching for a tear in the rift that would allow her to escape into the mortal realm. Understand, her powers are immense, but tied to the laws of this world, meaning she cannot destroy you herself in this world, but she could in another."

Winnie's mind was beginning to fill with more questions. "If she's as powerful as you say she is, then why do I remember things when it seems no one else does?"

Lor's expression turned thoughtful. "You weren't alone, Winnie. Boo remembered as well, though you never spoke with him. His powers are tied to this world, more than even he realizes. In time, he'll find that he's the protector of your group. His powers will continue to grow and literally reshape the team but that time for him is not now. The reason you remember parts of that time erased is because of your magic."

Winnie's brow furrowed. "I don't understand."

Lor continued, "In that moment, you were not only holding Jynx in your arms, but you also were holding the eraser you had magically imbued earlier. Hexus's magic was unable to penetrate the charm fully, due to your magic being in effect and her unknowing of it. The charm protected parts of that memory for you."

Winnie felt a sense of relief wash over her. "What about my book, though, and the engraving on Jynx's collar?" she asked.

Lor's expression turned serious. "Those two questions are tied to the same answer. Winnie, when you read the plaque in the celestial room, you unlocked the beginning of your destiny. You are what this realm calls, a Pure Light, a witch of light magic."

Winnie's eyes grew wide in horror. "A light witch? But light magic is banned for a witch to practice. What does that mean for me?"

Lor's voice was calm. "Casting light magic is only forbidden for a dark witch, Winnie, and you are not a dark witch. It's also the reason you struggle with your magic. You are not proficient in casting dark magic because you don't have the means to tap into the energy source needed to do so as your heart is pure. The reason your spell book is blank is that it belongs to you now. When you spoke those words, you rewrote the timeline yourself. The spell book customizes itself to its holder, and until the new owner unlocks the book, it's vulnerable."

"The reason you've inherited this powerful tome, Winnie, is due to the sacrifices and dedication of your lineage—the witches who've held this book before you, protecting it with their lives, including your parents. They've safeguarded its secrets for generations, and now it's in your hands. Hexus has been after this book for eons, aware of its immense power. Although she's unable to destroy it now that you've unlocked its potential, she'll stop at nothing to tap into its secrets. If she succeeds in gaining full control and uncovering its mysteries, the consequences would be catastrophic—she'd not only shatter the boundaries of the dream world but also reshape the very fabric of existence itself."

Winnie felt a deep resonance with Lor's words, and although she still had much to learn about her powers, she was grateful for the answers he'd provided. "Before you leave, Winnie, I must warn you," Lor said, his expression serious. "You will face many challenges in the coming days. Some will be magical, while others will be internal. It's essential to remember that while this path is yours to walk, you don't have to walk it alone. Rely on your friends when needed, trust in the bonds you've built, and listen to your inner voice in times of grief."

Winnie nodded, taking Lor's words to heart. As Lor's attention turned to Jynx, Winnie watched with interest. "As for you, little one, your path in this world is already linked to Winnie's," Lor said. "A time will come when that link will present itself, as both of you have already set those wheels into motion." With that, Lor began to slowly fade away, his voice echoing across the sanctuary walls. "I bid you farewell, defenders. Allow the light to be your guide."

As Lor disappeared, Winnie looked down at Jynx. "I'm a light witch," she whispered, still trying to process the revelation. She paused, letting everything Lor had said sink in. "We should get back," she said finally, opening her satchel for Jynx to jump in. "The others are probably wondering where we've been." With her crystal ball in hand, Winnie opened a portal back to Sweet Screams, eager to share her newfound knowledge with her friends.

As the portal opened inside Sweet Screams, Winnie stepped out, her satchel slung across her body, with Jynx peeking out of the top. "Let's go find the others, Jynx," Winnie said, walking away from the portal as it closed behind her. Jynx's eyes widened as she took in the colorful array of candies passing her by with each step Winnie continued to take. She reached out a paw in an attempt to swipe some but Winnie was just out of reach, and Jynx slumped back into the satchel with a soured look upon her face.

Winnie turned the corner and bumped into Boo. "I'm so sorry," she started to say, but Boo cut her off. "Oh, Winnie, it's you! I need to talk to you!" Winnie replied, "What's wrong, Boo? You look like you've seen a ghost," Winnie said, chuckling at the irony of her own words. Boo pulled Winnie aside and whispered, "I don't think today is really today." Winnie nodded knowingly. "I know, Boo. I was actually coming to talk to everyone about that."

Boo's expression changed from concern to surprise, and he followed Winnie to meet up with the rest of their group. As they approached, Wraps yelled out, "Hey, it's Winnie & Jynx!" The rest of the group welcomed them warmly making Winnie smile. After the greetings calmed down Winnie announced to the group, "We need to have a meeting guys." Freddy asked, "Is something wrong?" Winnie replied, "I'm not entirely sure but it's going to take a bit to explain."

The group decided to walk outside to the outdoor theater, where they could talk without disturbing anyone. Once seated, Winnie began to explain what had happened from the beginning. The others were skeptical, and Boo interrupted, "She's telling the truth, though!" The group looked at Boo in confusion, and he continued, "Something wasn't right when I woke up this morning. I didn't even remember going to bed. Do any of you?"

The group shook their heads, trying to recall their last memory.

Boo recounted his conversation with Flip from that morning, telling them about how he'd touched the mirror and had a strange reaction. "Flip said that my stare went blank and I was projecting something into the mirror," Boo explained. "He was able to see it, but it was backwards on his side." Boo's eyes widened as he relayed the details of Flip's description. "He said it was of us battling ourselves, but we weren't ourselves. And then there was this really pretty lady that appeared, and a monster caught fire, and there was a little girl crying in a cage." Boo's voice grew more frantic as he added each new detail, "OH AND JYNX DIED!" Jynx's head shot up out of Winnie's satchel with an indescribable look when Boo mentioned her death. The others sat on the edge of their seats, engrossed in Boo's story. Once he finished, Vaughn and Wyatt slowly began looking at each other and started laughing. "You really had us going there for a minute, Boo," Vaughn said, chuckling. "Yeah, I don't know how either of you kept a straight face this entire time," Wyatt added.

Winnie let out a small "huh?" Boo tried to explain, "But I'm not making it up. I'm telling the truth! It's what Flip said he saw." Winnie stepped in, "No, seriously guys, he is telling the truth. Well, at least I think he is. I don't really remember a lot of that, but I do remember the woman." Winnie's explanation seemed to only make Wyatt and Vaughn laugh even harder. Winnie continued her side of the story trying to explain what had happened

when they left that morning and why it took her so long
to arrive.

Vaughn and Wyatt continued to poke fun, even when
Winnie showed them the engraving on the back plate of
Jynx's emerald. "Man, you guys really went all out for
this," Vaughn said, grinning. "I'm impressed."

Winnie looked at Boo and said, "You know, Boo, I
read something once about the thing that happened to
you this morning. I think you may have created some
kind of memory echo with the mirror when you touched
it. I need you to try and do it again so they know we're
telling the truth." Winnie pulled out her crystal ball and
placed it in the middle of the table. Boo reached out and
touched the globe, and suddenly, his eyes went blank
once again. A multi-purple toned fight scene projected
itself inside the crystal ball.

Vaughn and Wyatt's laughter slowly subsided as they
watched the replay of the entire fight scene. They saw
everything Boo had described only in greater detail, and
their tone quickly shifted. "Who is she?" Wyatt asked, his
voice filled with a curious anger. Winnie explained what
Lor had told her, "Her name is Hexus." She continued,
unfolding the story piece by piece until every detail of
Lor's speech was finally told.

The group sat in stunned silence attempting to
process all of the information. Wraps spoke up, "Okay,
wait a minute. So, you're a light witch, and your spell
book is completely blank now?" Winnie nodded. "Does
that mean The Dream Diary is now just an actual diary
and not a spell book anymore?" Wraps asked again.
Winnie replied, "I don't think so, but maybe? Lor said it
would customize to the owner, and when I said the words
out loud, it apparently became linked to me."

Vaughn's expression turned serious. "But light
witches don't exist in the monster realms, Winnie. How
are you supposed to train to be one if one doesn't exist to
train you?" Winnie shrugged. "I don't know, but one
thing's for sure – we need to be better prepared before
going back into The Shadowfel. Otherwise, we may all

234

end up like Jynx did" and with that, she scooped up the crystal ball and tucked it back into her satchel.

What the Spell?

Later that night, the group reconvened at Freddy's, determined to hone their skills and prepare for the battles ahead. The crystal ball's revelation had driven home the reality of their situation – they were in over their heads, facing more than just personal demons. Freddy's place was still shrouded in Winnie's protective magic; a surprising feat given her magic was usually short lived. However, thanks to Boo's newfound ability to create memory echoes, they could now pinpoint their weaknesses.

The group began to work on their individual issues. Vaughn focused on self-reflection, recognizing the importance of understanding himself. He had always been driven to prove himself, but his impulsive nature often led to reckless decisions. Wyatt, on the other hand, was working on balancing his confidence with caution. Boo knew his weakness all too well – a lack of courage. He struggled to stand up for himself, and his counter had taken advantage of this vulnerability during their battle.

Freddy's dark side was a force to be reckoned with, and his inability to assert himself made him an easy target. Wraps, despite his clumsiness, seemed more put together in his shadow form, but his tendency to stumble into trouble was a liability. Winnie's counterpart, however, was a different story altogether. Her shadow form exuded power and confidence, traits Winnie knew she lacked. The fact that her counterpart wielded dark magic proficiently raised an interesting question though – if Winnie was a light witch, why wasn't her shadow form using light magic? Winnie pondered the mystery, sensing that the key to her growth might be hidden within that contradiction.

As the night wore on, the moon rose high in the sky, casting a silver glow over the landscape. The group, exhausted from their training, decided to call it a night and get some rest. One by one, they drifted off to sleep, but Winnie's mind wasn't ready to sleep. She was determined to unlock the secrets of the Dream Diary and understand her powers. Pacing back and forth in her room, she held the spell book open, flipping through its pages, but nothing seemed to work. She tried to summon the power of light, just like she had in the battle, but her hand remained still and quiet.

Frustrated, Winnie tossed the book onto the bed and sighed, "I don't think I'm ever going to figure this out, Jynx." She made her way to the door to turn off the light, convincing herself that a good night's sleep would bring a new perspective. Jynx hopped up onto the bed, snuggling against Winnie as they both drifted off to sleep.

But Winnie's rest was short-lived. As she slept, she began to toss and turn, her dreams filled with visions of the celestial room and the pedestal only this time it's where the Dream Diary sat. The dream began to take a dark turn. The lights flickered and died, plunging the room into darkness. The spiri's swarmed the walls, their eyes burning red as they writhed and contorted like living shadows. The lime green mist crept in, and a silhouetted figure emerged from the fog – Hexus, making her way to the pedestal.

Winnie tried to run, but her feet felt heavy, as if rooted to the spot. The spiri's seemed to be closing in, their twisted forms covering the walls and ceiling. The room went black, and Winnie was trapped, unable to move or see. But then, she heard Lor's voice in her mind, "Listen to your inner voice in times of grief." Winnie focused on the words, "Let the light be your guide" and suddenly a spark of power ignited within her. She raised her hand, and strands of light began to slowly weave from her arm, gliding through the darkness like growing vines of ivy.

The light moved like a living thing, defying the shadows and spiri's that tried to stop it. It crawled across the room, picking up the Dream Diary from the pedestal and guiding it back to Winnie's outstretched hand. As her fingers closed around the book, the dream dissolved, and Winnie sat up in bed, gasping for breath. Jynx stirred beside her, looking up with concerned eyes. Winnie's heart was still pounding but a sense of clarity washed over her in that heart pounding moment – the light wasn't something to be summoned, it was a part of her, waiting to be tapped into.

Winnie sat up in bed, her eyes fixed on the Dream Diary as she reached for it. As her hand drew closer, the symbol on the cover flashed brightly, and she jerked her hand back in surprise. But her curiosity got the better of her, and she reached out again, picking up the book. As she opened the cover, a soft light began to burn across the page, illuminating script that seemed to appear out of nowhere. Winnie's eyes widened as she read the words aloud, Jynx watching with equal fascination.

"I have known many hands, many voices, and many witches across the turning ages. Some sought wisdom. Some sought power. Some sought comfort in the margins of my pages. But only one before you ever traveled in light. She lived millennia ago — the first and only Pure Light the world had seen...until now."

The words continued to burn and shimmer across the page, revealing the secrets of her destiny.

"Do not fear the emptiness you saw before. I am not a book of ink and parchment. I am a mirror, a guide, and a vessel. As you grow, so shall I. You are a Pure Light, child of the Luminous Thread — a witch born not to bend shadows, but to break them.

Winnie couldn't take her eyes off the words that danced across the page, each character revealing more about her own.

"Where others wield fear, you wield clarity. Where others conjure darkness, you reveal the truth. Your magic does not strike. It illuminates. A Pure Light sees what is hidden, heals what is wounded, and bends light into power no shadow can swallow."

As Winnie continued reading, a sense of understanding surged through her.

"Your gift is rare... and dangerous to those who hide within the dark. That is why their books could never hold your truth. You were meant to learn from me. I will teach you to call the light, to shape it, to wield it as shield and flame. I will teach you to read the world's reflections — and to alter them. As your casting deepens, incantations will fall away. First a name will serve, and then even that shall fade."

The words grew more intense the further she read.

"But know this: Light is not gentle. It reveals. It burns. It transforms. As you grow, my pages will fill. As you falter, I will steady you. You are me—I am you. That bond can no longer be severed."

The final words resounded in her mind as if the book itself were challenging her.

"You are the second Pure Light I have known... for she who came before was Pure Light entire, and you are the first of a kind yet to be named — a name that will awaken the moment you do. The first changed the world, and now you must choose whether to mend it... or remake it. Welcome to your destiny, Winnifred Eldravaine — daughter of the First Light."

The book's pages, once a barren expanse of blank parchment, now stirred to life. Winnie's eyes widened as she flipped to the next page, and her gaze fell upon lines of elegant script that began to fill the emptiness. She leaned in, as she read the words as they formed.

"NightSprite," the page read, "Level I — Passive Light." Winnie's eyes scanned the description as her mind tried absorbing the details, "A living entity but not truly alive. It cannot speak, yet it listens. It cannot think, yet it understands. It will follow you, warm you, and watch over you. Treat it gently — for in its glow lies the first truth of who you are."

As she finished reading the description, Winnie's gaze drifted to the incantation that followed. Her voice trembled slightly as she read the words aloud. She wasn't exactly sure what it was she was calling but she also felt a sense of safety in its words.

> *"Light that listens, hear my plea,*
> *Shape that comforts, come to me.*
> *Warm the dark and make it right,*
> *Stay beside me, little NightSprite."*

A small trail of light burst forth from the open page of the spell book, rising into the air like a tiny, shimmering snake. As it hovered above Winnie and Jynx, it gathered into a concentrated ball of light, its gentle glow illuminating the room. The light orb began to flit about, bouncing off the walls, floor, and even Jynx, who made it clear that she didn't share the light's enthusiasm. Winnie spun around, laughing and trying to keep up with the orb's antics.

As the light orb darted around the room, Winnie's eyes shone with delight. "Oh my gosh Jynx, look at it — its soooo cute!" she softly squealed. Jynx turned her head, a snarl on her lip, and the light orb's smile grew even wider. Its eyes closed, and it spun around in circles, its glow intensifying. Suddenly, it vanished with a soft "poof."

Winnie's face fell, but only for a moment. "Wow!" she exclaimed, still grinning from ear to ear. She couldn't wait to see what other magic the book held. As she looked down at the book, she saw that the next page had already begun to write itself. "Starflare Orb," the page read, "Level I — Offensive Light." Winnie's eyes scanned the description, her voice growing more serious as she read aloud.

"A sphere of gathered starlight, fragile yet fierce. Cast it forth and let it burst, scattering shards of dawn across the dark. Use with care — even the smallest star can blind the night." Winnie's voice trailed off, and she turned to Jynx with a hesitant expression. "Oh, this one seems a little more dangerous than the last one, Jynx," she said, her voice laced with uncertainty. Jynx narrowed her eyes and puffed out air from her nose, as if to say "so you say."

Winnie backed away from the bed, her arm extended and her palm open. She took a deep breath and began to recite the incantation.

> *"Gentle starlight, softly spin,*
> *Cosmic shimmer drawn within.*
> *When you fly, your form will split,*
> *Break the night and banish it."*

As she finished the spell, Winnie realized she was still facing Jynx, who was sitting on the opposite side of the room. Winnie cried out, "Oh no!" but it was too late.

An orb of light burst forth from her palm, flying directly towards Jynx. Jynx's eyes widened in terror as she scurried backward, her back pressing against the wall. She stood up on her hind legs, her front paws pressed tightly in front of her. With a resigned expression, she turned her head to the side and closed her eyes preparing for what she was certain would be her second and final curtain call. But instead of a collision, the orb burst into a thousand tiny star trails that radiated outward, filling the room with a gentle, shimmering light.

Jynx opened her eyes to find several star shards embedded in the wall around her like tiny ninja stars. Her chest heaved with labored breaths, her lungs struggling to keep up with her racing heart. She was trying desperately

not to hyperventilate, but her ragged gasps betrayed her
growing panic. As her eyes darted back and forth,
evaluating her surroundings, her gaze drifted over to her
tail, and her stomach sank in horror. One of the star
shards had grazed the side of her tail, leaving a small trail
of blood that trickled down her fur like a tiny, crimson
ribbon. Jynx's eyes became fixated on the blood, and her
vision began to blur. She felt a wave of dizziness wash
over her, and before she could even process what was
happening, she slumped forward, her paws slipping out
from under her. She collapsed onto the bed with a soft
thud, unconscious.

Winnie rushed over to Jynx, apologizing profusely as
she tried to wake her. "Jynx, I'm so sorry! I'm so sorry!"
she cried, her voice shaking with worry. Jynx lay limp in
her arms, her eyes closed, and Winnie's heart sank. She
gently touched Jynx's tail, seeing the blood on her fur,
and her guilt deepened.

Winnie continued to try and rouse Jynx, her concern
etched on her face. As she sat beside her unconscious
companion, the book in front of her suddenly sprang to
life. The pages glowed with a soft light, and the next spell
began to scribe itself out.

"Warm Touch," the page read, "Level I — Healing
Light." Winnie's eyes scanned the description as her
heart filled with hope. "A soft glow summoned to the
palm, gentle as breath and warm as dawn. Lay it lightly
upon the skin, and let its radiance close what's small and
sore."

Winnie's eyes scanned the incantation that followed.
Jynx was still unconscious, and she was bleeding. Winnie
knew she had to try and help. She placed her hand gently
on Jynx's wound and recited the spell, her voice soft and
soothing.

"Gentle glow, so warm and bright,
Lay your touch upon this sight.
Close the wound where pain took hold,
And wrap the heart in healing gold."

As Winnie spoke the words, a light began to course through her veins, like beautiful scrollwork unfolding beneath her skin. It flowed down her arm and into her hand, filling her palm with a soft, warm glow. The light shone between Winnie's palm and Jynx's tail, and when it faded, Winnie moved her hand to reveal that the wound was gone. Jynx stirred, her eyes fluttering open as she met Winnie's gaze. "I'm so sorry, Jynx," Winnie said, her voice filled with regret.

With a wave of relief washing over her, Winnie decided it was time to call it a night. She was grateful that Jynx was okay and the ordeal had left both of them feeling drained. "I think it's time for bed," Winnie said, smiling softly at her feline companion. Jynx, still a bit shaken but clearly on the mend, nodded in agreement, or at least, Winnie took her blinking as a sign of approval. Together, they snuggled back into bed, Winnie pulling the covers up around them as they settled in for a well-deserved rest. As they curled up together, Winnie felt her eyelids beginning to grow heavy, and she knew it wouldn't be long before she drifted back off to sleep once again. With a contented sigh, Winnie let her eyes close, feeling the warmth and comfort of Jynx's presence beside her and the quiet sense of safety the book had wrapped around her.

Anyone Seen My Cloak & Crown?

Morning dawned earlier than expected, but Winnie's rest had been peaceful. A new day brought a sense of control and purpose, and she couldn't wait to share her news with the others. Her spell book was no longer empty, and she had three new spells to learn and train with. Her excitement, clearly noticeable, as she jumped out of bed and quickly got dressed, eager to show everyone the progress she had already made. Winnie and Jynx descended the stairs, expecting to find the others already up and about working away in the kitchen. However, the house was quiet, and the kitchen was empty.

"No one's up yet, Jynx," Winnie said, her face falling into a disappointed expression. Undeterred, she decided she'd just go ahead and fix breakfast for herself and Jynx. Jynx hopped up to the breakfast table, licking her lips as she watched Winnie move between the counter and refrigerator, muttering to herself. Her thoughts kept drifting between last night's events, the others still asleep upstairs, and the simple task of making breakfast. She pulled a few eggs from the fridge, still mumbling under her breath, and set them on the counter. "Jynx, do you want pancakes this morning?" she asked absently. Jynx perked up instantly. Pancakes? The answer to this question was always yes! She nodded so hard her fur bounced, but Winnie didn't seem to notice. She was already back at the refrigerator, grabbing more ingredients, lost in her own swirling thoughts.

A moment later, as if the first question had never happened, Winnie said, "How about some French toast?" Jynx's eyes went wide. Pancakes and French toast? She closed her eyes and swayed in her chair, a huge smile spreading across her face. This was shaping up to be the greatest breakfast of her life.

Winnie made another trip to the fridge, and Jynx followed her every movement with eager anticipation. This time Winnie returned with a carton of milk and a bowl—though from where Jynx sat, she couldn't quite see what was inside it. "Jynx, would you like a little fruit for breakfast this morning?" Winnie asked, still staring off into nothing. Fruit too? Jynx could barely sit still. Pancakes, French toast, and fruit—a feast fit for royalty.

She settled at the table, watching Winnie crack the eggs into the bowl while muttering to herself, completely unaware of the culinary promises she was stacking up. Winnie poured a splash of milk into the bowl, then grabbed a butter knife and plunged it straight down into the mixture. Jynx's eager anticipation shifted, replaced by a slow, creeping confusion. Winnie sat the bowl in front of Jynx, saying, "Here's your breakfast." The bowl contained a strange mixture of grapes, still on the stem, with eggs and milk poured over them. Jynx's mouth filled with air as she tried to keep from throwing up, and she knocked the bowl off the table, sending the contents crashing to the floor.

Winnie spun around with a scolding tone, "Jynx!" But as she realized what had happened, her expression softened. "Oh... Sorry, I was just thinking about last night again." Jynx sat at the table, her tummy rumbling, and Winnie promised, "Ok, ok... pancakes coming right up! I have to clean this up first though." As Winnie cleaned the mess, Jynx's expression changed to one of anticipation, and she began swaying back and forth in her seat once more.

Winnie made a large batch of pancakes, deciding to make enough for everyone. As she finished plating them, she said, "I have an idea." Jynx looked up at her with hopeful eyes, and Winnie continued, "I'll be right back." She ran upstairs to grab her spell book, leaving Jynx sitting at the table with one eyebrow cocked.

When Winnie entered her room, she opened her spell book and thought about how she could introduce everyone to her new powers and gather them for breakfast all at once. She decided to conjure up her NightSprite to wake everyone up. Reading aloud the incantation, the little ball of light emerged, hovering in the air as if dancing. Winnie asked in a soft and gentle tone, "Hey little NightSprite, I was hoping you'd go around the house, room to room, and wake up all of my friends and bring them down for breakfast?" The light spun around rapidly, smiling, and flew out of the room, ready to complete its task.

The little ball of energy quickly glided down the hallway, illuminating its surroundings with a warm, gentle glow. Its first stop was Freddy's room, where it hovered in the doorway, staring down at the little boy sleeping peacefully in his bed, teddy bear clutched tightly to his chest. The light's warm glow seemed to soften as it gazed at Freddy, and it floated down to the bed, beginning to fly around Freddy's face in a playful, whimsical dance. Freddy, still half asleep, rolled over and pulled the covers up over his head, blocking out the light. The little ball of energy's face contorted into a comical grimace, its glow flickering with disappointment.

Unwilling to give up on its task, the light fluttered back out of the room and made its way down the hall to the next room, which happened to be Vaughn's. However, when it entered, it was surprised to find the bed empty. The light glided through the air, its glow casting eerie shadows on the walls, as it made a beeline for the bed to investigate. But before it could reach the bed, it heard a noise coming from the bathroom. The door swung open, and Vaughn emerged, brushing his teeth. The little light, still moving with purpose, didn't see Vaughn in time and ran directly into him. Vaughn let out a loud "AH!" best he could with a mouth full of toothpaste, and the little light imitated his reaction in silence, its glow flashing in surprise. Vaughn quickly took his hand and smacked the little light up against the wall, shouting, "Something's in the house!" His voice echoed across the second story floor, startling and waking the others.

Vaughn picked up his pillow from the bed and began swatting at the little light like a flyswatter chasing a fly. The little light, once a jovial ball of energy, was now panicking and dodging swing after swing in fear of its own life. Finally, it found a moment to free itself from Vaughn's room and flew out the door and down the hallway, looking over its shoulder as it tried to get away from him. As the orb turned back around, it found itself face to face with Wyatt, who was emerging from his room, rubbing the sleep from his eyes and yawning. "What's all the noise out here?" Wyatt said, but before he could finish, he looked up and saw the little orb of light heading straight towards him. Wyatt's eyes widened in surprise and he too let out a loud "AH!" The little light, still running for its life, tried to brake but was too late and slammed right into Wyatt's face, pushing his head backwards and hitting the door behind him. Wyatt landed on the floor in a sitting position, dazed.

Vaughn hopped out of his room into the hallway, dragging a vacuum cleaner by the hose, which was running at high speed. He started running down the hallway, pulling the massive vacuum cleaner behind him, and let out a fierce battle cry. The little light, still trying to recover from its collision with Wyatt, sat on top of Wyatt's head, and saw Vaughn charging right at it. The little light backed up against the doorway, eyes wide with fear, but before Vaughn could reach it, the sound of the vacuum began to weaken and stop. Vaughn turned his head to see what was wrong and saw Winnie standing in the hallway at the top of the stairs, holding the power cord of the vacuum. "What in the world are you doing to my NightSprite?" she asked in a concerned tone.

Vaughn looked sheepish, and repeated, "NightSprite?" before admitting, "I thought it was some kind of ghost or something?" Winnie raised an eyebrow and asked, "...and you thought a vacuum was the best solution for that?" Vaughn dropped the front end of the wand to the vacuum down to the floor and replied in his defense, "Well, yeah – I mean, they've made several movies about it." The little light, still shaken, hovered above Wyatt's head before immediately flying back to Winnie's side, while Wyatt himself slowly got to his feet, rubbing his face.

Winnie's sympathetic gaze met her little NightSprite, and she said, "I'm sorry. I didn't mean for any of that to happen. Thanks for trying to help, though." The sprite's gentle smile returned, and it bobbed in the air, its eyes darting between the others in the hallway. With a soft "poof," it vanished, leaving Winnie to shake her head at the chaos. "Come on, guys, let's get some breakfast," she said, beckoning them to follow her downstairs. The promise of pancakes was all it took to distract Vaughn and Wyatt from the commotion, and they trailed behind Winnie, their stomachs growling in anticipation.

In the kitchen, Jynx was perched on the counter, licking the last bits of pancake from the platter. "Jynx, those were for everyone!" Winnie exclaimed. Jynx responded with a burp that spoke volumes about her priorities. Winnie chuckled and began making more pancakes, motioning for the guys to take a seat.

As Vaughn sat down and awaited his breakfast he revealed to Winnie that he may have come up with a plan to get her back into school. Winnie replied excitedly anticipating the details of his plan. "Yeah, but I don't think you're going to like it," he continued. "Why, what's the idea?" she asked nervously. Vaughn stood up and reached into his pocket, pulling out a piece of paper. He unfolded it and turned it around to reveal the flyer for the tournament that had been slipped under her dormitory door earlier on. "You've been carrying that thing around with you all this time?" She asked. "Well, yeah. I mean I was always kind of hoping you'd enter it anyway, and it says right here 'Only a ticket holder can enter'," Vaughn said. "How does that help me get back into school though?" she asked, still confused. Vaughn sighed, a heavy sigh, frustrated that she didn't understand. "The rules! If you enter the tournament and win, the Council of Night has to grant you one wish, remember? You can wish to be allowed to finish school then," he explained. "I don't know, Vaughn that seems like a long shot" She replied. "It may be a long shot, Winnie, but it may also be your only shot," he explained.

Just as Winnie was about to respond, a loud explosion rocked the house, making them all stumble. "What was that?" Wyatt asked. Winnie's eyes met Vaughn's, and they both knew something was wrong. Winnie asked in a panicked state of mind, "Where's Freddy?"

The three of them ran out of the kitchen and made their way up the stairs, Jynx in tow. As they reached Freddy's bedroom door, they could feel massive amounts of air gushing in. The four of them stood inside the doorframe, evaluating the situation. "The wall is gone!" Wyatt exclaimed. Winnie ran over to Freddy's bed, a shape of someone still lying inside of it. She pulled the covers back to reveal nothing but pillows and his teddy bear. "Freddy's gone!" she cried out, as she picked up the bear clutching it to her chest. Vaughn walked over to the jagged hole in the wall, the wind whipping past him. "That's not all that's gone..." Vaughn revealed as he looked out, "...so is the cloaking spell. Vaughn stood framed in the shattered remains of the wall, the wind howling past him like a chorus of warnings. He turned his head towards the others and spoke the words that would seal their upcoming fate: "She's found us."

Stay Connected to the World of Sweet Screams

Thank you for joining Winnie, Vaughn, and all of the others on their first adventure. If you'd like to keep exploring their world — and maybe bring a little of its magic into your own — you're invited to stay connected.

Step into the World

Our online shop is more than just a store — it's a doorway into the Sweet Screams universe. From signed copies to magical surprises, you can explore the world beyond the pages at: **www.SweetScreams.com**

Join the Community

Want behind-the-scenes peeks, updates, and a place to share your love for the story? Follow the Sweet Screams community on Facebook:
www.Facebook.com/SweetScreamsPresents

A World Growing Bigger Every Day
Construction begins this year on the first Sweet Screams store — a real place where the magic of the books comes to life. Follow along as it grows, and be part of the journey from the very beginning.

Your excitement, your imagination, and your support help shape the future of this world. And trust me — there's so much more waiting for you.

Acknowledgments

Thank you to everyone who simply supports my crazy plans and ideas, with special thanks to my parents. You're helping me create the physical Sweet Screams that I know this world will come to know and love.

To every reader who picked up this book or shared it — thank you for giving me the chance to share this world with you. Creating Sweet Screams has been one of the greatest joys of my life, and just knowing you've chosen to be a part of it means more than I could ever express.

This story began with nothing more than a logo — a simple idea for a store that changed shape as I did. What started as an ice cream shop soon morphed into a candy store, which sparked the world you now hold in your hands. Like the journey of my characters, my own shifted in ways I never foresaw, but the heart of its message never wavered: to create a world where differences become strengths, where the unseen become seen, and where every spark has the power to reshape the world around it.

As for what comes next... voices are powerful, and finding yours is no small feat. If you'd love to see this story continue, reach out, let me know. And for those curious about the road ahead, the group will soon set out to rescue Freddy while attempting to foil the witch's plan. With Winnie's only way back into school resting on a technicality, entering the Obsidian Crown tournament will expose her as a light witch — a risk she may have to take to stand against what's coming.

About the Author

David Todd Comer is a creator from Bluefield, Virginia, where he is currently working with his parents to build the first-ever Sweet Screams shop — the same world he brings to life in his writing. Before returning home to care for his grandmother, David spent ten years in Nashville, Tennessee, earning a Bachelor's Degree in Interior Design and developing the skills he's now using to transform his family's run down storefront into a place for everyone to enjoy.

David has never been an avid reader. He struggled to stay focused while reading, which in turn affected his comprehension skills — a challenge that, rather than discouraging him, became a quiet motivation. That struggle pushed him to prove he could still belong in the world of stories by sitting down, learning, and exploring a craft he once knew nothing about, mirroring the very trials his characters would come to face." In that process, David discovered joy in storytelling by imagining his world the way he sees it in his mind — like an animated series or film inspired by the art styles he's always loved, both now and from his childhood. He likes to imagine, that one day, this story might also reach others in that same animated form.

What began as a simple logo grew into a world built on belonging, courage, and the belief that you don't have to fit every expectation to be part of something magical. David strives in his day-to-day life to promote mental health, body positivity, and the idea that "normal" doesn't exist. He encourages others to chase their dreams even when the path ahead seems bleak. He believes we are all puzzle pieces in this life — each shaped differently, each meant for a place uniquely our own. Sometimes we try so hard to fit in where we think we should belong that we forget we're meant for somewhere else entirely. But it's okay not to fit where you don't belong; your place exists, whether you've found it yet or not, and the puzzle isn't complete without you.

www.ingramcontent.com/pod-product-compliance
Lightning Source LLC
Chambersburg PA
CBHW020753310726
48969CB00002B/524